"I devoured [this book] in a single sitting. The sense of dislocation – and location – made it seem like a dream of another life, all of it so lyrical and yet narratively acute. A wonderful achievement."

—Jonathan Lethem

"Masterfully ambiguous ... [The book] raises complicated questions ... but doesn't neatly wrap them up. Rather, it allows the ideological inquiries at the center of the book to linger and bloom for continued consideration."

—*New York Times*

"A riot and very compelling – quite dark, as usual, but funny too... Thomson is an extraordinary writer."

—Samantha Morton, *Observer*

"An outstanding, compulsive work from a rare talent. Rupert Thomson continues to make my jaw drop with each book."

—Irenosen Okojie

"An utterly absorbing and elegantly written novel about the deepest of existential questions: how we should live. Rupert Thomson is truly one of our most brilliant and original writers."

—Graeme Macrae Burnet

"A novel that turns a midlife crisis inside out, rewardingly ... the result, in Thomson's expert hands, is fast-paced and headlong; the book ends up rewiring the reader's sense of what's banal and what's not. A work about estrangement and solitude that's surprisingly rapid, engaging, light-footed."

—*Kirkus Reviews*

also by rupert thomson

fiction

Barcelona Dreaming

NVK

Never Anyone But You

Katherine Carlyle

Secrecy

Death of a Murderer

Divided Kingdom

The Book of Revelation

Soft

The Insult

Air and Fire

The Five Gates of Hell

Dreams of Leaving

non-fiction

This Party's Got to Stop

rupert thomson

how to make a bomb

a novel

HEAD of ZEUS

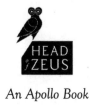

An Apollo Book

First published in the United States as *Dartmouth Park* in 2023 by Other Press

This edition published in the United Kingdom in 2024 by Head of Zeus Ltd,
part of Bloomsbury Publishing Plc

Song lyrics on page 256 from "The Boys in the Backroom"
by Frank Loesser, music by Frederick Hollaender, 1939.

9 7 5 3 1 2 4 6 8

A catalogue record for this book is available from the British Library.

ISBN (HB): 9781035908530
ISBN (XTPB): 9781035908547
ISBN (E): 9781035908509

Printed and bound in Great Britain by
CPI Group (UK) Ltd, Croydon CR0 4YY

FSC
www.fsc.org
MIX
Paper | Supporting
responsible forestry
FSC® C171272

Head of Zeus Ltd
First Floor East
5–8 Hardwick Street
London EC1R 4RG

WWW.HEADOFZEUS.COM

I

nausea

I

What triggered it was utterly innocuous
A young woman standing a few feet away from him took out a travel card and tapped it against the card reader, the gesture instinctive, automatic, like a reflex
There was also the noise the card reader made
A kind of beep
Then there was the tram's interior, the metal poles upright and painted orange, the seats upholstered in a practical, hard-wearing charcoal gray
Though he was sitting still, his head began to float sideways and backwards, the motion frictionless and easy, like an ice cube sliding across a pane of glass
But that wasn't all
A hand had wrapped itself around his brain, and it was squeezing
He was worried he might throw up or pass out
He was worried he might scream
He couldn't think
There was nothing left to think *with*

how to make a bomb

If he suddenly found what surrounded him unbearable, it was because it was artificial
Everything had been designed and manufactured, and he was trapped in it
He had also become aware of possibilities that might or might not have been explored
Behind that beep, a thousand other beeps
Behind that upright orange metal pole, a pole made out of something different, or molded into a different shape, or painted a different color
Somehow all the conceivable alternatives were still there, stacked up behind the version that had been decided on, and all of them unnoticed, overlooked
Except by him

He had boarded the tram at Nonneseteren
He was on his way back to London, after a four-day conference in Bergen
Studying the map above the window opposite, he counted twenty-five stops to the airport
The journey would take approximately three-quarters of an hour
He ran his eyes through the various stations
Paradis, Hop, Lagunen
In normal circumstances, he would have reveled in the foreign sounds

5

That afternoon they made him feel nauseous
Behind each station's name lurked all the names that station might have had instead

The tram slowed down
A series of electronic notes, a sort of jingle, and then a woman's voice
Kronstad
He lowered his eyes
How many women had auditioned for that role?
Like an image from a hall of mirrors, the queue of applicants curved off into a distance that seemed infinite
As for the voice itself, decisions would have been taken about character and tone
His mind began to spin and swirl with all the options, and once again he had the feeling that his head was leaving his shoulders, his neck as soft as chewing gum that has been chewed for hours
He had become the host for a sensitivity—a *hyper*sensitivity—that he couldn't regulate or even influence
He was tempted to get off the tram
He could sit on a bench and breathe the cold Norwegian air
Would it make any difference, though?
What if he felt no better?

He looked out of the window, hoping to distract himself, but the tram had stopped next to a billboard

how to make a bomb

He didn't notice what the product was, only that it began with
an *A*, and that the apex of the *A* was colored white, as if the
letter was a snowcapped mountain
This was the most unbearable thing so far
It was so obviously made-up
Dozens of ideas would have been discussed, presented, and
rejected in favor of the one that now confronted him
Behind the surface of reality lay other surfaces, other realities
Behind every single thing was something else

He brought his eyes back to the tram's interior, and there, as
before, were the seats and the poles
This is just a ride on a tram, he told himself, a ride on a tram in
Bergen
He hung his head again and closed his eyes
He could still hear the beeping of the card reader as new
passengers got on
The sequence of electronic notes
The female voice
Slettebakken

He opened his eyes and stared at the smooth gray floor
The smoothness was sickening
The grayness too
He couldn't close his eyes or keep them open
There was nowhere he could look

7

I might have to kill myself, he thought
It seemed like a perfectly reasonable response to what he was going through
It might even be the only solution available to him
How else could he make it stop?

Miraculously, he managed to hang on until he reached the airport

He stepped off the tram
The nausea was still there, though it was milder, more subdued
It reminded him of what happened when he took medication for a headache
The pain might lift, but it would leave a memory, a kind of afterimage
A place that was dazed and listless
Hollowed out

With an hour to spare before his flight was due to board, he found himself standing in front of a seafood restaurant called Fiskeriet
Here again the feeling was one of overload or surfeit
There was a prawn salad, a grilled salmon salad, a smoked salmon salad, a crab salad, and a salad with tuna, red onion, and black olives

how to make a bomb

And that was just the salads
There were also fish cakes and fish soup and fried fish and steamed mussels
Choice was one of the hallmarks of modern society
Choice was a kind of hell

He couldn't have said how long he stood there for, though there came a point when he attracted the attention of the woman behind the counter
If she thought he was behaving suspiciously, she would call Security, and then there would be trouble
He selected the dish that was closest to him—a prawn salad—then paid for it and took it over to a table
The woman seated nearby was dressed in a dark-blue blazer and a white skirt
She might have just stepped off a yacht
She had ordered a plate of fish-and-chips and a glass of rosé
He doubted it had been difficult for her

He took a breath, but couldn't seem to fill his lungs
It was as if he had been transported to a planet with a different atmosphere, and he was struggling to acclimatize
He picked up a wedge of lemon and squeezed a few drops onto his prawns
The woman in the blazer looked at him
It was the kind of look you give a lift door when the lift is on its way

Her mind was almost certainly elsewhere
He ate slowly, feeling he had made the wrong choice
Perhaps they were all wrong choices
Was he even hungry?
He forced himself to go on eating
He remembered a faint taste of salt water
Nothing else

Half an hour later he set off towards his gate

2

It was all right while he was in the air
As soon as the plane touched down, though, his symptoms returned
Welcome to London, where the local time is ten fifteen
He felt dizzy, winded
Oddly sick
How he got from the airport to the train he didn't know
He had no memory of that
He rested his head against the window, the darkness outside pressing close
The roar of wheels on the track
A woman opposite, shouting into her phone

how to make a bomb

Then the power station's chimneys, and the red lights on the top of cranes, and the furtive, oily glitter of the Thames

Once at Victoria he called an Uber
Your driver's name is Gulnazar
He waited on the pavement, by a café with an awning
The dim, damp streets
The delicate but unrelenting February rain
A black Toyota Prius sidled up to him
Philip Notman? the driver said through the open window
Philip nodded, then climbed in
They headed north

On Hampstead Road he saw a man clutching his coat lapels against his throat as he hurried past a row of shops
Paradise Café, Best One
Chicken King
Nobody ever missed a chance to exaggerate
Hyperbole was everywhere
A gap had opened up between the names of things and the things themselves
He hadn't been aware of it before, not properly, but now it was all that he could see and he felt he might get lost in it
He leaned back, closed his eyes

11

Two days earlier, in a museum in Bergen, he had stopped in front of a painting by Edvard Munch

A young woman was sitting on a bed, her clothes in a state of disarray

Perhaps she had slept in them, or perhaps, stilled by some memory or fear, she had yet to finish dressing

The look on her face was apprehensive, but also resolute

She had wept during the night, he imagined, and now, with day approaching, she was trying to be brave about what lay ahead

Munch had chosen tough, raw colors for her skin—the red of chafing, and the gray of dust or dirt

The painting was called *Morning*

Gradually, Philip's eyes were drawn to the top left-hand quarter of the canvas

A bottle and a glass stood on a round table near the bed

There was an inch of water in the bottle

The glass was empty

The young woman looked beyond the bottle and the glass towards an unseen window, the source of light in the room, and also, perhaps, a kind of gateway to the outside world, the root of her anxiety, but the bottle and glass, painted in the same rough creams and grays as the wall behind them, had a stillness and a transparency that she might have found comfort in if only she had been able to concentrate on them, give them the attention they deserved

They might comfort him as well, he realized

He could see them now, barely suggested, almost ectoplasmic, but undeniably and powerfully there

how to make a bomb

The image seemed like an antidote to everything that he had been through since boarding the tram in Bergen at four o'clock that afternoon

We're here, the Uber driver said

Philip opened his eyes
There was his house, eight steep steps to the front door, the porch light on
His wife, Anya, was expecting him
He stood on the uneven pavement and watched the Prius creep off down the road
It was after midnight
The rain had stopped, and the trees were dark and still
Sometimes a drop of water fell
His nausea had given way to numbness and fatigue
His feet were cold
It was all he could do to lift the latch and close the gate behind him
Climbing the steps, he reached into his pocket for his keys
He hoped Anya was asleep, and that he didn't wake her
He didn't want to have to talk

The night air pushed him into the hall
Downstairs, in the kitchen, the dishwasher was on
He could hear it churning, muted and watery, like the heartbeat of an unborn child

The air smelled of vanilla
Anya must have lit a scented candle earlier
All of this familiar, but not reassuring

As he stood by the door, a car's headlights swooped through the front room
A shout, a snatch of muffled bass
The surging of the engine
The nausea might have faded, but he felt it might return at any moment
He had no power over it
No power at all

He turned the porch light off and started up the stairs

3

There was Anya suddenly, with a cup of tea
He glanced at his phone
6:37
Anya was wearing a black T-shirt that belonged to him, though it had been washed so many times that it was gray
Her legs were bare

how to make a bomb

She put his tea down on the bedside table
So, did you have an affair?
He looked at her
I know what those conferences are like, she said
You're in a foreign city, everyone's from somewhere else, you have too much to drink
People get off with each other
He reached for his tea, but it was still too hot
Not this time, he said
She smiled, but it was faint, almost sad, as if she was touched by his attempt at lightness
As if she wanted to believe him
But really, Philip, she said
Did you?
He took her hand
No, he said, and it was true—though he felt that he had lied

At the reception on the opening night he had met a sociology professor from Cádiz
Her name was Inés Vaquero de Ayala
The way her lips moved when she was speaking, or even when she wasn't
Somehow he imagined they were numb
He had found himself looking at that part of her face when he should have been looking into her eyes, and he knew that she had noticed

He had wondered what it would be like to kiss that mouth, though the thought had been remote, almost abstract

Nothing had happened

No, he said again, and with a kind of wistfulness, as if part of him wished that he had in fact "got off" with the young woman from Cádiz
But you're right about drinking too much

Anya withdrew her hand from his and walked slowly, almost dreamily, across the room, like someone moving through water
Once again, he thought of the Munch painting, and how the artist had evoked the shimmer of dread or panic that sometimes overwhelms us when we wake, the feeling that we will be unequal to what is asked of us
Anya took off her T-shirt, then slid a drawer open and lifted out clean underwear
He talked about how expensive Norway was
One round of drinks—two glasses of wine and a gin-and-tonic—had cost him nearly forty pounds
Did you have to pay for drinks? Anya said, fastening her bra
Only once, he said
The square of sky framed by the window was still dark
It would be dark for another half an hour

how to make a bomb

Then it would be gray
Have you heard from Seth? he asked
Seth was their son
He was nineteen, and in his first year at university
I called him yesterday, Anya said
He sounded good
She pulled on a pair of black, wide-legged trousers
But, you know, with Seth
Her sentence stopped there, incomplete
He was aware of the house above and below him, a house they had bought with money she had inherited from an uncle in Wuppertal, they could never have afforded it otherwise, not on their salaries, and he had the same feeling he had had while standing in the hall the night before, a sense of familiarity but without the reassurance that usually comes with it

Anya gave him a kiss, then moved towards the door
I have meetings all day, she said, one hand on the door handle, but I'll be home by five or six
Okay, he said

He listened to her footsteps on the stairs

4

That morning, after breakfast, he climbed to the top floor of the house and opened Seth's door
Even though Seth had been gone for several weeks, his musky, melancholy smell hung on in the air
Since his early teens, he had struggled with depression
Philip stepped into the room
Blu Tacked to the wall above the bed were postcards of famous people
Lady Gaga, Samuel L Jackson, Kristen Stewart, Mikhail Bulgakov, Gerard Way, Zendaya, Margot Robbie, Neil Gaiman, Andy Warhol, Lorde
At least half of them had been unknown to Philip when he first saw them
He'd had to ask
Who's that?
And then again, Who's that?
Seth had been embarrassed for him
Dad
But there they were, the heroes and heroines, all in a row, like a kind of secular Last Supper

He sat down on the bed
His heart was quiet, almost stealthy, and his eyes had blurred with tears

how to make a bomb

Part of him stood some distance off and watched
What's happening to you? it said
You need to get a grip
In the past, he might have paid attention to that voice
Not anymore
The part he had to pay attention to, he told himself, was the part that was upset

He remembered how he used to wake Seth for school
Seth would have been thirteen or fourteen, and going through an emo phase
He had dyed his hair black in the summer holidays
Once, when Philip turned on the lamp next to the bed, Seth cried out in agony, and Philip thought of a vampire exposed to a beam of sunlight
Maybe you'd feel more comfortable, he said, if you slept in a coffin
With a lid, he added
Very funny, he heard Seth mutter from beneath the covers
We could go to the funeral director's at the weekend, Philip went on
See if they have any castoffs
It was the sort of joke that Anya hated
She thought it was tempting fate to mention death—or even harm—in the same breath as her son
If Philip was superstitious, it took the opposite form
Always put into words that which you are most afraid of

Always try to put it into words
Naming the dark thing lessens the damage it can do

Those mornings, though
He would stand at the foot of the stairs and call up the stairs
Ten-minute warning, five-minute warning, one-minute warning, and then, inevitably, We're going to be late
I'm doing my best, Seth would yell back
He would appear with a scowl on his face, his shoelaces undone, his earbuds trailing, like an alien disconnected from its life support
He would need reminding about his Oyster card, his school ID, his phone
He would need money
Philip would drive him to the bus stop, even though it was only half a mile away, then he would watch Seth through the windscreen as he crossed the road, his bulky schoolbag making a hunchback of him, his dyed-black hair unbrushed
Everything felt breakable—or not breakable, perhaps, but thin, like a membrane that could be punctured or torn open

Their family doctor referred Seth to CAMHS, Children and Adolescent Mental Health Services
He was prescribed an SSRI called Sertraline and started seeing a therapist for CBT
His existence had been reduced to acronyms

how to make a bomb

He belonged to a generation that was beset by peer pressure, diminishing attention spans, perceived social isolation, and constantly changing government targets, and all of it fed through a self-perpetuating technology that had a hectic, helter-skelter quality, and which he couldn't temper or escape
If he was depressed and anxious, was it any wonder?
Had it been this difficult when he—Philip—was growing up?
He didn't think it had
Would things improve as Seth got older?
He remembered Rilke's words
The future: time's excuse to frighten us

He stood up from the bed and walked to the door
Four years ago, he had painted the walls Imperial Yellow in the hope that Seth's spirits might be lifted by the color
It hadn't worked
The world had pushed and pulled at Seth until he unraveled, and when that happened, as it was bound to, it provided him with products and strategies to help him cope
It was like digging a hole and filling it in, except that the hole was never properly filled, and there had been nothing wrong with the ground in the first place
Philip looked inside himself and saw a fire burning deep down in the dark, a fire that was small and yet intense
He realized with a shock that it was rage

5

That evening, when Anya came home from work, Philip ordered a Chinese takeaway—half a crispy aromatic duck with pancakes, strips of cucumber and spring onion, and little tubs of hoisin sauce
He made a pot of jasmine tea, and they sat at the end of the kitchen table, at right angles to each other
Outside, it was raining again
He was conscious of having to push recent experiences to the back of his mind, of having to pretend that everything was the same as before, the same as always, but when Anya mentioned a chance meeting with someone she had known when she was young he was reminded of a dream he'd had in Bergen

In the dream he had woken to see a boy in his hotel room
It was Clive, a childhood friend
Philip woke from the dream, his heart beating hard, the T-shirt he was wearing damp around the neck
He was convinced that if he looked over the duvet he would see Clive at the foot of the bed
But Clive was dead
He had died in an accident in 1971
When he woke in the morning he thought of Clive, but no longer believed that he was there

how to make a bomb

A dream, he told himself
One of those dreams that feels real because it takes place in the room you're sleeping in
He parted the curtains and leaned on the window
Below was a paved area with modern office blocks, more like a precinct than a street
The sky was the color of zinc, the light flinty and sharp
I'm in Bergen, he told himself
The word sounded awkward, and the nerves throughout his body shook and rustled like dead leaves
What did the day hold?
At four o'clock that afternoon he had an event
He would be discussing his biography of Merovech, the founder of the Merovingian dynasty
Later, in the evening, there would be a dinner with various local dignitaries
He glanced at his watch
8:13
When did they stop serving breakfast?
He suddenly felt that if he missed it, things would spin out of orbit, come undone
In the bathroom he turned on the shower
His panic was as steady and insistent as the hot water drilling down in thin, hard rods
Back in the bedroom, a towel wrapped round his waist, he checked the time again
8:32
He couldn't decide what to wear—not that he had much choice

23

He had traveled light, just one small case

Still, he kept changing his mind, putting on items of clothing, then taking them off again, a racing or whirling in his head, the seconds thudding past as if on hooves

In the end, he settled on a black shirt and gray trousers

At five to nine he took a lift down to the lobby

Sitting in the breakfast area was Inés, the sociology professor from Cádiz

They had drunk wine together the night before

Outside, in the dark, wearing a red down coat with a fake-fur collar, she had offered him one of her Spanish cigarettes

Though he rarely smoked, he had accepted

The flame of her lighter showed him part of her face—one eye, a cheekbone, half her mouth—like something he was supposed to memorize

And here she was again, at a table for two, with her back against the wall and her head lowered, her eyes on her phone

Noting the black coffee and the bowl of fruit, he smiled because he felt he could have predicted them

Before he could say anything, she looked up

Philip, she said

Did you sleep well?

Something about the way she said his name, the fact that she was saying it, the fact that it was in her mouth

He wanted to keep hearing it

Her voice, his name

Not really, he said

What about you?

how to make a bomb

I slept like a baby, she said, then she was frowning
Can I say that—like a baby?
He nodded
Yes, you can say that
You can say anything you like
Her forehead cleared
Anything?
He smiled again, then gestured at the empty chair
Do you mind if I join you?
Please, she said
She was wearing a red blouse made from a gauzy fabric—
organza maybe, or chiffon
It seemed a bit dressy for breakfast-time, but he admired her
for it
Had she also had trouble choosing clothes?
I drank too much last night, he said
You also smoked, she said
He adjusted the position of his knife and fork
That was your fault
If I didn't give you a cigarette, she said, you would have asked
somebody else
You were desperate
I wonder if that's true, he said
She held his gaze for a few moments, then put her phone
facedown on the table
He watched her reaching for her coffee
I had a nightmare, he said
I haven't had a nightmare in ages

25

Philip?

Anya was looking at him, worry in the line between her eyebrows, cheap wooden chopsticks motionless above dark shreds of aromatic duck
Sorry, he said, you just reminded me of something
While I was in Bergen, I dreamed about a boy I knew when I was growing up
He lived on the same road as me
His name was Clive
I don't think you've ever mentioned him before, she said
Philip shook his head
He died
Anya put her chopsticks down
It happened years ago, he said, when I was nine
One morning, he woke to discover that a foot of snow had fallen
He met up with some friends and they took toboggans to the chalk pit
It was a place they often went to
Usually, they would half run, half slide down the steep slope that had been gouged out of the hillside, the loose chalk rumbling beneath their shoes
They called it "skiing"
That day, though, the slope looked smooth and someone had the idea of sledging down

how to make a bomb

They should lie on their stomachs, go headfirst
It was like a dare
He remembered an older boy yelling and whooping all the way to the bottom
It was Clive's turn next, but he hung back
He thought it might be dangerous
All the other boys made chicken sounds and Clive's cheeks flushed
All right, he said
He threw himself onto his sledge and pushed off with his feet
Instead of aiming down the middle, as the other boy had done, he took off at an angle
There was a dull noise, like two soft things colliding, and his sledge came to a halt
When they reached him, he wasn't moving
He had hit a rock and his whole face was smashed
The blood on the snow looked shockingly red, like a color that had only just been thought of
He looked at Anya
You feel responsible? she asked
He shrugged
I played a part in it
He wasn't sure what he had expected of her, sympathy perhaps, or a widening of the eyes as it dawned on her that he was guilty of wrongdoing, or even a crime, but the look she gave him had a quizzical or probing edge
You think I'm being self-indulgent, he said
Maybe, she said

She adjusted the emerald on her finger, then her eyes drifted to the window that overlooked the garden

He had told Inés the same story, over breakfast
Her response had surprised him too
The dream isn't about your friend, she said, and what you did or didn't do
It's about something else
Tell me, he said
Your friend appeared in the middle of the night, she said, like an archangel
He considered her in her theatrical red shirt
Like an archangel
It's the message that's important, she went on, not the messenger
But he didn't speak, he told her
He just stood there
There's still a message, Inés said
There's always a message

Anya stood up from the table
It's cold, she said
I'm going to light a fire

Later that evening, they lay on the sofa in the front room, both facing in the same direction, Anya's head a soft weight on his chest

how to make a bomb

I worry about Seth, she said
I worry too, he said
I was thinking about him earlier
He felt her shift
Were you?
This morning, he said, after you left for work, I went into his room and sat down on his bed
All of a sudden I realized I was crying
Well, not crying exactly, but I had tears in my eyes
Anya gave him a look from close up
Are you missing him?
Of course, he said, but it's not just that
He couldn't explain his tears—or rather, he felt that to attempt an explanation would take him into territory he wasn't certain of as yet
Instead, he offered something that felt approximate, tangential
I wish life wasn't so difficult for him, he said
I wish I could make it easier

The night slipped or shifted, like a lift dropping an inch or two inside its shaft

You seem different since you came back, she said
In the past, he had found it reassuring that he had never been able to hide anything from her
It was as if their relationship had come complete with its own in-built security system

With someone you could easily keep secrets from, there would be more incentive to deceive
Not that he had any desire to deceive her
All the same, you'd be left more open to temptation
He rested his cheek against her hair and gazed at the square, bright-orange screen of the wood-burning stove
That's a great fire you made, he said
She gave him another look from close up, as if she suspected him of changing the subject, then she settled back against him
How was the conference? she asked
You didn't tell me

6

He sat in the garden, under the damson tree
The sky looked hand tinted, sepia colored, like a photograph taken a century ago
The planes had stopped
It would be five hours before they started up again, and then the air would fill with a gravelly roar as they pushed, one after another, through the low cloud into Heathrow or Stansted
On the radio that evening a Conservative politician had been talking about uncertainty
It was a word you heard at least a dozen times a day, along with "deadline," "gridlock," and "cliff edge"

how to make a bomb

Even if you weren't feeling particularly uncertain yourself,
uncertainty crept into your psyche, your interactions with
strangers and even with good friends, your entire life
That was 2019 for you

He let his head fall back and looked straight up
Behind that sky was another sky, not light-polluted or loud
with aircraft engines, but depthless, uncluttered, black
Since returning from Bergen, he had sometimes wondered if
the nausea that often overwhelmed him could be a response to
the current political situation
He had rejected the idea
If he felt as he did, it was because he was asking a question that
was bigger than politics
A question no politician ever dared to ask
Is this really the best way to live?

While lying on the sofa with Anya, he had described how the
organizers of the conference had laid on various excursions and
activities for foreign guests
He had signed up for a tour of Grieg's house
Standing alone on a moss-cushioned promontory that
overlooked a lake, the house was called Troldhaugen, or Hill
of Trolls
The famous composer had lived there with his wife Nina for
almost a quarter of a century

The rooms had wood-paneled walls and gilt chandeliers, and the light that poured through the windows was so clean and clear that it felt rinsed
Visible from a veranda at the back were two green islands
Flatoyna and Ulvoyna
In recent years, a concert hall had been built in the garden, and once they had seen the house they were treated to a recital of piano works
The pianist was a young woman in a white blouse, her hair palest yellow, like the flame of a candle seen in sunlight
She spoke about each piece before she played it
Her English was flawless
Behind the piano, a plate glass window framed a view of tall pines and blue water
He had found the experience matter-of-fact but also poetic, and it had stayed with him, and when he thought of that day he felt oddly moved
How lovely, Anya said
I wish I could have been there
She paused
I know Grieg's music
I sang in *Peer Gynt* when I was seventeen
Not long afterwards she told him she was tired and she was going to bed
I'll be up soon, he said
A wind stirred the bare branches of the damson tree

how to make a bomb

Midnight in north London

He was aware of having kept something from Anya

Of all the foreign guests participating in the conference, only he and Inés had showed up for the tour

There had been a comical moment when they were waiting in the hotel lobby and a minibus that could have held thirty passengers pulled up outside

Hulga, their guide for the day, looked around wide-eyed

Only two? she said

Well, make yourselves comfortable!

He had exchanged humorous glances with Inés as they chose their seats

Though his feelings for her resembled those of a close friend and had a tenderness that seemed to preclude any sexual or erotic element, there was all the same something unusually intimate about being beside her as they wandered through those wood-paneled rooms, beneath those gilt chandeliers

There was something unusually romantic

It was almost as if they lived together in the house—or were being taken round it, perhaps, with a view to buying it

Did she feel it too?

He couldn't tell

Maybe it was just a fantasy, his imagination running away with him, the folly of a married man in his middle years—and yet there was no denying the fact that their eyes had met at certain moments

If required to defend himself, he would have claimed that he was reacting to the way she looked at him

---

How to describe that look?

In his memory, it happened when he stood to one side of her and
slightly behind her and she turned her head towards him, her
chin close to her left shoulder, her black hair falling past her face
Part of her right eye was visible, beyond her nose
Part of her mouth as well
That mouth, which seemed to rest lightly on her face, as if the
petal from some rare and voluptuous flower had been carried
on the wind and landed there
The look, though—what was it?
Not flirtatious
Not inquiring or amused
There was nothing in it that could be taken as evidence of
anything
It was like a text that refused to restrict interpretation
In the final analysis, he thought, it was the *fact* of the look—the
fact that she was looking when she might just as easily not have
done, and the fact that he was the object of that look
That was all there was to it
But it felt like a lot

Later, during the recital, there were other moments
The concert hall could probably have held three hundred
people, but they were only two

how to make a bomb

Inés took a seat in the row in front of him, a few yards to his right
Mostly, he watched the pianist, or else his eyes drifted beyond her, to the plate glass window
He couldn't remember when he had last felt so relaxed
When he noticed the words "Lunchtime Recital" on the itinerary, he had dreaded the prospect, but now that it was happening he didn't want it to end
Every now and then, his gaze fell on Inés
Though she sat quite still, he was sure she knew that he was looking at her
He hoped it wasn't a distraction
Ideally, she would find it welcome, like the glow you feel when the sun's behind you, shining on your back

After the concert was over, Hulga asked if they would like to spend a few minutes exploring the grounds
Inés answered before he had time to consult her
Yes, she said, I would love that
As they climbed down a flight of stone steps, he glanced back at the house, which rose above them, almost Gothic, behind a scribbled mass of bare branches
The path led to a groyne or jetty that reached out into the lake, and they walked to the far end
A chill wind that smelled faintly of iron pulled at their clothes
When they could go no further, Inés faced away from the water and lifted her arms into the air, as if to embrace the house, the hill on which it stood, everything around her

The gesture took him by surprise, it came from a part of her he hadn't yet discovered
They don't know what they're missing, she said
He laughed, perhaps because there was more in those few words than she intended, or perhaps because it was something he might himself have said, given how he felt

Sitting in his garden in Dartmouth Park, he thought about that simple, joyful sentence, how it had stayed with him and gathered meaning
The absence of other people had allowed him to experience a sense of lightness and abundance he couldn't have predicted, and slowly but inexorably that lightness and abundance had prompted the idea that what was lacking in his life might not be merely different to what he already had, but less
And loss, of course, could represent or prompt a gain
If you prune a rose, new buds appear

He drew his jacket more tightly around him

When he and Inés returned to the car park after their walk down to the lake, the same empty minibus was waiting for them, like a joke that was being told again because they hadn't laughed the first time
Make yourselves comfortable!

There was something really special about that, Inés said as they set off

With almost no one there to listen, the music felt more free

I thought so too, Philip said, especially when she played that peasant dance

Yes!

Inés's brown eyes gave off a light or power that bordered on the physical

The liveliness of it, she said, and not a single person dancing

Nothing except the music, the water, and the trees

All the way back to the city they talked about how strange it was that only two of them had accepted the offer of an outing to Grieg's house, and how lucky they had been

Hulga seemed delighted by their enthusiasm, as though it made up for any disappointment she might have felt at the lack of interest shown by the other foreign guests, but he was thinking that it wasn't just the fact that it was a much smaller group than it should have been, it was because it was him and Inés, that was why it had been so magical

If either one of them had failed to turn up, there would have been no atmosphere, no mystery, no point

The music, the water, and the trees

And us, he thought

And us

When Anya said, I wish I could have been there, it pulled him up short, because in his memory of that day, in that entire experience, there was no place for her

He looked at his watch

It was after one in the morning

He stood up from the bench and went back inside, taking care to lock the door behind him

When he climbed into bed, Anya turned and pushed herself against him, one hand on his head, the other on his hip
Your hair's cold, she murmured
He listened to the wind move round the outside of the house
I was in the garden, he said
I like the garden
It's peaceful out there, under the damson tree
But it's February, she said
He smiled
Go back to sleep

7

A few days later, in Kings Cross tube station, his nausea returned
It happened while he was on the escalator, going up
Something about the people standing on the right, two steps apart, the way they always did
Something about the aluminium treads, and how they flattened as they reached the top
How endlessly, unthinkingly, they fed into the floor

how to make a bomb

The Kings Cross escalators had been made of wood until the fire of 1987, when someone dropped a match and more than thirty people lost their lives
As he approached the ticket barrier, he retched, though he managed to disguise it as a coughing fit
He was sickened by the living, not the dead

Once in the British Library café, he sat at a table by the wall
He felt that he was stupid for having come
He shouldn't have even left the house
As he sipped his breakfast tea, someone said his name
It was Jess
He had met Jess seven years ago, at the drinks party following an inaugural lecture by a psychology professor
She was a postgraduate student with an interest in the subject
As they stood in the corner of the room, he had said something that she found funny, and her laughter had been so abrupt and full-throated that everyone looked round
In that moment, viewed from the outside, they appeared to be having a better time than anybody else
People who make you feel good are rare
If he had been allowed to choose which of his friends would surprise him by appearing in the café, he might well have chosen her

---

That morning, she was dressed in a black leather jacket and a pair of fourteen-eye Doc Martens, and her short, dark hair lay flat, a few spiky strands reaching down across her forehead
You've got a Fassbinder look about you, he told her
I mean, he was fat, and he had bad skin, but you know what I mean
She grinned
I thought you were in Norway
Last weekend, he said
He took another sip of tea
Something happened to me
Something odd
He told her about the nausea, and how it had undermined his ability to function, and how the feeling had persisted, albeit in a diminished form, in the days since his return
He could feel it even now, he said, like a flicker at the margin of his vision
It was there all the time, under everything
When he had finished, Jess kept silent for a moment, adjusting her severe, black-rimmed glasses with a forefinger and a thumb
If you ask me, it sounds like a panic attack, she said, or even a psychotic episode
He looked down at the table
He had thought she might accuse him of being out of touch with the modern world, of feeling left behind, and he had been ready to counter with arguments of his own
He hadn't expected her to tell him that he was mad

how to make a bomb

Setting aside the psychological implications, what she was
saying felt too reductive
There was a bigger picture, and she had failed to see it
Have you talked to anyone? she asked
He lifted his eyes to hers
She was serious
You think I need to? he said
She shrugged
You said it had recurred
I get traces of it, he told her, like flashbacks
She suggested that it might be a symptom of something
Why can't it just be what it is? he said
What it is? she said
What's that?
He picked up his paper cup and drank
A few moments of clarity
One hand pushed into her hair, she gave him a look that
searched his face, then moved away
He placed his cup on the table in front of him, but held on to it
You think I'm having some kind of breakdown, Jess?
She brought her eyes back to his
Honestly?
He nodded
Yes, she said
That one word pulled the trigger on their laughter, a laughter
that burst out of them at exactly the same time and exploded
into the high, white space above their heads

8

That evening, when Anya came home from work, he opened a bottle of wine and poured them both a glass
She told him she had emails to attend to, it wouldn't take long
One foot on the stairs, she paused
Was I dreaming, she said, or did you spend half the night in the garden?
He smiled
Not half the night, maybe an hour
But it's February, she said
I know, he said
That's what you told me when I came to bed
As he put his wine down on the kitchen table, the bottle and the glass in Munch's painting came to mind
How present they had appeared to be, despite the absence of clear edges, despite the ghostliness
What were you doing out there? she asked
Nothing much, he said
Just thinking

When Anya went up to her study, he moved into the living room
The evening before, while they were lying on the sofa, by the fire, she had told him that he seemed different, and he had chosen not to respond

how to make a bomb

He stood at the window, looking out
Lights showed in the tall house that backed onto their garden
As he watched, a woman in a room on the third floor reached up and drew the curtains
Something flipped and rolled in the pit of his stomach
It was an ordinary Tuesday night, but nothing about it felt ordinary
He had the feeling things could come apart quite easily

His twenty-something years with Anya had been unquestioning
He had met her at a summer wedding
A strong, strange wind had been blowing in the Wiltshire countryside that day, and no one felt the heat of the sun
A lot of people burned
The young woman who almost collided with him as he stood near the entrance to the marquee was skinny, with high cheekbones and long hair, and her face had a relaxed quality, as if she had been laughing only moments earlier
She pulled her hair away from her mouth
Sorry, she said
I was looking for my boyfriend
He smiled slowly, almost fondly
Look no further
He was surprised at himself
He was never normally so bold, especially with somebody who looked like her
Perhaps her mood had affected his

Something had passed between them, a recklessness, a giddiness, nothing would be taken too seriously or held against you, say anything you want
She grinned
You're not him, she said
But she didn't seem entirely sure
The sun was shining over his shoulder, into her face, and he could see a wrinkle on her nose and a thin crease at the corner of one eye, and then the eyes themselves, the light deep in them, they were the color of leaves on the bed of a stream, cadmium yellow, moss green, and ginger all at once, and that made him even bolder
I could be, he said
She was shaking her head, but the giddy, reckless feeling was still there
My boyfriend's name's Charles
What does he do?
He's a soldier
Philip scanned the field they were standing in, the hedges on three sides, the wooden gate propped open, a copse of beech trees in the distance
He's probably in camouflage, he said
That's why we can't see him
She was laughing again and looking at the ground, her glass held away from her so she wouldn't spill champagne all down her dress, and some of it slopped over and fizzled in the grass, then she placed her other hand against his chest, he was too funny, she had to stop him making jokes

And it was true, he felt funnier than he had in years—or maybe ever

A tall man walked over
He had the eyes of a sniper, small and shrewd, and he stood very upright, as if he had a broomstick wedged under his chin
You must be Charles, Philip said
I'm Philip
While shaking hands, he issued a silent warning to himself
If the soldier thought he was taking the piss, he would end up flat on his back with a cracked cheekbone or a broken jaw
It seems you've met Anya, Charles said
Philip looked at her
The laughter was still on her face, or just beneath, which made it look unsteady
Anya
What do you do? Charles asked
I'm a stuntman, Philip said
Anya choked on her champagne and turned away
She told him later that it went up her nose
Really? Charles said
What films?
You know that James Bond movie, Philip said, the one where his Aston Martin goes through a crash barrier and into a ravine?
Charles nodded
I remember

Philip knew for certain that Charles didn't remember, he couldn't have done, Philip had made it up, but the scene was sufficiently generic to have that crucial ring of authenticity
Also, people would often rather lie than admit to their own ignorance
That was me, Philip said
I was the driver
He described how he had wrenched the door open at the last moment and leapt from the speeding car
I landed awkwardly, he said, and broke my wrist
The soldier's eyes were gleaming
He was in awe of him, perhaps he felt they had something in common, they were both men of action after all
Heroes really
Philip was contemplating his left arm
It still troubles me, he said, on damp October mornings

Not long afterwards, they were interrupted, and he didn't see Anya again until the dinner and the speeches were over
It was dark by then, and everyone was drunk
The chill of a summer night in England, dew on the grass, a moon with fuzzy edges
Anya was under the pink lights, where the music was
"Rock 'n' Roll Star" came on
As Liam Gallagher sang about needing some time in the sunshine, Anya bent forwards, shaking her long hair in front of her face

how to make a bomb

There was no sign of the soldier
Ah, the stuntman, she said when Philip went and stood in front of her
How's the wrist?
She had left the dance floor and was leaning against a pole at the side of the marquee, a glow to her skin, hair dark with sweat
Do you live in London? he asked
Yes, she said
She seemed surprised by how serious he had become, and how direct
I'm going to write to you, he told her
Is that all right?
You mean letters? she said
He nodded
I love letters, she said
No one writes them anymore
I do, he said, and nodded to himself, like someone making a vow, then he turned and walked away

The bride, a friend of his, gave him Anya's address

In his first letter, he wrote about the young woman he had met at a country wedding
He talked about her wit, her looks—how cool she was
He could have been describing a third person
He wanted her to see herself as he saw her

It wasn't lost on him that he was competing with the soldier
You shouldn't be with him, the letters were saying
You should be with me
He filled them with anecdotes, funny things he had seen or heard, he did his best to entertain her, suspecting that a sense of humor was the one weapon the soldier didn't have
At first he signed the letters "Stuntman," but gradually, as the tone became more personal, and he began to ask her whether they could meet, he started using his own name, he started signing the letters "Philip," and it was strange how intimate it seemed suddenly, to write his name, perhaps because it had been introduced so intermittently, and so late
It was almost as if he had become two people—"Stuntman," who was forward and amusing, and who noticed everything, and "Philip," who was quieter and more emotional, and noticed only her—and the task that faced him, the conundrum he had set himself, was to reconcile the one with the other, to turn them into a single person, someone she would happily go out with, someone she might even love

It took about three months

At last she agreed to meet him in a pub in Hampstead, up the road from where she lived
He settled by the window with a pint of Guinness
He was waiting for a young woman he still longed for, but couldn't properly remember

how to make a bomb

When she walked towards him a quarter of an hour later in a
black ribbed jersey and black leggings, it took him a moment to
realize that it was her
He had these images of her—the sun reaching into eyes the
color of wet leaves, the bright laughter that spilled out of her
and the fizz of champagne on the grass, her sweat-darkened hair
falling across her face as she danced beneath the disco lights—
and they were so ingrained in him, so vivid, that he had trouble
adjusting to the young woman who stood before him

Once he had bought her a drink, she leaned forwards, over the
table
So what do you really do? she asked
He smiled
I hope you're not going to be disappointed, he said
I did a degree in engineering, but I jumped tracks when I was in
my early twenties
These days I teach history at King's
No way, she said
It turned out that she was an academic too
She had almost finished her masters in German literature, and
would soon be taking up a position as a junior lecturer
He told her that when they first spoke, at the wedding, he had
noticed something, not so much an accent as a cadence or an
intonation
She was from Berlin originally, she said, though she had lived in
London for the past twelve years

Over a second drink, she felt sufficiently at ease to bring up the subject of her boyfriend
The soldier's away, she said, but that doesn't mean
No, of course not, he said quickly
In his letters, he always referred to Charles as "the soldier," a strategy designed to turn him into something abstract and impersonal, to take away his magic
To make him easier to leave
Now Anya was calling him "the soldier" too
It was going better than he could have hoped

Ten days later, they met in a different pub, and this time she stayed longer, and then, during the first week of December, she told him her relationship with Charles was over
She took him back to her flat in Belsize Park, and she made gimlets with Rose's lime juice, a recipe she had lifted from *The Long Goodbye*, and they ended up in bed together
You have to tell me everything, she said
I don't like being in the dark
Of course, he said
Always
As he lay next to her in the middle of the night, he remembered struggling to stay awake
He wanted to go on lying next to her, and know that he was lying next to her

To close his eyes would be an act of complacency
A squandering
He remembered thinking that he had never been happier, and that things would be different from now on, and he wasn't wrong

Yes, his years with Anya had been unquestioning, he thought as he turned from the living room window and reached for his wine
He hadn't been unfaithful, and hadn't felt the need to be
Was that the definition of happiness, not even feeling tempted?
Sometimes other men would tell him how lucky he was—*you and Anya, you're so perfect together*—and he would smile and shake his head and say luck had nothing to do with it
He had fought for Anya, he would say
He had fought against a soldier, and he had won

9

One night in March, as he and Anya were sitting down to eat, she repeated what she had said a week or two earlier, when he returned from Norway
You're different
I can't seem to talk to you

She was looking straight ahead, towards the garden, her glass of wine untouched
Or maybe it's you who can't seem to talk, she went on, or when you talk I don't know what you're saying
Instead of changing the subject, as he had before, or pretending that he didn't understand, he found he was nodding
I know, he said
His clarity had come at a price
The feelings of nausea, whether low-level or full-blown, were with him all the time
It was true that he was different

I might have to go away, he said
Anya looked at him
Again?
He hardly registered her surprise
He was too surprised himself
The idea that he might have to leave hadn't occurred to him, not until that moment
Is it for the book? she asked
He was supposed to be writing about Priscus of Panion, a fifth-century historian, and he had made some headway before the conference in Bergen
He had made none since
No, he said
This is something else
Anya downed her wine in one, then reached for the bottle and filled her glass again

how to make a bomb

He had seen her behave like this before, when she was nervous or upset
You told me you wouldn't keep things from me, she said
You made that promise to me once
I know, he said
There were tears in her eyes
He reached across the table and put a hand on hers
Anya, he said
Though he was holding her hand, he sensed that she had withdrawn from it, she had to protect herself against him, safeguard something in herself
If I tell you, he said, you'll think I'm mad
She shook her head
Just tell me
He decided to be as straightforward as he could
It's reality, he said
I'm finding it unbearable
She sat back in her chair and folded her arms
Is this one of your jokes?
No, he said
How he wished he hadn't tried to put it into words
He had known that it would come out wrong
His eyes were lowered, he was staring at the table like someone guilty or ashamed
The woman he loved was watching him
He could feel it

And then he sensed a change in her, almost like a shift in the barometric pressure
When he lifted his eyes, she was standing over by the sink, with her back to him
Are you sure you have to go? she asked
You don't have to make it so dramatic, he told her
It feels dramatic, she said
She was still facing away from him
I need to work something out, he said, that's all
I don't think I can do it here
She began to stack their dirty plates into the dishwasher
Do what you have to do, she said

II

deep song

I

His EasyJet flight touched down in Seville on a Thursday morning at the end of March
The temperature was 22 degrees Celsius, his iPhone said
Zero % chance of rain
He put his sunglasses on and took a taxi to Santa Justa railway station
His Spanish was rusty, but the driver spoke to him as if he was fluent in the language
Everything seemed effortless
Once in the station, he checked the departures board
There was a train for Cádiz in twenty minutes
He bought a ticket and took an escalator to the platform, one level down

Leaving London had not been easy
The nausea hit him the moment he arrived at Gatwick airport
As he stepped onto the shuttle that connected the South Terminal to the North, he was exposed to the shrill

beep-beep-beep of the closing doors and a series of infantilizing health and safety announcements
The journey itself was over in a matter of seconds, the shuttle's whole existence seeming unnecessary and overelaborate, like a mickey-take or a pastiche

He was reminded of his last trip on a Virgin West Coast train
When he pressed the LOCK button on the toilet door, he had activated a prerecorded female voice
She began to go through items that he shouldn't think of flushing, her list including wet wipes, gum, old phones, junk mail, sweaters, dreams, and goldfish
It wasn't just the feeble attempt at surreal comedy that he objected to
It wasn't just the woman's chirpy tone
It was the fact that you were forced to listen to her say the same thing *every time you went to the toilet*

Luckily, the journey to the North Terminal was over before he knew it, but he had forgotten about Duty Free, the glitzy, tyrannical no-man's-land that lay between Security and the Departure Lounge
If you wanted to get to your gate—and frankly, how else were you going to fly?—you had no choice but to run a seemingly endless gauntlet of wines and spirits, perfumes, tins of biscuits, souvenirs, and toys

Staff with artificial smiles tried to lure you in with their special offers and their discounts
Three for the price of two, 50% off
Buy one get one free

Give me 100% off, he wanted to shout at the top of his voice
Give me three for the price of none

But the aspect of Duty Free that he despised the most was the path that wound its way past the promotions and the shops, how it was made up of one lazy curve after another, a meandering that wasn't actually a meandering at all, but a progress that was deliberate, enforced, and also underhand
You weren't supposed to notice it, you see?
It was intended to lull you into feeling that you were acting of your own free will
Had the route through Duty Free been dead straight, like a Roman road, he could have hurried along, not looking to the right or the left, but its serpentine nature prevented that
It slowed you down, right down
Some marketing supremo had thought of it
Some guru of industrial design
And he couldn't even keep his eyes lowered because the ground beneath his feet was a shiny black and silver, and inlaid with fragments of glitter
It was integral to the concept, part of the manipulation

how to make a bomb

You could be forgiven for thinking that you'd been admitted to some kind of exclusive nightclub
You were in a VIP area, an inner sanctum
You felt like a star
And stars need fragrances and alcohol
Stars need toys
The feeling of dizziness and disconnection was intense, and he had no idea how he survived
He could have collapsed on that terrible sparkling floor, in that bright and windowless consumer dungeon
He could have had a stroke in there
MAN DIES IN DUTY FREE

Once he was out the other side, he went to the Departure Lounge toilets, locked himself in a cubicle, and sat on the closed lid with his head clasped in his hands
No announcements, no special offers, just drabness, and water trickling, and the pungent mingling of shit and bleach
He wasn't sure how long he sat there for or how he eventually made it to his gate
The stewardess who scanned his boarding pass gave him a look
I was feeling a bit faint earlier, he told her
I'm fine now, though

He glanced out through the window of the train
An empty motorway ran parallel

Beyond the road was land and more land, some of it arable and green, the rest a desiccated yellow
Spain
The manufactured world was less in evidence
Maybe that was why he felt at ease
He saw a water tower, a railway crossing, a red truck heading south
Later, on a ridge, he saw a bull in silhouette
He knew he was looking at an advertisement for sherry, but it was so basic and so stark, so utterly archetypal, that the possibility of other versions didn't occur to him
In that sense, it resembled something natural
Maybe there was a political aspect to his nausea after all
What if he was responding to how the earth had been engulfed, suppressed, obscured?
We were surrounded by things we hadn't asked for, and didn't want
Things that upset or damaged us
The thought of his son flew across his mind like a crow across a field, or like the shadow of a cloud, then it was gone

2

Cádiz startled him with its whiteness
Most of the buildings were white, and they had white shutters too

how to make a bomb

Even the light was white
He had booked four nights at the Parador, a sleek four-star hotel at the tip of the peninsula
After that, he didn't know

His taxi driver, a young man with a shaved head and a sleeve tattoo on his right arm, asked if he was on holiday
Not really, Philip said
It's more like I'm exploring an idea
The driver tipped him a look in the rearview mirror
What idea's that?
Philip thought of Seth again
I don't like the way we live, he said
Things need to change
The driver was still looking at him in the mirror
Are you an anarchist?
Philip laughed
I'm not sure, he said
Perhaps
An anarchist would never say "perhaps," the driver said
He would say "of course"

Philip was distracted by the sight of one of the giant rubber trees Cádiz was known for, the trunk oddly fluted, the twisted roots clutching at the ground
Some local people liked to claim that Christopher Columbus brought the *Ficus macrophylla* back from the New World

According to experts, though, the trees dated from the early nineteenth century

My problem is this, Philip told the driver
Everything I see around me has been thought about
Everything has been *made*
The driver said he didn't understand
When I see a car, Philip said, I start thinking about all the decisions that went into it
Behind that car are many other versions of that car
It's the same with a commercial on TV or that T-shirt you're wearing
I have a sense of duplication, a feeling of superfluity, it's too much to take in, it's like a kind of bombardment
How wonderful, he thought, this shift from English into Spanish
The words seemed to be offering themselves
Duplicación, superfluidad
Bombardeo
And there's an even deeper and more fundamental question, he went on
Did that car need to exist in the first place?
He paused
If I'm looking at a tree, there's only a tree
If I'm looking at a river, it's the same
It's more restful, the driver said
Yes, Philip said
That's a good way of putting it

how to make a bomb

On a wall not far from your hotel, the driver told him, there's a graffiti that says *To build another society, you have to destroy this one*
Philip nodded
I agree
Perhaps you're an anarchist after all, the driver said
Philip leaned forwards in his seat, his mouth close to the driver's ear
If I was an anarchist, he said, I wouldn't say "perhaps"
The driver laughed

Philip was pleased by everything they passed on that short taxi ride—a small square bristling with palms, the Moorish arch on a shuttered window, a strip of blue sea at the far end of a narrow street—and the pleasure was immediate, unthinking
How long will it take, the driver asked, to explore this idea of yours?
I bought a one-way ticket, Philip said
You're serious, the driver said
Philip nodded again
The taxi pulled up outside a building he recognized from images he had seen online—pale-blue mirror glass, biscuit-colored concrete, steel
Behind your hotel, the driver said, are many other versions of the same hotel
He turned in his seat and gave Philip a grin
Philip grinned back
You learn fast, he said

3

That evening, he wandered through the old part of the city, looking for somewhere to have dinner
Light oozing, dun-colored, from the streetlamps, the walls of the buildings cracked and crumbling
A low-tide smell of rock pools and wet sand
He had emailed Inés a few hours earlier, letting her know that he was in Cádiz
As yet, she hadn't replied
It was possible that she would ask what he wanted
He didn't really have an answer
All he knew was that he couldn't separate the fact that he had met her and spent time with her from what had happened to him on the way to Bergen airport

He found himself in a small square, the windows of the houses outlined in bright-yellow paint
There was a shrine to the Virgin made from ceramic tiles
There was also a restaurant
A waiter showed him to a table that stood against the front wall
Or would you prefer to sit inside? the waiter asked
Philip shook his head
After studying the menu, he ordered *pimientos de padrón* and *boquerones en vinagre* and half a liter of Albariño
The wine came first, followed by the water and the bread

how to make a bomb

The air was warm for the time of year, the sky a deep, unlikely blue
From where he sat he could watch locals passing through the square
Anya would like this place, he thought
He had to remind himself why she wasn't there, but the momentary lapse did nothing to diminish the happiness he felt
The anchovies arrived, fanned out like the petals of a flower, their creamy flesh tinged with light brown and a trace of pink
The peppers came next, piled in a heap
Tiny salt crystals glittered on their glossy, dark-green skins
As he filled his wineglass for the second time, his phone vibrated on the table
An email had arrived

Philip!
What a surprise
Are you free for lunch tomorrow?
Come to the Faculty of Medicine at 2 pm
Inés

She had said she was surprised, but she didn't sound surprised
This seemed in character
He saw her as someone who was difficult to ruffle or wrong-foot
He looked away into the square

They would have lunch, and then—then what?
He didn't have the first idea
Up until the conference in Bergen, his life had been ordered and predictable
There was the teaching, the research
The writing of articles and books
He had always prided himself on his ability to establish and adhere to a routine
Even when he was on sabbatical, as he had been since the beginning of the current academic year, the weeks and months that lay ahead could be envisaged
Now, though, the future had been wiped clean, like a blackboard following a lecture, and anything could be written there
Anything at all
He poured himself another glass of Albariño
The carafe was almost empty

After the lecture he had given in Bergen, Inés had approached him while he was signing books
She stood close by, not saying anything, but not leaving either
He suggested they go for a drink when he had finished
He had seen a bar called Tempo Tempo, he told her, it was further down the street, he could meet her there
She said she would wait for him, then turned away, drawn into conversation by one of the conference organizers

how to make a bomb

Twenty minutes later, he found her outside, under a shop awning, smoking
It had begun to rain
The look she gave him as she brought her cigarette up to her lips had a tacit quality, as if they were involved in something that couldn't be talked about
Something no one else was privy to
He felt a little like a spy
I enjoyed your talk, she said
This Merovech, he's the first in a line of great kings, and yet he seems to be hidden in clouds of uncertainty
I think that's what attracted me, he said
The scarcity of the sources, the reliance on scraps and hints
The need for speculation
He moved under the awning to shelter from the rain
What's your next project? she asked
I'm writing about a fifth-century historian called Priscus, he said
Very little remains of his work, and almost nothing is known about his life
Short book, she said
He laughed
She dropped her cigarette on the ground and as she stepped on it to put it out, her hair fell forwards, across her face
Bringing her head up again, she simultaneously pushed her hair back and blew smoke into the dark, beyond the awning
Klaus asked if he could join us, she said
I couldn't say no
Philip's mood dipped

This was their last night, and he had been hoping to have her to himself
After all, it was quite possible that they would never see each other again
Maybe he won't stay long, she said
If he was interpreting her correctly, she was telling him that they would outstay Klaus—or at least she hoped they would—and also, perhaps, that she wouldn't be making Klaus feel too welcome

Klaus was a philosopher from Munich
He wore suits that looked too tight for him, especially under the arms and round the thighs, and his head was so closely shaved that it seemed to have been polished
Philip had noticed him gazing at Inés
What if the philosopher was also eager to be alone with her?
He might prove stubborn, hard to shift
Of course, they could elude him altogether by changing their plans and going to a different bar, but Philip wasn't sure he wanted to be the one to make that suggestion
It was precisely his determination not to be pushy or overt, he suspected, that had drawn her in
Ambiguity was an essential component of their relationship, and also of the intoxication, and he was unwilling to sacrifice it, even if his last night with her was compromised as a result

It was a Saturday and the bar was packed, but they found a flight of stairs at the back that led to a mezzanine
Separated from the crowd below by slender wooden railings, the mezzanine had an exclusive feeling, though in fact it could be used by anybody
Once they had settled at the far end, Inés in an armchair, Philip at right angles to her, on a sofa, he perceived another advantage
If Klaus walked in, he would be faced with a crush of people, and might not realize the mezzanine existed
He reached for his drink and looked across at her
I never asked you
Are you with someone?
There was a poet, she said
She made a vague, dismissive gesture with her glass
Before that, I was seeing a flamenco guitarist
He was older
I used to listen to flamenco when I was about fifteen, Philip told her
Sabicas, Tomatito—Paco Peña
One of Inés's eyebrows lifted, and a shadow of amusement, like a smudge, appeared at one corner of her mouth
You were romantic?
I don't know, he said
Maybe
He put his wine down
But you're on your own now
Yes, she said
What about you?
She paused, eyes lowered

There's a wife, no doubt
No doubt, he said
If he was repeating her words, it was because he liked the way she used the English language, not because he was laughing at her
And she's beautiful, of course, she said
He glanced sidelong, through the slender wooden railings
The music in the bar grew louder
Outside, the night was slippery and black
No moon

When he looked back at Inés, she had placed her drink on the low table and crossed her legs
I'm sure your wife is beautiful, she said
He sensed that she was pursuing the subject in order to dispense with it
That which remains overlooked or disregarded has a certain power, but once it has been acknowledged, even in a cursory way, it can be set aside and you can concentrate on what matters
He could hardly blame her
After all, he was the one who had taken the conversation in this direction

It's strange how comfortable this feels, he said
She touched her lips gently, almost cautiously, with the tips of her fingers, and her eyes glittered in the half light of the mezzanine like pieces of dark glass

how to make a bomb

Her black hair shone as if she had just walked straight out of a lake
People are mysteries, he went on, but not at the beginning
Lowering her eyes again, she reached for her wine
I've lost you, haven't I, he said
She smiled
I'll tell you if I'm lost
For the first time she seemed to be flirting with him, though he might have been mistaken
In any case, he didn't want anything to happen—or rather, the thing that he *did* want to happen was already happening
Sometimes you meet someone, he said, and you feel you know them
There's an ease, a quickness
An unspoken understanding
He leaned forwards, his forearms on his knees
The effect was to bring her closer
It doesn't really make sense, he went on
You've spent almost no time with each other, your backgrounds have very little in common, you come from different cultures—and yet
She was to his left, the distance between them charged and humming, like the air beneath a pylon
To put it the other way round, he said, you can spend years with someone and suddenly realize you don't know them at all
People grow away from each other, she said
Maybe it's that, he said, or maybe there's a sort of taking for granted that we mistake for an affinity or a rapport

Maybe we become complacent, forget to pay attention
Inés was nodding
He asked if she would like another drink
My turn, she said

Watching her move through the crowd below, he felt proud that he knew her, and that he was with her, but this struck him as unearned, presumptuous
As if to reprimand himself, he moved his gaze beyond her to the plate glass window at the front of the bar
Outside, a man rode his bicycle through the slab of red neon that glowed and trembled on the street
He watched the reflection heal itself
Someone had told him that Bergen was the wettest city in Europe, with an average of 239 days of rainfall every year
Bergen was known as "the city of rain"

On her way back to the mezzanine, Inés lifted her eyes to his
She had known he would be looking
As she appeared at the top of the stairs, he glanced through the railings and saw Klaus standing by the door in a green suit
He had the sudden urge to throw himself full-length on the floor and pretend he wasn't there
At that moment, though, Klaus looked up and saw him
Klaus has arrived, he told Inés as she approached
Her face didn't alter

how to make a bomb

Klaus, he said when the philosopher appeared, can I buy you a drink?

A gin-tonic, Klaus said

Inés made a move as if to go to the bar herself, but Philip put a hand on her arm

You've just been, he said

He was telling her that he felt confident enough to leave her on her own with Klaus

Only later did it occur to him that she might have wanted to be spared

When he returned five minutes later, Klaus was nodding in agreement with something Inés was saying

His skull shone like a billiard ball, and his suit trousers were stretched tight across his thighs

Philip thought of supermarket mince and how it seems to press against the cellophane it's packaged in

Did all the men in Munich wear suits that were a size too small?

He had never been to Munich, and had no desire to go

The conversation was desultory for a while, though never awkward, darting from one subject to another and alighting finally, and unexpectedly, on the phenomenon of chemsex

It was Klaus who brought it up

Does it feel dangerous? Inés wanted to know
Is that why you're drawn to it?
Dangerous? Klaus said
He passed a hand across his shaved head
You mean, for my health?
Emotionally, Inés said, and gave Philip a subtle, glancing look which Klaus didn't notice, and which Philip wasn't sure how to interpret
If he was right, she was indicating that Klaus had failed to understand something basic, something that he—Philip—already understood
There's no emotion, Klaus said, only sex
He glanced at Philip, hoping for support, perhaps, but Philip wouldn't have taken sides with him against Inés, even if he had agreed
Klaus talked about the drugs he used—GHB, GBL—and how they made you feel
The access to a euphoric state, the shedding of inhibitions
The increase in your sexual appetite
You were in an unfamiliar apartment, he said, with strangers
There was no need for commitment
No one had any expectations
You were free
What if you want to see those people again? Philip asked
You don't, Klaus said
There are more people
He was describing rich possibilities, endless choice
Why then, Philip wondered, did his words sound so oppressive?

how to make a bomb

Inés leaned forwards, one hand clasped in the other, her manner intense, almost forensic
So you consciously separate sex from emotion, she said
Klaus stared at her
I don't have to separate anything from anything, he said
They were never together
You haven't ever been in love? she said
Lust only, Klaus said
Inés asked how old he was
I'm forty-nine, he said
And before there was chemsex, Inés went on, what happened then?
Klaus was smiling, not dismissively, but in a good-natured way, as if he was indulging a favorite student, and was entertained, or even flattered, by her struggle to comprehend
Sex and drugs, he said, they've always been available, of course, but it wasn't so well organized
So the world is better than before, Inés said, in that respect at least
The irony seemed lost on Klaus
Imagine living in the fifties, he said
What a nightmare
Not long afterwards he rose to his feet, telling them he was going back to the hotel
He turned to Philip and gave a little bow
Thank you for the drink
No GHB this evening? Philip said

No random sex?
In Bergen? Klaus said
I don't think so
Perhaps you're underestimating Bergen, Inés said
Klaus leaned over and kissed her on the cheek
Do you know something that I don't?
Inés didn't answer
Philip watched Klaus disappear down the stairs and reappear in the crowded bar below
Were you bored? Inés asked
Only a bit, he said
She smiled
You hid it well
He didn't notice
He wasn't looking at me, Philip said
If the observation surprised her, she gave no sign of it
Their glasses were empty again
One for the road? he said

He looked up from his restaurant table and out across the square
Here he was, in her city, and given the size of the place it was possible that she might, at any moment, walk past that shrine to the Virgin, past those windows framed in yellow
A thrill went through him at the thought of what he had done
What he was doing
Catching the waiter's eye, he signaled for the bill

On the way back to his hotel, the streets were warm and narrow, and saturated with a dingy, ocher light
Domestic sounds came from the houses—the clink and clatter of people having dinner, a game of football on TV, a baby crying
Unlike London, Cádiz had no background roar
He knew there was a beach nearby, and sometimes felt he was picking up the murmur of the waves
To walk through a city and be able to hear the sea!
He would like to have called Anya, but he didn't think she would understand why he was so happy
The only thing she would understand was that his happiness excluded her
Who wants to be told something like that?

One for the road
As he stood at the bar at Tempo Tempo, Inés moved past him, putting two fingers to her lips to signal that she was going for a cigarette
Once outside, she turned close to the plate glass window and cupped a hand around her lighter, then she stood facing down the street, her cigarette held to one side of her mouth, as if to minimize the movements she would have to make to smoke it
Two hundred and fifty kroner, the barman said
Philip paid and took the drinks up to the mezzanine
Our last night, he thought
Tomorrow he would fly back to London and she would fly back to Cádiz, and normal life would start again

Inés came and sat down, smoothing her skirt beneath her thighs
She looked at him with that open, receptive gaze that allowed for so many different interpretations
So you feel like you know me, she said, even though we only met three days ago
She had returned to the point they had been at when Klaus appeared, as if she viewed his presence as an interruption and had already edited it out of the evening
But it might equally have been the graphic nature of their conversation with Klaus, he thought, that had sent her back to this gentler and more subtle ground
You know how you read poetry when you're young, he said, and you hardly understand any of it, and yet the words have an effect on you?
The look she gave him now was like a smile, but one that was being held inside
That's how it feels, he said

He glanced sideways, through the wooden railings
Most people in the bar were drunk
A young blonde woman in a silver crop top was dancing among her friends, her pale arms in the air above her head, her elbows delicate, almost vulnerable
It's late, he heard Inés say
I should go back
When he turned to face her, she was already putting on her red down coat

how to make a bomb

His heart dropped inside him at the thought that it was nearly over
There was the short walk to the hotel, and maybe breakfast, if he was lucky, and that would be it

They left the bar and set off through the cold, wet streets
They saw almost no one
She told him she was looking forward to returning to Cádiz
She didn't think she could live in a place like Bergen, where there was so much water and so little light
He asked if she had always lived in Cádiz
How strange, he thought, to be asking the routine questions at the end rather than the beginning, and yet they had a kind of depth or richness now, informed as they were by everything that had gone before
No, no, she was saying
I grew up in Madrid and I'll probably live there again one day
Cádiz is very conservative
Not much goes on
Enough for now, though, he said
Yes, she said
Enough for now

When they entered the hotel, they found Klaus and two other conference guests having a nightcap in the lobby
They would have to pass the three men to reach the lift
Feeling he should be polite, Philip stopped

As they stood chatting, he saw Inés remove her coat
Was she thinking of joining them?
Jealousy snaked through him, but he instantly reproached himself
He had no right to feel anything like that
He had no claim on her
At the same time, if he was startled or dismayed by her decision, if he saw himself as being deprived of her, or even betrayed, it was a measure of how he felt about the evening he had spent with her, not to mention all the other moments they had shared
However hard he might try to persuade himself that his interest in Inés was intellectual or platonic, it seemed his emotions weren't exactly uninvolved
He noticed that the men had also watched her taking off her coat, as if the act had significance for them as well, as if they too saw it as an announcement or an opportunity
But then she calmly folded the coat over her arm, said goodnight to Klaus and the others, and moved on towards the lift
He smiled at the men, then followed her
The episode with the coat now felt like a feint or a bluff, though he doubted that had been her intention
His back was turned, but he could sense Klaus and the others watching
Did they think he was sleeping with her?

Once in the lift, he reached out and pressed two buttons—4 and 6
He pressed them quickly, as if to prove the men wrong

how to make a bomb

Or perhaps he was hoping to shield himself from temptation
He knew her room was on the sixth floor
She had mentioned it at the drinks party on the first night
I can see the mountain, she had told him, and then she had
gone on to describe the wooden houses, how they were built
into the steep slope, one on top of the other, and how it almost
gave her vertigo to look at them
You're obviously much more important than I am, he said
All I can see is office blocks, a few parked cars
He paused, then said, It's only VIPs who get the mountain view
She had laughed at that
In the lift he glanced at her and saw no expression on her face,
though he knew she had seen him press the buttons without
waiting to be asked
He had made the decision himself, and already regretted the
finality of it
What if he had simply pressed 6?
To go to her floor first, even though it was higher up, could
have been viewed as a courteous or thoughtful act
Also, it would have given him a few more seconds
He wanted to prolong the ambiguity
On the other hand, she might have seen it as presumptuous
She might think he was assuming that she would invite him to
her room
A series of glimpsed or cinematic images came to him
The red of her short skirt and the black of her hair as she leaned
against the wall outside her room, the corridor stretching away
beyond her, an EXIT sign at the far end

The mountain framed in the window, lights on in the houses, as she bent quickly and plucked two vodkas from the minibar, the little bottles chinking in her hand
Her bare arms raised, her elbows pointing outwards, as she stood before the bathroom mirror, pinning up her hair, her beauty more than equal to the merciless white light
In the small space of the lift he turned to face her
You took your coat off, he said
I was hot, she said
She looked at him
You're not hot?
He shook his head
I'm fine
He watched the numbers change as the lift ascended
When they reached the fourth floor, there was a ding and the door slid open
It was happening too fast, too soon
Once more, he turned to her
Her face was close to his
He kissed her on both cheeks and then stepped back
Good night, he said
Sleep well
Then he was in the corridor, and the silver door closed over her, like water closing over somebody who's drowning

Back in his room, he took off his coat and threw it on the bed
He stood at the window, looking out

how to make a bomb

No mountain ridge, no wooden houses clinging to its slopes, just the neutral paved area in front of the hotel, a kind of precinct, a dead space
You're the VIP, she had told him on their first night
You're the one who has written all the books
She had been laughing as she spoke, everything about her glinting and alive
The images that had come to him in the lift had stayed with him
They were as vivid and haunted as Edward Hopper paintings—the solitary figures, the atmosphere of loneliness, the drab yet pungent colors
He felt like a Hopper painting himself
Man in a Hotel Room at Night
He picked up the remote for the TV, pressed the power button, and started flicking through the channels
A news bulletin about fishing in the North Sea, a sitcom with violent canned laughter
Golfing highlights from somewhere in America
He turned the TV off again and stared at the blank screen, a shadowy figure in a dark shirt
He couldn't remember what happened next
He must have taken off his clothes and thrown himself down on the king-size bed
He must have slept
At some point he imagined he heard someone knocking
He imagined opening the door
Inés was standing in the corridor outside

I'm sorry, Philip, I couldn't sleep
Can I come in?
But the knocking he had imagined, the knocking that he longed for, never came

There was the stark modern shape of the Parador ahead of him
He walked up the wide steps and through the lobby with its gleaming surfaces and its Milanese-style sofas

Once in his room, he lay down in the dark
The bed heated up
The air closed round him, and his lungs felt tight
He looked at his phone
12:38
He moved across the sheet until he found a patch that was still cool

There are more people
What Klaus had said that night in Tempo Tempo had been so offhand, so nonchalant
A statement of the obvious—to him, at least
Apps like Tinder, Bumble, and Hinge resembled the catalogs that households used to receive in the post, only the products were human beings now, and they cost nothing

People were voluntarily and eagerly self-marketing
This is what I have to offer
But there was a reductive element, wasn't there?
A person had become a source of pleasure, like a bar of chocolate
You want 55% cocoa or 90%?
You want praline?
Supermilk?
As for the mystery that he—Philip—had talked to Inés about before Klaus arrived, presumably Klaus would have considered the entire discussion not only beside the point but laughable
What difference did it make if you knew someone or not?
All that mattered was negotiation and consent
It was about the number of holes, and which ones were available
To live with the same person for years and allow that person to become a mystery would constitute imprisonment for Klaus
To be bound by that loose but resilient feeling known as love would be anathema
He didn't need it or understand it
He had no time for it
There are more people

Philip looked at his watch again
2:17
Had he slept at all?

4

His dreams had a sticky, tangled quality
On waking, he struggled to free himself, his mind filled with lurid, glinting green, a river winding through a jungle, the wing of an insect seen up close
His phone said 5:41

He slid the window open and went out onto the balcony
It was beginning to get light
An Olympic-size outdoor swimming pool lay below, with two smaller pools nearby
Mist swirled across their still, gray surfaces
Beyond them was the bay
The air was fresh, almost raw, and smelled of fish grilled on a bed of coals
There was no horizon, only a blurring, a kind of haze
Out of such weather anything might come
Longships from a thousand years ago, their oars dipping to the water, then lifting again, blades dripping
A sea monster with scarred flanks and gaping jaws
A mermaid's song
He felt no nervousness or fear, only a quiet expectancy

---

how to make a bomb

Back in his room, he lay down again
The previous morning, when he said goodbye to Anya, she had been remote
It was as if he had left three weeks earlier, when he first told her he might have to leave
As if she was already used to the idea of him being gone
Usually when he went on a trip she came to the front door to wave him off, but this time she stayed at the kitchen window, with her back to him
Beyond her was the garden, emerging from the dark
The unmowed lawn, the bench salvaged from a chapel, the small white petals on the damson tree
He remembered thinking that the blossom had come early
Goodbye, Anya, he said
Goodbye, she said, not turning round

He closed the front door behind him, then he opened it again, hoping for one last glimpse of her
The hall was empty
Though he felt the urge to go back into the house, he resisted
He knew what she would say if he reappeared
Did you forget something?
He would shake his head
I just wanted to say goodbye
You already did that, she would say
Sometimes there was a literal quality about her, an impatience with anything that seemed inefficient or sentimental

I wanted to say it again, he would say, attempting a smile, and she would give him an exasperated look
Goodbye's a word you only need to say once, she would tell him
That's the whole point of it

Out on the street his Uber was waiting, and yet he couldn't bring himself to move
How long did he stand there for?
No more than a minute, though it felt like an eternity
In the end, he had no choice but to pull the door shut and turn away
Afterwards, he wondered whether Anya had noticed how long it took for him to leave the house
If so, what would she have thought?

He lay on the bed in his room
Through the open window came the revving of a car, the muffled boom as a wave broke against the base of the seawall
The low, weary barking of a dog
None of the sounds were foreign in themselves, but the air they traveled through to reach him made them seem unfamiliar
The happiness of the night before flowed into him again, a happiness that seemed to flower out of nothing

5

He stood outside the Facultad de Medicina, a tasteful, modern building with a façade of brick and concrete
A single palm tree rose at an angle from the cobbled square
Inés had said two o'clock
He was early
Sitting on a bench, he watched the students come and go
Above the faculty building, the sky was an even, flawless blue, and he remembered her remarking on the lack of light in Bergen
He tried to imagine her walking out of the door and down the steps
Somehow he couldn't

He turned his face up to the sun and closed his eyes
Wanting to support her at the conference, he had attended a lecture she had given
Her subject was immigration into Spain in the years since the country joined the European Union in 1986
Her habit of reaching up occasionally to touch her lips gave the peculiar but charming impression that she was given pause, or even moved, by her own words
He approached her afterwards as she was gathering her sheets of typescript into a folder
He told her how much he had enjoyed her talk
She gave him an ironic smile

You didn't fall asleep?
Philip?

He opened his eyes
There she was, in a tailored black jacket, dark-blue jeans, and sunglasses
He stood up and kissed her on both cheeks
Under the fragrance she was wearing was the smell of cigarettes and coffee, a smell he remembered from their days in Bergen
You looked so contented sitting there, she said
He smiled
I was thinking about you, actually
Aware of how that sounded, he qualified it by adding, About your lecture at the conference
You were bored to death, she said
Admit it
They were laughing
How easy and natural it felt, he thought, to be standing with this woman in the warm spring sunlight

She turned away, and they began to walk across the square
When did you arrive? she asked
Yesterday, he said
He told her about the pleasure he had taken in the train journey from Seville, and in his first impressions of Cádiz, and in the restaurant that he had found
I've been there, she said

how to make a bomb

The food is good
She led him out of the square and into a maze of narrow streets
It's a small town, she told him
Everyone knows everyone

A solid wooden door opened onto a dark interior that smelled of aged cheeses and meat that had been cured or smoked
He followed her into the garden at the back, and they sat beneath a date palm, in the shade
She had taken off her sunglasses
In the Spanish light her eyes looked different, the irises more brown than black, the whites more white
When I last saw you, she said, you didn't tell me you were planning a visit to Cádiz
I didn't know, he said
It came as a complete surprise to me
She opened the sparkling water and poured them both a glass
What brings you here?
There was no wariness in her face, and no suspicion
It hadn't occurred to her that his sudden appearance in the city might have something to do with her
Then again, he wasn't sure whether his sudden appearance in the city *did* have anything to do with her
While he found it hard to disentangle her from what had been happening to him, he was still unclear as to how exactly she might be involved
Sitting across the table from her, in that sunlit garden, he wondered if she might be able to clarify things for him

At the very least, she could act as a kind of judge
She was certainly bright enough

I have to go back to our time in Norway, he told her

After their drink in Tempo Tempo, he had slept surprisingly well, and when he got up the next day, he remembered that she was leaving on the morning flight
Wanting to say goodbye, he had looked for her in the restaurant area
There had been no sign of her
He had breakfast, then waited in the lobby
At nine thirty, she stepped out of the lift with her case, her coat already buttoned
She sat with him for a few minutes, but they weren't able to talk properly, as the lobby was filling up with other departing conference guests, and they were interrupted by Klaus, and also by a French economist
Before too long, Hulga began to usher people towards the minibus
Inés stood up, and they gave each other a hug
She told him that it had been a pleasure to meet him, and he wished her a safe journey
Ordinary words, but the feeling that underpinned them had not been ordinary, though he didn't mention that to her, not at the time, and not now either
As he watched her walk to the minibus with the others, he wanted to shout "Make yourselves comfortable!" but she was

already out of earshot and nobody else would have understood the joke
He watched the minibus until it passed the railway station and vanished round the corner

Inés lit a cigarette, then leaned back in her chair, legs crossed
What a memory you have, she said

It's important for me to remember it in detail, he told her, because I think it has something to do with what happened next
He broke off
A slim, dark-haired man in a T-shirt and jeans was walking in their direction, and he was moving with such speed and grim determination that it seemed he might turn the table over and send the plates and cutlery and glasses whirling up into the air, like a juggling act gone wrong
He came to a standstill and stared at Inés
His face was pale beneath his stubble, and his eyes looked wet
She asked him what he wanted, her voice dispassionate, removed
She called him Álvaro
Words tumbled out of the young man so rapidly that Philip had difficulty understanding
At first, he thought this Álvaro might be a student of hers—she had given him a low mark, perhaps, and he was feeling aggrieved—but then he saw how calm and implacable she looked, and suddenly he understood that they had been in a relationship and that she had ended it

She turned away from Álvaro, eyes lowered, and put out her cigarette
When she looked up again, she asked him to leave
He tried to remonstrate
Just go, she said
Her voice was quiet, but it silenced him, and his head dropped, and he backed away

She apologized to Philip, then poured some wine into her glass
That was the poet I told you about, she said, when we were in the bar in Bergen
He didn't like you being here
He was jealous
Jealous? Philip said
He thought you were his replacement, she said
Is that the right word?
Philip nodded
She was so fluent that he often forgot that English wasn't her first language
You'd never have known, except for an airiness around her *h*'s
When she said "he," for instance
She reached for her packet of cigarettes
He said some things about you
It wasn't very pleasant
Like what? he asked
She hesitated
You're sure you want to know?
He nodded again

how to make a bomb

I'm curious
Okay, she said
He said you were old
He said I could do better
Philip laughed
What she had told him ought to have hurt, but these were thoughts that he had already had, and he was glad the poet had put them into words
It saved him the awkwardness of doing it himself

As he considered the role that he had been ascribed, that of Álvaro's "replacement," he realized that something significant was missing from his account of the last morning in Bergen
When he hugged Inés, he had been acutely aware of the puffiness of her red down coat, and her beneath it, just beneath
There had been feeling on both their parts, more than he would have expected
There had even been a suggestion of abandon
He had thought to kiss her on the cheek, but he was suddenly too close
He kissed her hair instead, her hair was in his mouth and also in his eyes, he felt almost smothered, deliciously so, then they let go of each other and he stepped back, and that was when she said, It was a pleasure to meet you, and he said, Safe journey
If he had failed to mention the embrace, it was because he was worried that he might have read too much into it

In bringing it up, he would seem to be trying to make a point, or pursuing an agenda, and that would give Inés the wrong idea
He wasn't thinking of leaving his wife or even of having an affair
That wasn't why he had come
All the same, it was one of the memories of Bergen that he treasured most, and it might even be relevant, since it could have contributed to the intense feeling of disconnection that overwhelmed him later

In drifting off into his own thoughts, he had stopped listening to her
I'm sorry, he said, what was that?
I don't see you as being old or young, she told him
To me, you don't have an age
He was flattered, but he couldn't think of a reply
But Álvaro, she said, he interrupted you
You were in the lobby
You were saying goodbye to me
My flight wasn't until the evening, he said
I had hours ahead of me
He paused
How I wish I'd left that morning, like the rest of you
She tapped some ash into the ashtray, blue smoke curling past her wrist
But then you wouldn't be here, perhaps

how to make a bomb

He eyed her steadily, his head at a slight angle, amusement in his eyes and round his mouth
It was a look he might have learned from her
She glanced at her phone, then stubbed out her cigarette
I'm really sorry, Philip, but I have to go
I have a class
He looked down at his empty coffee cup, the breadcrumbs on the tablecloth, his teaspoon clean, untouched

When he looked up again, he was surprised to see a gentleness in her, something approaching fondness, as if she had noticed his disappointment, and was moved by it
What if we resume this evening? she said
In that moment, the feeling that went through his heart was like a long, slow pulse, like the flush of color in a face when someone blushes
You're free? he said
She wrote her address on a napkin and handed it to him
The old-fashioned way, she said
Come at nine o'clock
He studied the napkin
Her handwriting was precise and elegant, with little flourishes around the capitals, suggesting someone capable of both extravagance and discipline
You pay attention to things, she said
It's something I've always liked about you
He laughed
She asked why he was laughing

You saying "always," he said
We only met in February

Out on the street they said goodbye and he began to walk away, not having the slightest idea where he was going, but then she called his name and he turned round
She was standing on the pavement in a fall of sunlight
How strange that I know her, he thought
It feels like such a gift
If you have time, she was saying, go to the Torre Tavira
It's the best view of the city

6

Cádiz from high up
The flat rooftops that spread out below him were scarlet or rose pink or the pale yellow-gray of sand and formed a maze of interlocking rectangles and squares, the streets between them only visible as straight, dark gashes
You might think a giant had reached down with a knife and cut into the city randomly
The whiteness that was so apparent at ground level was diminished, or even hidden altogether
Nearby, he could see other watchtowers

how to make a bomb

They had been built by merchants in the eighteenth century,
when Cádiz was the first landfall on the continent for ships
arriving from America
In the distance, and all around, the bright-blue glitter of the
bay
The way the color of the rooftops hid the color of the buildings
beneath seemed loaded with significance, and he found himself
studying the view, as if it was a puzzle that could be solved, but
nothing came to him

Towards five o'clock he returned to his hotel room, where he lay
down on the bed and fell asleep
He woke an hour and a half later in a panic
There was something he should be doing, or something he
hadn't done
He leaned up on his elbows, heart beating hard
The gray blind drawn down against the plate glass window, a
foot of fading daylight near the floor
Outside, on a balcony close by, a woman was talking on the
phone in Spanish
He lay back again, his head sinking into a stack of pillows
Let it all go, said a voice inside his head
Empty yourself
Then see what you fill up with
It won't be the same things as before
It will be new things
Things that astonish or confound you
Things you couldn't have imagined

7

He managed to pick up a bottle of Ondarre Blanco from a small supermarket, but lost his bearings in the labyrinth of streets behind Avenida Campo del Sur, and it was almost half past nine by the time he arrived at the address Inés had given him
He pressed the bell and the door clicked open
She was on the top floor, she told him through the intercom
She was sorry but the lift wasn't working
He would have to take the stairs

When he reached the fifth floor, he paused to catch his breath
The door to her apartment stood ajar, and he could hear piano music that he thought he recognized
He entered a hallway paved with worn, unvarnished terra-cotta tiles and lit by a Moroccan chandelier made of alternating orange-and-blue glass panes
At the end he turned right, into a spacious living room
Inés came towards him in a black sweater and white jeans, her hair damp from the shower
Sorry I'm late, he said
I had some trouble finding the street
I'm glad, she said with a laugh
I was late getting back from work
This music, he said

how to make a bomb

She moved a strand of wet hair away from her face
It's Grieg, she said
He smiled, then handed her the wine

There were dark wooden beams on the ceiling and the same unvarnished tiles on the floor
On the whitewashed walls were framed black-and-white images of performers from the world of flamenco
He recognized Diego el Cigala
The famous singer had the ink-dark eyes and untamed hair and beard of a prophet or a musketeer
Two French windows with stained glass fanlights led out onto a terrace
Between them were tall shelves stacked with books
What a wonderful place you have, he said
She put a glass of chilled white wine into his hand
I was fortunate to get it
A friend moved to Mexico City and said I could live here
Will your friend come back? he asked
Unlikely, she said
He got married and had a child
His life's there now

She opened the French windows and he followed her outside
The night was cool and the sky was clear
There were even stars
A city where you could see the stars and hear the sea!

He drank from his glass
The wine slid through him, its coldness bright, almost silver, as if he had swallowed a sword

He walked to the end of the terrace and leaned on the parapet
There, surprisingly close, was the cathedral, with its two baroque towers and its yellow-brown dome sitting snugly on the roof like an acorn in its shell
Fifty yards away, and some distance below, a man in a short-sleeved shirt was smoking on a wrought-iron balcony
A woman came out of the room behind him and put her arms around him and laid her cheek against his back
The man stayed still for a few moments, then flicked his cigarette into the dark
Philip watched the glowing tip arc down into the street

It's not so bad, Inés said, the view
She was leaning on the parapet right next to him
He turned to face her
There's something I have to say
His sudden change of tone seemed to amuse her, intrigue her too, and he had the feeling that she thought she knew what was coming
She didn't, though
Perhaps I should have told you before, he said, when we had lunch today, or when I wrote you that email yesterday
You're a master of suspense, she said

how to make a bomb

Like Hitchcock
He laughed
I'm sure you know this, he said, but I really enjoyed meeting you in Bergen
We seemed to have so much to talk about
I felt we could talk forever, you and me, and other people, there wasn't any room for them, they just got in the way
He looked for the couple on the balcony below, but they must have gone inside
It sounds extreme, he went on, but that's how I felt
It's how I feel now
But I thought I should put your mind at rest
I don't want anything from you
She was looking at him steadily, and something had gone out of her face
You don't *want* anything from me?
He shook his head, but felt less sure
No, he said
She turned away and lit a cigarette
Her face in profile now, she inhaled, the red tip crackling, then blew the smoke into the dark air that hung over the street
I thought you should know, he said
I wanted you to understand
Still not looking at him, she put the cigarette to her lips again
Okay, she said
But her voice had a flat or stoic quality, and whatever had left her face had not returned
It had been a mistake, perhaps, to attempt to address the ambiguity

---

Later, as they ate the shrimp tortilla she had cooked, she asked if he had really come all the way to Cádiz to tell her that he didn't want anything from her
Though she was mocking him a little, her question betrayed a genuine curiosity, and a continuing bewilderment
He put down his knife and fork and touched his napkin to his mouth
Something happened to me, he said
I need your help with it
She watched him closely, but didn't speak

On that Sunday morning in Bergen, he told her, after she had left with all the others, he had plunged into a state of desolation that he couldn't explain
He remembered looking at his watch
It was five to eleven
The time made him feel queasy
Something about the precision of it, the specificity, the way the watch hands overlapped
And then those recurring *v*'s
Five to eleven
The words had a stubborn clumsiness, like the concrete blocks that protect the coast against erosion
They sounded more like obstacles than language

---

how to make a bomb

He took the lift to the fourth floor, then stood at the window
in his room and stared at the paved area in front of the hotel
What was he supposed to do with all the hours that lay
ahead?
He wanted to leave, but couldn't
His flight wasn't until seven thirty in the evening
He was surprised at himself, this was so unlike him, as a rule he
was full of ideas, never bored or at a loss, but even his surprise
registered as a dull sensation, seemingly observed rather than
experienced, like an explosion on TV
He forced himself out of his room again
Along the corridor
Into the lift

Once outside, he set off in no particular direction, and with no
purpose other than to kill as much time as possible
Only three days before, he had explored the new city with his
eyes wide-open, looking in alleyways, and in shops, and in the
windows of people's houses
He had photographed the street art—a bearded man with a
crown on his head, a woman holding an enormous fish
He had even found presents for his wife and son
There was none of that engagement or alertness now
He was in a weird double bind
Imagine having nothing to say, but being unable to listen
Imagine being incapable of dying, but no longer wanting to be
alive
He ate lunch in a café

He had no memory of who served him or what he ordered
By half past one he was back in the hotel
He lay down on his bed in all his clothes and shut his eyes
He woke at a quarter to four
Darkness had fallen, and his feet and hands were cold
He felt tranquilized, but also panic-stricken
He knew what it was like to be Gulliver, set upon by unknown forces, pinned down by countless tiny ropes
He undressed and stood under the shower
He let the hot water beat on his head until the bathroom had filled with steam
When he had put his clothes back on, it was time to go

It should have been a relief to be on the move at last, but he had become aware of the journey that lay before him
He could imagine it in all its detail
The tram to the airport, the flight to Gatwick, the shuttle from one terminal to the other, the train into Central London, the tube or taxi home
He wanted the whole thing over with
At the same time, he knew he would have to see it through, stage by stage, moment by moment, and he had the terrible feeling that he might view whatever came next with the same dread or apprehension

Once on the Bergen Light Rail, the dread or apprehension seemed to rush towards him out of that imagined future

how to make a bomb

As he described the experience, Inés leaned closer, her chin propped on one hand, her dark eyes fixed on him
He must have talked for fifteen or twenty minutes, and when he finally came to the end she was still in the same position, as if the slightest movement might have put him off
That's it, he said
I've told you everything

She poured them both another glass of wine, then reached for her packet of cigarettes and her lighter
And you think what happened to you has something to do with me? she said
He nodded
I've felt that all along
That's why you're here, she said, in Cádiz?
Yes, he said
Still holding the cigarettes and the lighter, she rose to her feet and walked to the far end of the room
After a few moments of standing with her back to him, she turned and walked back again
You give me too much credit
You think? he said
She lit a cigarette and leaned against the wall, her right elbow resting in her left hand, her cigarette held just to one side of her mouth
What you describe sounds like an extreme reaction to abandonment, she said
We left for the airport, you had to stay

You were suddenly alone
He listened with great care to every word
She was thinking out loud, but he liked how her thoughts unfolded, one into the other
Perhaps those circumstances, she went on, people leaving and you having to remain, perhaps it connected with an old memory you have
Some ancient wound
The effect it had on you could be related to that original event
What happened in Bergen acted as a trigger
While her theory about some ancient wound might be valid, he instinctively felt there was more to it than that
Maybe it's the other way round, he said
She moved back to the table and sat down opposite
How do you mean?
Maybe the state of mind I was in allowed me to see something, he said, something I wouldn't ordinarily have been able to see
He asked for a cigarette
She gave him one and lit it for him
You're making this about me, he went on, because I'm the one who told you the story, I'm the one it happened to, but what if this isn't about me at all?
What if this is about everything *apart* from me?
Okay, she said slowly
So you believe you've seen something that is true and therefore valuable
Something that feels—I don't know—*pure*
It was as if he had been holding his breath and now he could let it out

how to make a bomb

I knew you'd understand, he said
What are you going to do? she asked
For the first time that evening his mind was blank
He looked into her bright, urgent face, hoping he might find an answer there
What would you do, he said, if you were me?
She drank some of her wine
I'd probably try to hold on to it, even if it frightened me
You'd hold on to it? he said
If you think you've seen something that's valuable and true, she said, why would you let it go?

I don't know your plans, she said later, as she showed him to the door, but I'm going to Jerez tomorrow evening, to a flamenco club
If you'd like to come, you'd be welcome
He stared at her in disbelief, and also with a kind of wonder
He had been hoping to see her again, but felt that he had already taken up enough of her time
She misinterpreted his silence
Maybe it's of no interest to you, she said with a smile
After all, you're not fifteen anymore
No, no, he said
There's nothing I would rather do
Great, she said
I'll pick you up at half past six
Good night, he said over his shoulder as he started down the stairs, and thank you

She was still watching him from her apartment doorway
Good night, she said

8

He took a meandering route back to the Parador, choosing streets at random
In the old part of Cádiz it wasn't possible to be lost for very long
Sooner or later, you would reach the end of the land
The water would correct you

In telling Inés the story of what had happened to him after she had left, he had chanced on an argument that his friend Jess might have found persuasive
Now that he thought about it, his experience in Bergen had been similar to that of someone who had dropped acid
One of the roles of the thalamus, a small egg-shaped structure in the center of the brain, was to screen out information it considered extraneous, which prevented people from becoming overwhelmed, and made it easier, or even possible, for them to function
While on the tram, his thalamus had been neutralized or circumvented, and he had been subjected to a flood of data, a kind of deluge

But it wasn't evidence of a breakdown on his part, as Jess had claimed
On the contrary
The off the cuff analysis he had given her was accurate
He had been privileged with a rare moment of clarity
He had seen the world unfiltered
As it really was

He turned the corner into a street called Calle Ángel and came across a man slumped on the pavement
The dim light of the streetlamps yellowed his white hair
He looked to be in his seventies
A woman of about the same age crouched beside him, one hand on his shoulder, a silver bracelet glinting on her thin, tanned wrist
At the sound of Philip's footsteps, she glanced round
He had the strange feeling that he was exactly where he was supposed to be—or, stranger still, that his presence had been requested
What happened? he asked
Were you attacked?
A husky laugh came from the woman
He fainted, she said
I think he drank a little too much wine
There's a taxi rank a few streets over, Philip told her
I could fetch a taxi
I can walk, the man said
He was trying to struggle to his feet

The woman gripped him by the arm, restraining him, then turned to Philip and signaled that he should go

When he approached Calle Ángel again, a few minutes later, in a taxi, the woman was leaning against a coffee-colored wall, smoking a cigarette
Her partner sat on the curb with his elbows propped on his knees
He had a truculent look, as if the situation had been imposed on him, as if it was all someone else's fault
Philip opened the door for them
Their names were Vernon and Allegra, the woman said as they climbed into the back
They were staying at the Parador
Philip told them he was staying at the Parador as well
I'm in the oil business, Vernon said
Olive oil
It was almost certainly a joke he had told before
Andalucía's the biggest supplier of oil in the world, Vernon went on
Bigger than Greece, bigger even than Italy
Vernon, Allegra said, you're boring the poor man
She eyed Philip from beneath her heavy lids
My husband always assumes that everybody shares his passion
She spoke in a drawl, her voice dehydrated, as if all the music had been extracted or suppressed
It was like a voice from another era, he thought
From ancient history

how to make a bomb

Then suddenly he knew what it made him think of, and the realization sent a shiver through him
She sounded like an oracle

Vernon had turned to face his wife
This reminds me of Bali, he said, the time I nearly knocked myself out, remember?
His truculence was gone, and he seemed transported, in a kind of rapture
It happened about ten years ago, Allegra told Philip
He walked into part of a beach hut
I had to repair his eyebrow with butterfly stitches
Vernon was laughing
You could have lost an eye, Allegra said
Philip asked if they had brought any butterfly stitches to Spain with them
We didn't think we would need them, Allegra said
We didn't know it would be so dangerous
They were all laughing as the taxi pulled up in front of the hotel

Back in his room, Philip slid the window open
As they waited for the lift, Allegra had thanked him for being so kind
I hope we'll see you tomorrow, she had said
He stepped onto the balcony
Lights were still on in the swimming pool below, and the rectangle of blue fluorescence hovered in the dark

This was his second night
He had two more
Then what?
Like the pool, his question appeared to exist in isolation, without a context
Like the pool, it appeared to glow
This not-knowing might be a part of it, he thought
He should dispense with structure, and open himself up to possibility and chance
That way, surely, something would emerge

9

When he woke the next morning, the weather was colder and mistier
He left the hotel early, wearing a jacket and a scarf
On Calle Sacramento a man stepped out of a bar with a bucket and threw the contents across the pavement, then took a broom and began to chase the soapy water into the gutter
The brisk strokes of the brush seemed to follow Philip as he turned the corner into Calle Concepción
That was how quiet it was
The light had a gauzy feel, and a pale-gold sun hung in the gap between two buildings, sharp-edged and circular, like a blank medal on a dull-gray uniform

how to make a bomb

A dog ticked past, glistening with sores
Stopping at a café near the Mercado Central, he sat outside and ordered a *ración* of churros and a glass of hot chocolate
The waitress had a chipped front tooth
She called him *cariño*
My dear
The churros were crisp and sugary, and the hot chocolate was as dense as a milkshake

As he looked out across the Plaza de la Libertad, he remembered something Inés had told him in Bergen, during the drinks party hosted by the mayor
When she went to a city for the first time, she always tried to interact with it on some basic level
She would do the kind of thing she'd do if she lived there
On a flight to Kiev the previous year, for example, a button had fallen off her coat
She searched the streets around her hotel and finally found a place that did invisible mending
The man in the shop couldn't match the missing button, so she asked him to replace all the buttons on her coat
The strange thing was, she preferred the new buttons to the old ones
It's like a transaction, then, Philip said
Usually, it involves a skill or a craft, she told him
Money often changes hands, but the gift can't be measured purely in financial terms
Something of the place passes into you

On his way back to the Parador, Philip saw a barber's shop
I could have a haircut, he thought
It might not be as tangible as buttons on a coat, but it would be an interaction nonetheless
When he walked in through the door, though, the barber told him that he was booked up for the entire day
What about tomorrow? Philip said
The barber shook his head
I'm also booked up for tomorrow
He paused
And the day after
You're very popular, Philip said
The barber shrugged
Two streets away, he said, the look on his face at once humorous and melancholy, you'll find a barber who is not so popular

Smiling, Philip followed the directions he had been given and came across a young man leaning against a railing, a lit cigarette between his thumb and forefinger
He told the young man he was trying to find a barber's shop
It's right here, the young man said
Philip looked him up and down
You're the barber?
The young man nodded, then inhaled
He had a peculiar way of smoking

how to make a bomb

Cocking his head and turning his hand so the back was uppermost, he seemed to poke the cigarette into his mouth
It was like watching a key being inserted into a tricky lock
Are you free? Philip asked
I will be, the young man said, when I've finished smoking
Philip leaned against the railing and stared at the white building opposite
Weak sunlight colored the top floor
Lower down, the façade was stained a brownish orange, where a pipe had leaked
In the writings of Priscus, Philip recalled a passage that described how the youngest son of the king of the Franks appeared in the marketplace in Rome, his golden hair pouring over his shoulders
It was an image so vivid that it had always stayed with him
In a house nearby somebody coughed
The barbers of Cádiz, he thought

At last the cigarette butt bounced into the middle of the street and the young man turned towards an open doorway
Philip followed him inside
When he was sitting in the chair before the mirror, a black cloth fastened around his neck, the young man asked him what he wanted
It's up to you, Philip said
Do whatever you think is best
He would put his trust in this young man
All outcomes were good

Sensing the barber preferred to work in silence, a silence broken only by the buzz of the razor and the deft, rapid snipping of the scissors, Philip didn't attempt to talk
Once, though, as the barber stood between him and the mirror, trimming the hair around his ear, he thought to ask his name
Lazarus, the barber said
I'm having my hair cut, Philip thought, by a man whose name is Lazarus

Half an hour later, when Lazarus had finished, he used a round hand mirror to show Philip the back of his head
His hair was shorter than it had been in many years, but the fact that he no longer looked entirely like himself seemed appropriate
That was why he had left London, wasn't it
To undergo some kind of change
Once again, he thought of Inés at the drinks party hosted by the mayor of Bergen
The strange thing was, I preferred the new buttons to the old ones

10

It was twenty to one by the time he climbed the steps to the Parador
As he entered the lobby, his phone rang
Sitting on one of the Milanese-style sofas, he stared at the phone's small screen for a moment before he pressed ACCEPT
Anya, he said, how are you?
I miss you, she said
He looked out across the lobby's polished floor
I miss you too, he said
It wasn't true—or rather, if it was true, it was true in another world, a world that was parallel to the one he had been living in for the past three days
He still loved her, but the emotion was distant, almost poignant, like arriving at a bus stop to see the bus pulling away without you
He wondered if she sensed a kind of shortfall
It's raining here, she said
She didn't sound at all downcast or resentful
He let his breath out slowly

Perhaps because he was relieved he talked about the blue skies, the palm trees, the smell of grilled fish, the weather-stained white buildings
He talked about Vernon and Allegra
He talked about Lazarus

You had a haircut? Anya said
It's really short, he said
You probably wouldn't recognize me
As soon as the words were out of his mouth he wished he could take them back
He had drawn attention to a change in him when there had been no need
He could so easily have failed to mention it
It's odd, he went on quickly
It looks much darker
Anyone would think you were on holiday, she said
His eyes drifted towards Reception, where new guests were checking in
Before he could summon a response, she spoke again
Are you leaving me?
He saw the bus again, but this time her face was in the rear window, a pale apparition that became smaller with every second that passed
No, he said, of course not
He was feeling dazed
When are you thinking of coming back? she asked
Are you coming back?
You're asking the wrong questions, he said
You wouldn't ask if you were me? she said, scathing suddenly
You wouldn't want to know?
He looked down at his shoes and sighed
How about "I've no idea"? she said
How about "Not yet"?
All right, he said

how to make a bomb

All right what?
Not yet
What do you mean by that? she said
Having coerced him into responding on her own terms, and in her own language, she was taking issue with his answer
He shook his head
You're going to have to trust me
That's all I can tell you
She made a noise that was either exasperation or stifled, bitter laughter
I don't seem to have much choice
He pictured her standing at her study window, arms by her sides, hands loosely clenched, as if she was steeling herself for something, a crowded room she was about to walk into, a cold, dark lake she had to swim across
This was the sometimes guarded but always brave and loyal woman he had married
I love you, he said
You mustn't ever think I don't
She was still standing at the window, gazing out
Brown hair, clear skin
He felt he had to hold on to the image or he wouldn't be able to talk to her
You can do without me for a while, he said
You'll have the house to yourself
She interrupted him
I don't understand
You're not telling me anything
Her voice was loud in his ear, unsteady

I'm telling you as much as I can, he said, and then he said, It's only been two days
When's your flight back? she asked
He said he didn't have one
She began to cry

Looking up, he saw the lift doors open
Vernon and Allegra stepped out into the lobby
Anya, he said, don't cry
Allegra had seen him, and she was moving towards him, Vernon following behind
I have to go, he said
I'll ring you soon
He took the phone from his ear and ended the call, but not before he heard Anya say something through her tears, something he didn't catch

What happened to your hair? Allegra asked
She was wearing a yellow cardigan over a white dress and sunglasses that covered half her face
I had it cut, he said
The barber's name was Lazarus
Vernon's laugh was short and sharp, like a cough
He had a plaster stuck on his forehead at a jaunty angle
Philip asked how he was feeling
Much better, Vernon said
I still don't have the faintest idea what happened

how to make a bomb

One moment I was walking along quite happily, the next
moment—he moved his forearm from a vertical position to a
horizontal one—I was flat on my face
Allegra placed a hand on Philip's arm and asked if he had eaten
He shook his head
We'd like to buy you lunch, she said
Vernon has reserved a table at El Faro, one of the finest
restaurants in the city
Philip didn't feel he could refuse

Twenty minutes later, as he studied a weighty menu bound
in chestnut leather, he found that he was still bothered by the
phone call with Anya
Though he had done nothing wrong, he could hardly pretend
to have been honest
But how to explain a relationship as subtle and unenacted as
the one he had with Inés?
You seem preoccupied, Allegra said
Philip took a drink of water
I was wondering about your accent
I grew up in Athens, she told him, but my father was Lebanese,
from Beirut
My mother came from Crete
A town called Rethymnon
The Cretans don't think of themselves as Greek, Vernon said
They're like a different race
More fierce
There's a word for it, Allegra said

Kouzoulada

It's a kind of craziness or passion

Vernon was nodding

They still have vendettas there

Allegra leaned towards Philip and spoke in a low voice

I don't believe you were thinking about my accent

You were thinking about something else, something more—how to say it?—personal

Allegra, Vernon said, we're trying to thank the man for his good deed

Stop grilling him

Allegra's smile was knowing and also mischievous, but she dropped the subject

When their main courses arrived, the conversation circled back to Crete

During their early years together, Vernon told him, they would often visit the island

They would rent a Vespa in Heraklion and set off along the coast

They took a night flight once, landing at dawn

By the time they reached the mountains, they were tired

They stopped the bike and slept on the ground, among the rocks

You slept, Allegra said

I drifted

There was just the warm wind blowing and the smell of sage and the blue sea far below

how to make a bomb

She let out a sigh

We had lunch in Rethymnon, with Allegra's mother, Vernon said, then we rode on

He explained that Allegra's mother lived in an apartment by the old Venetian harbor, but she also owned a house on the south coast, in a village called Agios Nektarios

Allegra turned to Philip, her eyes a curious, searching pale brown beneath their heavy lids

Have you ever been to Crete?

No, never, Philip said

He split open the salt crust on his sea bass

The white flesh underneath was moist and succulent

It's the most beautiful place, Allegra was saying

Stark and primitive, but beautiful

She adjusted the wide silver cuff that encircled her left wrist

There's almost nothing there, and yet there's everything

Philip felt something fizzle through him

In all his dealings with this elegant old couple, he had been acting in good faith, with no hint of an agenda, and yet he couldn't help feeling that what he was hearing was significant

At the very least, he was being steered in a certain direction

The evening before, on Calle Ángel, it had occurred to him that Allegra sounded like an oracle

Perhaps that wasn't as far-fetched as he had thought

When we were young, Allegra was saying, we'd stay for weeks on end
Later, when my mother sold it, we bought a house of our own, in a nearby village
He asked what the house was like
The walls are stone, Allegra said, and there are blue shutters on the windows
The front door's blue as well
There are fig trees
In the summer the air smells of ripe figs
And sheep droppings, Vernon said
He laughed
You eat and read and swim and sleep, Allegra said
The sun is very strong
You get so brown, you look like wood
We hardly go there anymore, Vernon said
We're too long in the tooth
He finished his coffee
It stands empty for most of the year
An idea came to him, and came with such force that it threw him forwards in his chair
Maybe you should go, he said
Philip remembered something Inés had come out with as they were driving back from Grieg's house
With almost no one there to listen, the music felt more free
Maybe life in Crete would have that quality
The simplicity, the naturalness—the nothing that was everything

It would be like taking all his recent thinking to its logical conclusion
I'd love to go, he said
His heart was beating fast at the thought of the offer, but he didn't believe Vernon would follow through on it
Between them they had polished off two bottles of Belondrade y Lurtón, the most expensive white wine on the menu
It was just the drink talking

In the taxi back to the Parador, Allegra told him they would be returning to England the following day
Hopefully, I'll see you before you leave, he said
At breakfast, perhaps

Back in his room, he realized that Vernon and Allegra had showed no interest in him at all
They had only talked about themselves
He didn't see it as indifference on their part, though, or narcissism
It was more like a subtle form of tact
Somehow they had understood that, despite his willingness to come to their rescue, despite his attentiveness, he wasn't quite himself
Apart from Allegra's one probing remark—and she had been concerned, he felt, rather than intrusive, despite what Vernon had said—they had chosen not to subject him to any scrutiny,

preferring to entertain him with their own flamboyant
thoughts and stories
Still, it gave him an eerie feeling
It was as if there was nothing to find out, nothing to know, as if
he had become nebulous, indeterminate
Was that why it had been so difficult to talk to Anya?

11

At half past six he was waiting on the hotel steps when a white
car pulled up, Inés behind the wheel in a soft black leather
jacket and sunglasses
Your hair's different, she said when he got in
He passed a hand over his head
Do you like it?
She nodded
You look—I don't know—not so English
That's how I feel, he said
Not so English
You're mocking me, she said
He smiled at her
Only a bit

how to make a bomb

As they set off, he described how he had been inspired by her, and she seemed surprised and flattered, not just that he had remembered what she had said at the drinks party in Bergen, but that he had acted on it
He told her about the first barber, who had been popular, and the second barber, Lazarus, who had not
She turned to look at him
Perhaps this is another message, she said
He didn't follow
The name given to the barber, she said, it's a name that is also intended for you
You have come back to life

In the last of the sunlight, they crossed the Puente de la Pepa, the big bridge that linked the old city to the mainland
All the windows were open
Cool air poured into the car
Inés drove fast, as he had guessed she might, but took no unnecessary risks
Her black hair flickered round her face
You're staring at me, she said, though her eyes were on the road
I'm grateful, that's all, he said
He looked out of his window, east towards Puerto Real, the sprawl of docks and warehouses orange in the sun
It was a Wednesday in early April, and he was on his way to Jerez de la Frontera
Could he trust the happiness that was rising through him once again?

There was the time his mother came back from a shopping trip in Brighton
He would have been fourteen
She had been to Habitat and spent almost seven thousand pounds on cushions, vases, rugs, and lamps
There was wonder on her face as she walked in through the door, but there was also fear
What have I done?
When she asked him to come downstairs and help her carry things inside, he must have said something because all of a sudden she was in a temper
Don't you want to see what I bought for us?
Aren't you even going to look?
I'm sure it's all lovely, he said, but *seven thousand pounds*?
That evening he had to create a space she could step into, a space where she could view her actions objectively, a space where she wouldn't be exposed to ridicule, embarrassment, or shame
In the morning she returned every item she had bought
A few days later, she told him she had been taken over by a force that was much more powerful than she was
It was like being possessed, she said
She had felt so happy as she wandered through the shop, selecting one beautiful thing after another
I felt so happy
She was crying when she told him that
Was something similar happening to him?

Was the exhilaration that he was feeling a form of derangement, like the nausea?
And what about the fierce blaze he had seen inside himself when he thought of Seth and the damage that the world had done to him?
What about that white-hot burning deep down in the dark?
What about that rage?

He was so lost in memories and speculation that they were driving up a hill into Jerez before he knew it
We're here already? he said
Inés looked at him, her sunglasses pushed up into her hair
It's only half an hour
She found a place to park, and they began to walk
The streets seemed hushed and secretive, the buildings rising sheer and white on either side, with ornate metal grilles over their windows
He had a sense of what it might be like to live behind those forbidding walls, inside those shuttered rooms
The pleasures would be simple, quiet
A decanter of red wine with dinner, a glass of black sherry afterwards
An opera on the radio, broadcast live from New York or Milan
A library of rare books
Crisp sheets on a four-poster bed
He would sit on a high terrace in the sun and dream of travels to distant countries and meetings with unfathomable strangers

He would acquire knowledge and see almost nobody
He would die in his sleep

Inés took him to a bar in a square filled with tall plane trees
Outside, a light rain began to fall
You remember last night, she said, when you said you didn't want anything from me?
He nodded
I don't like the idea of being a cliché
She asked him what he meant
A married man goes to a conference, he said, and meets a woman who's younger and unattached
He paused
If this was a TV drama, we all know what would happen

She reached for her drink, then leaned back in her chair
It's only a cliché, she said, if you look at it from the outside, if you generalize about it
But you can't generalize about such things
To generalize is a form of diminishment
She looked down into her drink
Also, it's not very intelligent
It lacks nuance

He smiled at her words
Go on, he said

how to make a bomb

If you look from the inside, she said, if you focus on the particular, you might see something unique
You already suggested that yourself, in Bergen
You talked about people seeming to have nothing in common on the surface, but overlapping in unlikely and unintended ways
She put her glass on the table, then used the same hand to tuck her hair behind her ear
When you said you didn't want anything from me, she went on, I had a problem with that
It felt kind of—what's the word?—proprietorial
But I turned up unexpectedly, he said, out of the blue
She interrupted him
That's my point
If you had stayed in London, there would be nothing to discuss
Now you're here, though, don't you think I also have a say?
I was trying to reassure you, he said
She was shaking her head
A man flies two thousand kilometers and appears on a woman's doorstep and what's the first thing he comes out with?
I don't want anything from you
How does that sound to you?
He didn't say anything, and nor did she, but he felt he could read the expression on her face
Finally, we're getting somewhere
It was as if he was a student of hers, one of the slower ones
She glanced at her phone
We should go

The rain had stopped
Old people stood in doorways, looking up into the night
Inés led him through the streets with the sure-footedness of somebody who knew them backwards
He understood that she had no desire, for the moment, to pursue the subject of what he might or might not want from her, and what her thoughts on that might be
He also understood that the subject was by no means closed, and that there was more to be said
There would be a time for that, and it would be a time of her choosing

12

The Tabanco el Pasaje was a skinny, L-shaped place, with stark white lighting and green walls
When they walked in, it was already packed
They had to edge their way through the crowd to reach the bar
On a low stage at the far end were a singer and a guitarist, both seated on simple wooden chairs
Two *palmeros* stood behind them, clapping
The singer wore a porkpie hat made of straw with a black ribbon round the crown

how to make a bomb

He had mournful eyes and thin wrists
The guitarist was dressed in a faded denim shirt, and his matted
gray hair hung to his shoulders
Behind the four men, fixed to the wall, were posters advertising
bullfights
Inés asked him what he'd like to drink
Above the bar, on a narrow strip of a shelf, was a row of glasses,
each no more than two inches tall, and each containing a
different type of sherry
The colors ranged from the dark molasses-brown of oloroso
through the glowing yellow-gold of amontillado to the almost
transparent tones of fino, and the prices varied from one euro
to one euro fifty
Amontillado, he said

Before too long, he was on his third or fourth
His Spanish seemed to have improved, and he found himself
talking to Ramón, a burly man of about his own age
You can't understand flamenco, Ramón was saying, without
understanding *cante jondo*, or "deep song"
Cante jondo had a great deal in common with the primitive
chants and incantations of the Indian subcontinent
There was an interest in enharmonics, which mirrored birdsong
and the calls of animals
There was a strict adherence to a restrained melodic line, and
the consistent, almost obsessive use of a single note
There was also the *voz rajada*—the cracked voice

The flamenco of today had grown out of *cante jondo*, he said, and out of a mysterious collision between the culture of Andalucía and that of the Roma people, who arrived in the late fifteenth century, after they were driven out of India
As a musical form, it drew on centuries of persecution and oppression
Was it any wonder if the themes were anger, hatred, guilt, despair, jealousy, defiance, grief, and pain?

Ramón went on to talk about the lyrics, and how they tended to be anonymous
Or, as Lorca once put it, they floated on the wind
It was always night
Love was stronger than death
The sound of weeping could be heard behind locked doors, through fastened shutters
Ramón quoted a few lines about a man asking his lover to bind his hands with her long black hair after he had died
Women's hair, he said, was often mentioned

Perhaps because Philip stopped listening for a few crucial moments, or perhaps because there were some words he didn't understand, but suddenly—or so it seemed to him—Ramón was telling him that he had been unfaithful to his wife
After seven years of marriage, he had slept with another woman, she was a flamenco dancer, irresistible, her hair a

how to make a bomb

striking blend of red and black, like blood drawn straight from a vein
His wife had learned of it, as wives always do
She didn't say anything for several days, though her behavior was different
Philip wanted to know how
Her face had no expression, Ramón said
She was cold

As if to warm himself, he ordered two more drinks

A week passed, and he thought he'd got away with it, but then one night he came home very drunk
It was late, and he went to bed without speaking to his wife
He woke up screaming
She had cut one of his fingers off while he was sleeping
In the harsh light of the bar Ramón raised his right hand in front of Philip's face
Most of the forefinger was missing
You know what she said to me? Ramón said
Philip shook his head
At least there's one part of you that filthy whore won't have
What did she do with your finger? Philip asked
I don't know, Ramón said
I never saw it again

Time slackened and doubled back on itself and though he was still talking to Ramón he had the feeling it was later, much later, and there was more that he had completely failed to grasp
Inés appeared, asking whether he was hungry
She could order anchovies, she said, and maybe some sausage, and there were also wedges of *payoyo*, a hard goats' cheese, topped with quince jelly
Food wasn't something he could contemplate just then
He saw the stump on Ramón's right hand and thought of how Ramón had never seen his finger again and didn't even know where it was
Perhaps his wife had thrown it in the trash
Or fed it to a dog
The green walls tilted, and the air around his head felt hot
I have to go to the toilet, he murmured

He seemed to be falling, not walking, and the bar swirled past him like the world seen from a merry-go-round
A black door swooped towards him, then flew sideways
Was that the toilet?
He fetched up on a tiled floor, his head between his knees
Later, he gripped the smooth edge of the sink and stared into the mirror, but the mirror kept sliding away, sliding away, and he didn't recognize the man he saw in it
The hair was wrong
He ran the tap and splashed cold water onto his face
He drank some too, and some of it spilled down his shirt, it didn't matter, it would dry

how to make a bomb

A man came in behind him
The man said something he didn't understand and stood at the urinal, then left again
After a while, he didn't know how long, the mirror stopped moving on the wall
You're all right now, he told himself
You'll be all right

He pushed through the crowd and out through the back door into an alley
Five or six people stood about
A woman wearing a white dress with butterflies all over it, the singer in the porkpie hat
Smoke from their cigarettes hung in the glare of a security light
He sat on a doorstep, his head lowered, his forearms resting on his knees
He couldn't see Inés, but knew she couldn't be too far away
She wouldn't leave without him
He drew cool air into his lungs, his forehead cold and damp
The dizziness was almost gone
The world seemed steadier
All the same, he thought he would stay where he was

He had been outside for about ten minutes when he heard a voice in the air above him
I've been looking for you everywhere

He knew from the boots and jeans that it was her
She knelt in front of him
Are you okay?
I felt strange back there, he said, but I feel better now
I met a man who only had nine fingers
Ramón, she said
He asked if she had a cigarette
She gave him one and lit it, then she lit one for herself

They sat on the doorstep, smoking

Ramón was telling me about flamenco, he said
How it's rooted in oppression
I think I knew that, but all of a sudden it connected with the things that have been going through my mind
When you're obsessed with something, she said, you become a magnet
If you're in love, for example
All the love songs that you hear seem written just for you
Smiling, he tapped some ash onto the ground between his shoes
I really liked what you said last night—you know, about keeping hold of what is valuable and true, even if it's frightening
I'm not sure it's enough, though, just to keep hold of it
What do you have in mind? she asked
He sighed
I don't know yet

She flicked her cigarette away from her, the butt landing on the far side of the alley
It's a lot to go up against, she said

A few minutes later, she mentioned that they had been invited to someone's house
There'll be more flamenco, she said
Maybe dancing too
She glanced at him through the loose strands of hair that fell across her face
Or would you prefer to drive back to Cádiz?
He looked into her eyes
Like a limo's tinted windows, they were opaque, hinting at a life that was different, glamorous, beyond imagining
I don't think I want the night to end, he said

13

They set off through the town
The rain was falling again, as fine as mist
The paved streets gleamed
Ever since you arrived, she told him, you've been reminding me of something
He felt ready for anything that she came out with

Whatever happened would add to him, nothing would be extraneous or wasted
It's *Don Quixote*, she said
He laughed
I've never read it
She walked a few paces before saying, But you know what it's about
Only what everybody knows, he said
The windmills
The full title was *The Ingenious Gentleman Don Quixote of La Mancha*, she told him, which was generally believed to be ironic
In the decades after the book was published, people thought of Don Quixote as a self-deluded fool
Later, in the nineteenth century and the first half of the twentieth, literary opinion shifted, and he was seen as more heroic, someone who was battling against a mundane and prosaic existence
He constantly misreads situations and gets things wrong, but his mistakes are understandable, forgivable
More recently, she said, he seems to represent a quest for personal identity
Through a period of madness, he recovers his true or deeper self
It's always one man against the world, though
He's mocked and ridiculed, he's the victim of violence, but he remains single-minded, faithful to his vision
She paused to consult a map of the city on her phone, then they moved on
It won't be easy for me, will it? he said
No, it won't, she said

Her answer was so swift and certain that it sent a little twist of fear through him
She stopped outside a tall, sand-colored house
This is it, she said

14

She rang the bell, and a hatch opened in the wooden double door, the small, square opening protected by an iron grille
A man in his early twenties let them in
His eyebrows had been shaved, then penciled in, which gave him a startled look, though his manner was calm, funereal
Crossing a tiled hallway, Inés and Philip entered a vaulted space
The house used to be a convent, she told him
This would once have been the chapel

Thirty or forty people had gathered in the room, some sitting at tables, others standing around in groups
The guitarist from earlier was seated on a chair, his right ankle balanced on his left thigh, his instrument wedged up against his chin
As he played, he bared his teeth, as if in pain
A woman in a shiny black skirt and a black blouse stepped into the space in front of him

Her mascara was so heavily applied that it seemed her eyes were caged
Heavy silver hoops dangled from her ears
She turned slowly, almost hydraulically, and clicked her fingers
Her dark hair hung down her spine in a thick plait, like a rope that might be used to ring a bell
It was impossible to tell her age, only that she wasn't young

After each long, sung phrase, which took her to the very end of her breath, she plucked at her skirt, hitching it up, and turned in a tight circle, stamping fiercely on the floor and flinging her head back, as if rejecting an offer or a possibility
The people in the room let out cries of approval and encouragement
To Philip, the timing of their cries felt arbitrary, and he realized how little he understood, how ignorant he was
Inés put her mouth close to his ear
Perhaps you already know this, but the traditional environment for flamenco is not a bar or a theater, but an intimate gathering like this, where everyone's involved
It's called a *peña*

The guitarist started playing again, and a woman with long, blonde dreadlocks appeared
She wore a midnight-blue dress down to the ground and blue eye shadow and a silver choker around her neck
There was a wide gap between her two front teeth

Philip didn't understand many of the words, since she was singing in caló, the language used by Roma people, but Inés told him it was the story of a woman who had been mistreated by her man
He was weak, he wasn't good enough for her, he came to a violent end
She still loved him, though, even after he was dead
The woman might have been treated badly, Philip thought, but she had survived, and the man had not
The fact that the love that had caused her so much pain was being sung about was both a symbol of her triumph and a reason for celebration
The song was evidence
A kind of proof
He remembered what Ramón had said
Love is stronger than death
It's always night

The next time he looked for Inés she was sitting on a sofa in the corner
The man she was talking to had the hair of a clown, all wisps and clumps, and he was smoking a stumpy black cigar
He wanted to be on his own with her again
He wanted to be driving through the dark—south, to Cádiz
As he approached, her face lifted to his
She asked if he was tired
He nodded
Is it all right if we leave?

I have a better idea, she said
She spoke to the man with the cigar, who inclined his head as if gracefully assenting to a request, then she rose to her feet and touched Philip's arm
She led him out of the chapel
Instead of making for the front door, she turned towards a flight of stairs
We can stay the night, she said over her shoulder
He felt nervous, but he followed her
What did she have in mind?
I drank too much, she said by way of explanation
I don't think I can drive

The staircase walls were lined with blue-and-white tiles up to waist height, and every floor was sealed off from the floors above and below it
There were no landings, and no windows
The convent's hermetic design embodied the complementary ideas inherent in a cloistered existence
There was an emphasis on interiority and devotion, the solitude one might experience in a monastic cell
At the same time, it looked outwards, taking the form of a fortification that provided protection against the world, the devil, and the flesh

When they reached the fourth floor, they passed through a varnished wooden door and on into a dimly lit passageway

how to make a bomb

Orange glass lamps hung from the ceiling
There was the smell of plaster and old stone
He had left behind the world he knew and might not find his way back
Did that matter?
The nervousness he had felt on starting up the stairs was cushioned by a dreamlike or narcotic sense of suspension, as if the act of ascending had involved divestment, a casting off

In silence, they moved through a kind of antechamber
There was a sideboard topped with pale marble and a tall, dark wardrobe with an upright mirror built into the door
In the foxed glass he looked stealthy, insubstantial
He was marooned between where he was and where he used to be, he had failed to materialize properly
He was neither here nor there

Beyond the antechamber was another, smaller room
Inés turned on the lamp
Two twin beds stood side by side on the bare tile floor, a wooden cross hanging on the whitewashed wall between them
We're not the only people staying, she told him
There are many bedrooms
She was standing over by the door
Are you going back downstairs? he asked
Just for an hour, she said

15

He went to the window and parted the heavy velvet curtains
The building opposite had a tomb-like façade
Its walls were sheer, and its shutters looked to have been closed for years
It was less like a house than a mausoleum
He opened the window
The building was so close that he could almost have reached out and touched it
He leaned on the sill and peered down
The narrowest of alleyways
Leaving the window open a few inches, he drew the curtains again, then he undressed, switched off the lamp, and climbed into the nearest bed

The sheets were cold and smelled of carbolic soap
He pulled the blankets up to his neck
He couldn't hear the music, only the tapping of rain in the alley and the creak of drainpipes and gutters
There are many bedrooms
He remembered nights in Bergen, how he lay on his back, one arm behind his head, and thought of Inés two floors above, on the other side of the hotel, the side that faced the mountain
He imagined a knock, and then her voice calling through the door

how to make a bomb

Philip?
He imagined putting on his hotel bathrobe and going to the door and opening it
What would she have said?
I couldn't sleep
Or, *I was feeling lonely*
Or, *There are people having sex in the next room*
He would have invited her in
Then what?
He had taken the fantasy no further
It had felt too hazardous

All of a sudden, Inés was in the room and taking off her clothes
He must have slept, then woken
She stumbled against a piece of furniture and let out a whispered curse
Joder
She had left the light off
She was trying to be considerate
It was so dark with the curtains drawn that he couldn't see her at all at first
Only when she was half-naked could he begin to make her out, her skin the most subtle form of illumination, all shadows and glimmers
Almost monochrome

Wearing only her underwear, she got into the bed that was closest to the door

He thought he heard her shiver

There was quiet for a few moments, then a rapid, oddly frantic rustling

She had turned onto her side, and she was looking at him

Philip?

Her voice was soft, as in his fantasy

Are you awake?

Not really, he said

There was a silence, then she spoke again

I'm cold

Yes, he thought with a smile

That was also something she might have said if she had appeared at the door of his hotel room in the middle of the night

I was cold

He was aware of his excitement, but it was subdued, low-level, a machinelike hum

He didn't say anything

Do you mind if I get into your bed?

There was nothing suggestive in her voice—she made it sound like a perfectly reasonable request—but his heart was beating faster than before

We don't have to do anything, she said, just sleep

There's not much room, he said

She seemed encouraged by the fact that he had spoken

It will be warmer, she said

Aren't you cold?

A little, he said, though he wasn't

how to make a bomb

She left her bed and slipped into his, then she lay down, facing away from him
He was aware of their bodies in the dark, the places where they touched
The small of her back against his belly
The back of her thighs against the front of his
Her hair smelled of the flamenco bar they had been to—cigar smoke, sherry, anchovies in vinegar, and something more buried, more difficult to pinpoint, like the bass note in a perfume
He felt himself stiffening against her
You're making this impossible, he whispered
He thought he heard her laugh—a quick, quiet exhalation
I'm sorry about that, she said
Then, moments later, You think you can sleep?
I'll try, he said

She drifted off before he did
He heard her breathing change and deepen
His left hand was under his cheek
He put his right hand on her hip and left it there
She murmured, but didn't wake
She was so near
Death could take me now, he thought
I would be happy
Still hard, he lay quite motionless and breathed her in
The smell of her hair

Her skin
He breathed her in with every breath

16

When he woke again, he was alone in the room
He could hear the shower running
He rolled over into the part of the bed where she had been lying, into the warmth she had left behind
He remembered what she had said during the night
Sorry about that
She hadn't sounded sorry
There had been a kind of relish in her voice
Some mischief too
She knew her power
I don't want anything from you, he had told her
His body had contradicted him

As he lay there, his phone rang and he saw that it was Anya
How could he answer, with Inés only a few feet away, in the next room?
What if Anya heard her voice?

---

how to make a bomb

He went and stood by the open window, hoping that the sounds coming from outside would disguise any sounds coming from within
Anya, he said
I'm sorry about yesterday, she said, getting upset like that
It's me who should be sorry, he said
She asked him where he was
He hesitated
Still in Cádiz, he said
Is that a guitar, she said, in the background?
He opened the window wider and looked down into the alley
Someone was playing a *bulería*, but he couldn't tell where it was coming from
This part of Spain is famous for flamenco, he said
Will you take me one day? she asked
Of course, he said
One day
No, she said, I know you
It'll never happen

A door opened behind him and Inés stepped out of the bathroom wrapped in a white towel, her black hair dripping
He pointed to the phone and put a finger to his lips
She nodded
I didn't know you liked flamenco, he said to Anya, turning back to the window
I like lots of things, she said
He asked if she had heard from Seth

She told him that she hadn't
Maybe no news is good news, he said, aware that he was sounding hopeful, then he fell silent
They had been talking for less than five minutes and he had run out of things to say
Not for the first time, the idea of returning worried him
He could hardly go back to his old life
Once you know something, you can't unknow it

And suddenly, almost uncannily, Anya seemed to sense the direction that his thoughts had taken
Listen, he heard her say
If you need some space, I understand
He stared at the blank wall of the building opposite
There had been occasions in the past when she had startled him by stepping back
He had worried that she might be losing interest in him, or even disposing of him altogether
That didn't seem to be part of her thinking, though
It was more as if she considered it unfair or vulgar to impose herself, and this came naturally to her, since she liked her own company better than anyone he knew
When he first met her, at the wedding, she had been so forward, so present
She had been traveling at the very front of who she was
Only later, when she was his girlfriend, did he realize how untypical her behavior had been
But why that day? he asked her once

Why then?
He thought she might say that it had something to do with meeting him—the power of the moment, an unexpected chemistry—but she just gave a little shrug and said, I don't know, I can't remember, maybe I was drunk
He smiled as he stood there by the open window
Outside, the guitarist had stopped playing
I'll ring you tomorrow, he said
I should know more by then

17

Down eight flights of stairs, Inés in front of him, her hair still wet, their footsteps light on the worn stone
Not a sound from other floors or other rooms
It's early, she told him
People are sleeping
He pulled the front door shut behind them
In a café round the corner they sat outside and ordered coffee and brioches
She put on her dark glasses
The sunshine seemed washed clean by the rain that had fallen a few hours earlier
She didn't ask about the phone call
It was none of her concern

They drove out of Jerez, down a sloping, tree-lined avenue
What will you do? she asked
I don't know, he said
Tonight's my last night at the Parador
At least, it's meant to be
Trees rushed past, a blur of green
Everything's happening so fast, he said
Shifting down a gear, she rounded a roundabout
I'd invite you to stay, she said, but
No, no, he said quickly, I wouldn't want to bother you like that
You've already given me so much

Looking sideways, through the window, he felt an ache in his throat, a nostalgia that he couldn't explain
Do you feel sorry for me? he asked
Sorry? she said
Why would I feel sorry?
Perhaps you think I'm going through some sort of crisis, he said
Perhaps you think I'm lost
It was a while before she answered
Is that so bad? she said
By now, they were on the A4, heading south
It's true, he said
It doesn't feel bad

---

how to make a bomb

The flat land stretched away to a range of mountains that were mauve and gray
There was so much emptiness in Spain, so much distance

Somewhere along the line, it seems to involve faith, he went on
It's like stepping into the pitch dark or into blinding light, and not knowing where your foot will fall
You have to believe there's something there
You don't know what it is, though
He was still looking through the window
A hawk flying across a field of yellow grass, a farmhouse with its roof half-gone
That should be exciting, shouldn't it? she said
He turned his head
Her black hair flickering around her face, her right wrist resting at midnight on the steering wheel, her fingers dangling, relaxed
You're astonishing, Inés, he said
I love you
She looked at him quickly, then looked away
His declaration had startled her, it was so sudden, so extreme, and yet, at some level, she seemed to understand

Driving to Cádiz in the spring sunlight, after a night in a convent
The silence of centuries on the stairs and in the rooms

The smell of old cloth, ancient stone
Her bare back as she lay beside him in the bed, her bra straps thin and black against her skin, her breathing deep
Cigars and rain and sherry in her hair
His heart as full as it had ever been, but also light, untethered
His eyes prickling from lack of sleep
What had he thought?
He knew what he had thought
To those who ask for nothing, everything shall be given

They raced past Puerto Real, with its rusting shipyards and its low, pale warehouses, then took the smooth, fast curve up to the Puente de la Pepa
It felt like so long since they had left the city that he was fooled into thinking he was coming home
This wasn't home, though
This was ground that was unstable, shifting
Territory that was wholly new
She asked if he was going back to his hotel
He gave a grim nod
I suppose

She stayed in the left lane as she came down off the bridge, making for the tip of the peninsula
They passed white apartment blocks with striped awnings on their terraces

how to make a bomb

They passed a public garden
Chessboard paving stones and rows of palms
Walks along the bay
In the windscreen, the Parador appeared
Not now, he thought
Not yet
He was afraid his happiness depended on her being near
How could he endure the next few moments, let alone the
distance that would open up between them?

When she parked in front of the hotel, he faced her with a kind
of trepidation, as if looking at her was forbidden, as if he might
be turned to salt or stone
Thank you, he said, for everything
Everything? she said
He knew what she meant, but couldn't allow himself to think
of it
He kept his eyes and mouth level
They could have been playing a game in which the slightest
change of expression on his part would cost him points
He got out of the car, then leaned on the open window and
looked in
You might not have seen the last of me, he said
She looked at him through her dark glasses, her eyes
unreadable
Good, she said

As he hurried up the hotel steps and through the door, the sun bounced off the glass in big, bright chunks
The laminated green faux-marble panels on the walls
The slats of dark wood higher up
A deep exhaustion swept over him, he could almost have fallen asleep on his feet, but he forced himself on across the lobby, towards Reception
Good morning, said a woman in a crisp white shirt
He asked for his room key
She turned away from him and when she handed him his key it came with an envelope
Your friends wanted me to give you this, she said
He opened the envelope
Inside was a postcard of a house
The card was signed "Vernon and Allegra"
He had forgotten all about trying to see them before they left for England
Are they still here? he asked
They checked out an hour ago, the woman said

18

Back in his room, he sat on his bed and read the card
They had looked for him at breakfast, Allegra said, and in the lobby afterwards

how to make a bomb

They were sorry not to have been able to say goodbye
Once again, she thanked him for being so thoughtful and so kind, and apologized for what she called "the business with Vernon"
She hoped they hadn't caused him too much inconvenience
The house pictured on the card was the house that they had mentioned over lunch
If the idea still appealed to him, it was his for as long as he wanted
They wouldn't be going until the middle of September
She gave him the address and told him to ask for Mrs Zoumpoulakis, who lived in the village and looked after the keys
Houses don't like to stand empty, she said
Should he take them up on their offer, he would be doing them a favor

The card still in his hand, he looked straight ahead and saw himself reflected in the blank, black screen of the TV
Only a couple of hours ago, as they sped down the hill towards the motorway, Inés had asked what he would do, and he hadn't had an answer
Now this, from nowhere
He laughed once, out loud, then turned the card over
The house was built from stone, as Allegra had described, and all the wooden features—the front door, the window frames, the shutters—were painted a chalky pale blue
They wouldn't be arriving until September, Allegra had said
That gave him the whole of spring, if he wanted it
The summer too

His brief stay at the Parador had opened out into something that felt almost limitless
Also, life in the village would be simpler
It was the logical next step

His weariness gone, he took out his phone and called Anya
I can't talk now, she said
She sounded short of breath, as if she was walking fast
Anya, he said, this will only take a second
I'm going to Crete
I'll go tomorrow, if I can get a flight
He paused
You don't have to worry
I'm not having an affair
There was silence on the other end
How long will you be there? she asked eventually
I'm not sure, he said
I've been given an opportunity, something I couldn't have predicted or imagined
She asked what she was supposed to tell people
What you always tell them, he said
He could hear traffic behind her voice
She would be hurrying down the hill, past the Boston Arms and the Spaghetti House, on her way to the tube
Or else she would be crossing Euston Road, not far from where she worked
Philip, she said, I really have to go
His phone was still pressed to his ear, but the line was dead

how to make a bomb

It had been selfish of him to ring the moment that he had any kind of certainty
He had sounded convincing, and also honest, perhaps for the first time since returning from Norway, but it would have done little to reassure her
The call had been for his benefit, not for hers
He lay back against a stack of pillows, looking at the card again
He imagined the heat, and the stillness, and the grating of cicadas in the trees
He imagined the blue air trembling
He closed his eyes

On waking, he had a shower, then put on his hotel bathrobe and ordered room service
He spent the next hour and a half on the phone
There was a flight from Seville to Athens at two thirty the following afternoon
He would change planes in Barcelona
That night he would stay in Piraeus, where he had reserved a single room in a small hotel
The next day, he would take the boat to Heraklion
From Heraklion to Vernon and Allegra's house in the village of Kalivaki it was about three hours by car

---

He wrote a note to Vernon and Allegra, thanking them for the card and for their generous offer
He hoped to arrive in Kalivaki towards the end of the week
He would be happy to pay rent, he said, or else he could work on the house if things needed doing—and things always needed doing, didn't they, with houses
Next, he emailed Inés, telling her that a miracle had happened
He would be catching the 9:40 train to Seville the following morning
Was there any chance of seeing her before he left?
He pressed SEND, then he called Seth
The first two times it rang and rang and went to voice mail
The third time Seth picked up
Dad, are you okay?
Philip couldn't help smiling
Whenever he called, Seth acted as if it was some sort of emergency, as if their whole house had gone up in flames, or someone had been diagnosed with cancer
I'm fine, he said, everything's fine
How's Manchester?
I can't really talk now, Seth said
In the background people were roaring with laughter
He heard Seth say, It's my dad
Are those your friends? he asked
But Seth was busy talking to someone and didn't seem to be listening to him
Still, if Seth had friends he was glad
He spoke into the noise, like a person shouting into the wind

I love you, Seth, he said
I love you very much, and I've been thinking about you
I was just calling to tell you that
You're sure you're okay, Dad?
Seth's voice was suddenly up close again, inside his ear
I'm okay, Philip said, really
I'll call again soon

The sun was setting over the Bay of Cádiz, the western sky a blaze of pink and orange
As he leaned on his balcony, his phone buzzed
It was an email from Inés
She had a faculty meeting that evening, she said, and a dinner with colleagues afterwards, but she was free for breakfast
Perfect, he wrote back

19

By half past seven the next morning, he was sitting in the breakfast area with a *café con leche*, his mind empty but alert, expectant
Inés arrived at ten to eight
Watching her approach, he was reminded of the first time he saw her, at the party hosted by the mayor of Bergen

She had moved towards him with a smile
When she reached him, she held out her hand, her arm very straight, and said simply, I'm Inés
Had that really been only a month ago?
So much had happened since
This morning she was wearing a black knee-length dress with small buttons up the front and a pair of white trainers
Thank you for coming, he said
She put her phone on the table and sat down
How are you today? she asked
He remembered the drive back from Jerez, and how he had told her that he loved her
In retrospect, his outburst felt like an exaggeration, though that didn't mean that he regretted it, or that it wasn't true
He had been in a euphoric state—the avenue of trees, the lack of sleep, Inés behind the wheel in her dark glasses—and she seemed to understand that his skin was thinner than usual, and that his feelings were closer to the surface
I'm fine, he said

She stopped a passing waiter and asked for a *café solo*
The tilt of her lips and chin
The low, almost intimate voice she used
It gave him pleasure to see her do the ordinary things, just as it had at the beginning

---

how to make a bomb

So what's all this about a miracle? she said
He showed her the postcard, then told her about Vernon and Allegra, and how he had run into them after having dinner at her apartment
He described how Vernon had hurt himself, and how he had helped them to get back to the hotel
They had seemed disproportionately grateful
He had only done what anyone would do
Inés disagreed
Most people wouldn't have been so considerate, she said
Besides, isn't it wonderful when the world treats us with a generosity we don't think we deserve?
He was smiling
You know what it's called when the world does that?
Luck, she said
He nodded
I thought you'd know

He looked away from her towards a plate glass window, its bottom half filled with the blinding glitter of the sea
He wasn't sure why he was looking away
It was out of despair, perhaps
He had a sense of how little time was left, and it was so little that it might as well be less
He was giving himself a foretaste of the future
A future that didn't have her in it

I'm going to miss talking to you, he said, still staring out over the bay
I'm not sure how I'll manage
He reached for the postcard and shook his head
Crete, he said
She leaned forwards, over the table, and put a hand on his wrist
Go there and enjoy it
He looked at her again, something that was still possible
He nodded again, more slowly

She let go of his wrist and leaned back in her chair, though she didn't take her eyes off him
Will you write while you're there? she asked
He remembered Ramón's description of *cante jondo*—deep song—how it grew out of adversity and triumphed over it
Perhaps he could come up with his own deep song
Something that had the same grim roots, the same passion, the same transforming influence and power
You think I should? he said
She shrugged
It's just a thought
She lowered her eyes for a moment, and when she lifted them again she said, Who knows, I might even visit you
He longed to take her seriously, but he knew he shouldn't
She was just trying to make it easier for him to leave

how to make a bomb

Five minutes later, they walked down to the lobby, where he collected his suitcase
The taxi was already waiting
He handed his case to the driver, who stowed it in the boot, then he turned to Inés
He couldn't think of anything to say
He was worried he might cry
The taxi driver stood with one hand on the door, the other on his hip, untroubled by the time that it was taking
He knew all about goodbyes
You're not going to tell me you love me again, are you? she said
He smiled, then kissed her cheek
She smelled the same as always—sunlight, coffee, cigarettes
He remembered how she had left her bed and slipped into his, how he had felt her against him in the dark
He remembered how she had looked at him and said, You've seen something valuable and true
The words still resonated
She had given him more than he could ever have expected
He was in her debt
I'm not sorry I came, he said
She put on her sunglasses, then glanced beyond him, down the road
Why should you be sorry?
He got into the taxi, but left the door open and looked up at her
Thank you, Inés
He paused
Have I been thanking you too much?
Perhaps, she said, but gratitude's a virtue, isn't it
She smiled, then said, That's Cicero

The taxi pulled away
Through the back window, he saw her standing on the pavement, her sunglasses, hair, and dress all black, her trainers white
Was that it? he wondered
Was that the end?

20

The bus from Athens airport to Piraeus took almost two hours, and it was close to midnight by the time he arrived at the Hotel Olympus
He stood on the narrow street, the light like melted caramel
The air smelled of cement dust and diesel oil
Since leaving Cádiz, a space had opened up inside him
He had to keep swallowing
A half-hearted breeze pushed past, carrying a whiff of grilled meat
Keftedes or souvlaki
He wasn't hungry, though
He had eaten during the three-hour layover in Barcelona

how to make a bomb

In the cramped lobby, with its yellow wood-chip wallpaper, was a hatch and a small shelf that acted as Reception
A young man in a Pink Floyd T-shirt sat inside, his face close to the pages of a graphic novel
Passport, he said, not looking up
Philip pushed his passport through the hatch
The young man tapped his details into a boxy, mushroom-colored computer that looked like a relic from the eighties
One night? he said, holding up a finger
Philip nodded
He saw that the young man had written his surname as
NOMAN
You spelled my name wrong, he said
The young man looked at him
His eyes were bloodshot
Probably he'd been smoking weed in the back room
Never mind, Philip said
The young man handed him a key
Attached to the key was a knob of greasy wood with the number 316 burned into it
Third floor, the young man said
You can take the lift
Philip asked what time breakfast was served
No breakfast, the young man said

On his way up in the lift, Philip wondered why he had booked himself into such a cheap hotel

He unlocked the door and switched on the light
Above the single bed was a painting of a dog with soulful eyes and a pink tongue
He stood his case on the floor near the window
The view was of the blank sidewall of an apartment block
Below, on the waste ground between the two buildings, were a cement mixer and a heap of dumped black plastic bags
It looked like the kind of place you'd find a body
A nearby TV blared Greek music

Stepping back into the room, he sat down on the bed, which sagged under his weight
He thought of the time he and his mother took a train to Eastbourne, where her cousin Mabel lived
We're on the lam, she'd told him
She had a rattled, hectic quality, and the silver glitter in her eyes reminded him of the disco balls he had seen on *Top of the Pops*
Beggars can't be choosers, she said as they arrived at Mabel's perfect little white front gate
She was doing her best to sound nonchalant, but it was November, and they were cold, and she couldn't keep the nerves out of her voice
Mabel had a porcelain face that hid what she was thinking
She put him in the box room, and he spent most of the first night trying to fit himself around the lumps in the mattress
They had only been there a few days when he was woken by the slamming of a door downstairs

how to make a bomb

He heard his father's voice, full of good cheer, as if the Christmas lights were up already, and then his mother's, quieter and yet defiant
Later, his father began to shout
You're not leaving, you hear me
You're not bloody leaving

He lay back on his bed at the Hotel Olympus, legs crossed at the ankle, hands folded on his chest

By Christmas, they were renting a flat in Brighton
Are we on the lam again? he asked his mother when they moved in
She stood beside him at the window, one hand on his head, the dull-gray sea outside
You're such a clever boy, she said
She never stopped trying to convince herself that life was an adventure, but sometimes, when she thought he was asleep, he would hear her sobbing in the bathroom
The following September, she sent him to boarding school
He was frightened, but he kept his fear to himself
People would ask him if he was all right, and he would nod
It's nothing, he would say
His mother wanted to believe in the light-entertainment version of the world, with its buzzers and its prizes and its tinny fanfares, and he couldn't bear to tell her it was all made-up
If he crushed her urgency and sparkle, what would be left?

He woke on top of the covers, all his clothes still on
The room felt damp, and his mouth tasted sour
The bare bulb was shouting at him from its grimy paper shade
He looked at his phone
2:07
He undressed slowly and switched off the light
Lying in the dark, his thoughts turned to his son
All the things he dreaded came down on him—the feeling of being at fault, the feeling of being useless, the feeling of not being something, or being the wrong thing
It was almost dawn before he fell asleep again

21

The next morning he walked for hours in the shadow of stained gray-white apartment blocks
He drank a coffee at a zinc counter by the port
Later, he found a stationery shop and bought an exercise book, its cover flimsy, shiny, royal blue
He liked how foreign it looked, and how the Greek words on the front and back excluded him
Despite what he had said to Inés, he had no desire to write anything as yet

how to make a bomb

His ideas should be fluid, he thought, and constantly evolving, not butterflies in a display case
Pinned, unchanging
Dead

He stopped for lunch in a small place near the Zea Marina
The walls were the color of mint ice cream
There was a Greek soap on TV
He ordered a plate of fried squid and a half bottle of retsina
Like Philip, most of the diners were men, and most were eating on their own
As the waiter was prizing the top off his retsina, the door to the restaurant opened
A stocky woman with dyed-blonde hair paused to remove her sunglasses
The men shifted on their chairs, but didn't look at her
He put her age at roughly seventy

She took the table next to his and when their eyes met she spoke to him in Greek
I'm sorry, he said, I don't understand
She tucked her sunglasses into a snakeskin clutch bag
Is this your first time here?
Her English was flawless, with almost no accent
Yes, he said
It's the best restaurant in Piraeus, she said
She caught the waiter's eye

Isn't that right, Kyros?
Maybe best restaurant in Athens, Kyros said
I come here every day, she told Philip
Kyros drew the cork on a half bottle of white wine and poured her a glass
I'm just passing through, Philip told her
I'm on my way to Crete
The land of the minotaur, she said
She raised her glass
Ya mas
Ya mas, he said

She was Swedish, he found out, from Gothenburg
That was why her English was so good
She had been living in Piraeus for a long time
She had married a Greek man, a theater director, the love of her life, but he had died eight years ago
He asked if she ever thought of going home
To Sweden? she said
He nodded
No, she said
This is my home now

Her name was Kristen, and when they had finished lunch she said that he was welcome to come back to her apartment for a coffee
She lived just round the corner from the restaurant

how to make a bomb

He took her up on her invitation
He had nothing else to do
Her building was one street back from the harbor
The lift, which looked as if it dated from the fifties, shook and rattled as it climbed to the top floor, but Kristen didn't seem to notice
Unlocking her front door, she showed him into a spacious living room that was filled with driftwood, flokati rugs, and vases made of colored glass

While Kristen prepared the coffee, he stepped onto the terrace
In the gap between two apartment blocks were moored speedboats and yachts, all jammed together
He thought he could smell the water, dense and still and smeared with oil
He felt a shiver of anxiety, as in a dream where he was supposed to be somewhere but he was in the wrong place and the journey would take too long and he had no hope of getting there
He checked his phone
3:45
He had hours before the ship departed
It was only a twenty-minute walk to the ferry terminal, and the Hotel Olympus, where he had left his case, was on the way

When Kristen appeared on the terrace with a tray, he put his phone on the table and sat down

She poured the coffee from a silver pot
Are you all right? she asked
You seem nervous
I didn't sleep too well last night, he said
He described his hotel—the stoned receptionist, the lumps in the mattress, the potential crime scene under the window
He had been hoping to make her laugh, but she had a hand over her mouth
Why did you stay in such a terrible place?
I don't know, he said
It was all very last-minute
He looked down into his coffee and had a momentary feeling of vertigo, as if he had shrunk to one-hundredth of his true size and was about to dive into the cup from a great height
I seem to have left my wife, he said, the words tumbling out, unprompted
Was that what was happening?
Surely not
Instead of returning to Anya, though, he was increasing the distance between them
Perhaps that explained his unease
Perhaps he was trapped in a kind of dream or trance, and he was waiting for someone to wake him up, and that was why he rebounded from one stranger to another, talking to almost anyone who crossed his path
He didn't want reassurance or support
He wanted to be discouraged

how to make a bomb

She's not here with you, Kristen said, in Athens?
He shook his head
She's in London
She has no idea where I am
He paused
I've been worrying about her
Kristen sipped her coffee
It seems to me, she said, that it's you we should be worried about, not her
She looked off into the sky
We tend to overestimate our own importance
In relationships, I mean
We're convinced that we're the ones who hold everything together
If we leave, the other person will fall apart
It isn't true
She paused
People are stronger than you think
Your wife is probably stronger than you think
Her chuckle was low and husky, as if she had been a heavy smoker when she was young
After all, she went on, there was a time before you
Perhaps there will also be a time after you
She leaned forwards, reaching for the silver pot
More coffee?

III

the land of the minotaur

I

He was on the deck of the ferry, watching the lights of Athens sink into the night, when he felt in his jacket for his phone
It wasn't there
After checking all his pockets, he bent down and opened his case
He went through the contents, unzipping every compartment, no matter how small, then he sat back on his heels
Fuck, he murmured
He could feel the shudder of the engines through the soles of his shoes
His head was burning, as if he was too close to a heat lamp
He knew what he had done
His phone was on the table on Kristen's terrace, next to the silver coffeepot
He had forgotten to pick it up

Kristen seemed like a good person, and he felt sure that she would look after his phone for him, but how was he to contact her?

how to make a bomb

He didn't have her number, and hadn't made a note of her address

If he thought hard enough, he might be able to recall the name of the place where she ate lunch every day

He could see the mint-colored walls, the TV in the corner

If the name didn't come to him, he would find an Internet café and google it, then he could write to her, care of Kyros the waiter

In the meantime, he had lost the ability to communicate with anyone

He stood at the rail and turned his face to the wind

Out there, in the dark, were the islands

Aegina, Poros, Hydra—and beyond them, the Cyclades

The windmills of Mykonos

Volcanic Santorini, with its glistening black beaches

And further south, the largest and most rugged of them all

The land of the minotaur, as Kristen had called it

And what was the myth of the minotaur, he thought, if not a demonstration of what happens when you start meddling with the natural world, when you dare to mingle gods and men?

Initially, it was a story about shame—the shame of King Minos, who deceived Poseidon, and the shame of his wife Pasiphaë, the adulteress—but it was also a cautionary tale

If you interfere with nature, you will suffer consequences

In the twenty-first century, we treat our suffering with drugs that are manufactured at the expense of the environment, their waste products contaminating the water and the air alike

Sickness, medication, pollution, sickness
We have created a vicious circle in which we have agreed to live
Our own poisoned labyrinth

Once he found his cabin, he washed in the basin, then took off his clothes and climbed into the bunk bed
His phone was part of the complex, unnecessary overlaying of reality that sickened him
It bound him to a version of the world that he objected to, and the agony he had felt at its loss was proof of the insidious power of the bond
In leaving his phone on Kristen's terrace, he had unwittingly acted in accordance with his new beliefs
He should be happy it was gone
Lulled by the distant pounding of the engines, he closed his eyes
He was heading south, over the Aegean Sea
South, to Crete

2

Early morning in Heraklion
The light was so bright that the shade looked aubergine, and the streets were loud with motorbikes and car horns and pneumatic drills

how to make a bomb

Planes seemed to scrape the rooftops as they took off
The airport was only a mile to the east
Tucked between two closed shops he found a small place that served deep-fried dough balls soaked in honey and dusted with cinnamon
They served Greek coffee too
He drank one cup, and then another
After paying, he asked the man behind the counter what the little balls of dough were called
Loukoumades, the man said, then he repeated the word, so Philip would remember
My breakfast, Philip told him
The man laughed, revealing big, stained teeth

The city gave the impression of being hardworking and careless of its appearance, and Philip warmed to the matter-of-factness and the jumble, the complete absence of pretension
Without his phone it took longer to find a car rental business, but by eleven o'clock he was sitting at a desk with a man called Spiro
When Spiro took his details, he seemed impressed
Philip, he said, like Philip Collins
Philip stared at him
You must know Philip Collins, Spiro said
Everybody knows
He began to sing, but Philip didn't recognize the song
In the Air Tonight, Spiro said
Easy Lover

Philip began to laugh
It's *Phil* Collins, he said
No one calls him Philip
Spiro was shaking his woolly head and grinning, as if he knew better
Crazy English, he said
Philip had only walked into the place five minutes before, but Spiro was behaving as if they were old friends
He told Spiro he was looking for a car that was small and practical
He would need it for a month, maybe longer
Spiro was grinning again
Phil, he said, I have small cars, big cars, any car you want
You need Roadside Assistance?
Only six euros a day

He had imagined that he would spend some time in Heraklion, seeing the sights—there was the tomb of Kazantzakis in a tower on the outskirts, and the Archaeological Museum housed, among other treasures, a delicate ivory bull-leaper from Knossos—but once he was behind the wheel of his Fiat Panda he felt the urge to keep going
He sped along the coastal highway, heading west
The city piled up in his rearview mirror, a messy clutter of white, as if a writer, unhappy with his work, had crumpled sheet after sheet of paper and tossed them onto the ground
Before too long, the road began to climb
Seen up close, the bare rocks had the look of oxidized metal

He parked on a gritty verge and turned the engine off
The silence was immediate and vast
In the middle distance, a bird of prey soared on an air current, moving across the view so smoothly that it might have been sliding along a greased rail, then everything was still, just oyster-colored sky and rust-brown land
He took a deep breath and let it out slowly
Once he reached the house in Kalivaki, he would travel no further
Whatever had to be decided would be decided there

3

After an hour he dropped back down to sea level, and the road became wider and faster
The scarlet of the poppies on the hard shoulder was so luminous and startling that the color looked enhanced, unreal
The sky had cleared
Up ahead, mountains appeared to float in the haze, snow on their steep flanks
He stopped at a service station and bought two corn rings and an iced frappé, then he drove on
To his right was the north coast
Its long, straight beaches gaped at the horizon, and resort towns blended, one into the next

There were tourist hotels, nightclubs, pizzerias, supermarkets, cocktail bars, and diving centers
He even saw a Jehovah's Witness Kingdom Hall

By three in the afternoon he was in Rethymnon
He spent half an hour in an Internet café, where he wrote an email to Anya telling her that he had arrived in Crete, and also that he had lost his phone
That done, he googled cheap restaurants in Piraeus
In five minutes he had tracked down the place with the mint-green walls and made a note of its name and address
Out on the street again, he bought a postcard and addressed it to Kristen, care of Kyros the waiter
He told her that he had left his phone on her terrace and asked if she would be kind enough to look after it until he returned
How easy it was to say "returned," he thought
How difficult to imagine

To the west of Rethymnon, the road ran alongside a wild beach
The waves broke a long way out, bands of deep blue and turquoise crumpling into creamy white
Later, there were eucalyptus trees
At Vrises he turned inland
Once, in the rearview mirror, he glimpsed the sea, now far below, and a memory came to him
He was sitting at the kitchen table with his mother
It wasn't his fault, she said

how to make a bomb

He was who he was
She was talking about his father
Their Brighton flat was on the third floor at the front, waves creasing and uncreasing in the window
I don't regret it, she went on
How could I?
I have you
He understood that she was using his existence as a counterweight to her many disappointments and misfortunes, but it was a misrepresentation of the facts
She gave birth to him first, her troubles happened after
It's all right to have regrets, he could have said, you don't have to keep pretending that life is better than it is, but the force in her gaze made it hard to disagree with her, and he was only about fifteen at the time
Then she offered something that had him thinking differently
He became a mystery to me, she went on, but not one that I wanted to solve
The things I didn't know, I didn't want to know
She looked away from him
The tendons stood out in her neck
When I first met him he was a mystery as well, but I wanted to know everything, I was twenty-one, and him telling me things, it made my heart go fizzy, like a Sherbet Fountain
You remember Sherbet Fountains, Philip?
They used to be your favorite
She let out a sigh
Somewhere along the way, she said, that changed

The fizzing in her heart, she meant
Do you still love him? he asked
Oh, love, she said in a strange half-laughing, half-crying voice
That's the last thing to go
Everything else disappears—the staying up all night, the lying in each other's arms, the talking, the looks, the way you click, even something as basic as liking each other—but love's still there somehow
It's like the last person at a party
The music's stopped and the houselights have been turned on and there are empty bottles everywhere
Someone's probably been sick
Love's still there, though, on the dance floor, all alone
She sighed again
So yes, Philip, she said, I still love him
For what it's worth
The road wound its way along one edge of a gorge, the ground falling steeply away, then rising again
Trees and shrubs clung to the wall of shattered rock on the far side
There was no sense of scale
He felt that if he stretched out an arm he would be able to touch the leaves
The windows in the car were open, and he could smell wild sage and sheep droppings
There was also a mineral smell, keen but ancient
The smell of the earth itself

He passed through a village called Imbros
In front of an abandoned house was a horse with a black coat and a mane that looked silver blonde, almost metallic
Feeling he had seen a creature from a fable or a myth, he was tempted to stop, but the sun was already low in the sky, and it was still half an hour's drive to Kalivaki

4

At last, the land opened out, the road descending across a barren slope in a series of lazy curves
The Libyan Sea stretched before him, smooth and glowing, copper-sulfate blue
If he had driven straight on, he would have found himself in a town called Hora Sfakion
Instead, he turned onto a smaller road that dipped down into a gully, then doubled back on itself
The sky to the north and east was growing dark, and the orange strip on the horizon had a burnt look
Night was closing in
The road narrowed still further, then crossed a stone bridge and rose steeply towards a sign that said KALIVAKI in Greek, and also in English
The sign was dented and rusty, riddled with bullet holes
People had been using it for target practice

He slowed as he entered the village
Houses with whitewashed walls and dark-blue shutters crowded in on both sides
He passed a *kafeneío* that was open
Half a dozen men sat outside in the glare of a fluorescent light
Up ahead was a plain white church with a double nave and a stone tower that housed a single bell
The road bent round the church, then tilted downhill
The houses thinned out
He was through the village before he knew it
He did a U-turn, then drove back up the hill and parked next to the church
When he locked the car and stood on the road, something dark and angular jinked through the space behind him
A bat, he thought
He felt observed, but saw no people
Painted down the side of a building opposite, the crude black letters stacked vertically, was the word ROOMS
The air stood tall and quiet above his head

He started back towards the *kafeneío*
His knees ached after the drive, and his stomach felt hollow, but he wanted to find the house before he had dinner
He felt the need to see it for himself, with his own eyes
Though he had made the long journey to the village, he was beginning to think that he might be deluded, or that he might

have misunderstood, and that nothing was actually on offer at all, or even real
Kristen had called Crete "the land of the minotaur"
What if he was some kind of Theseus—a Theseus who hadn't thought to bring an Ariadne, a Theseus with no sword, no thread?

A dog lunged at him, teeth bared, muzzle slobbery
Fear prickled at the base of his skull
Luckily, the dog was tied to a metal ring in the wall, its owner having used a red electric cable
He moistened his dry lips with his tongue and kept walking
His footsteps echoed on the road

By the time he reached the *kafeneío*, all the men were staring at him
They didn't seem hostile, but they weren't welcoming either
I'm looking for Mrs Zoumpoulakis, he said
One of the men leaned over the table and crushed his cigarette out in a cheap tin ashtray, then he glanced up at Philip, smoke leaking from his mouth, and said something in Greek
Sorry, Philip said, I don't understand
The man wore glasses with mauve-tinted lenses, and his hair was such a lustrous black that it drew attention to his pale, pockmarked skin
Mrs Zoumpoulakis, Philip said

Can you show me?
The man looked at his companions, and they looked at him, and once again their faces were expressionless
Finally, he stood up, signaling that Philip should follow him

Just beyond the bend in the road, the man climbed three or four steps to a dimly lit establishment
There were half a dozen tables, but no customers
The man stopped inside the doorway and shouted a few words into the empty space
He looked at Philip and his head tilted back, one swift gesture that was like a nod in reverse, then he turned and left
Philip understood that he should wait where he was
A curtain of plastic beads suggested a doorway to another room
Outside, a Toyota pickup went by, red brake lights pulsing as it passed the church

At last, the bead curtain parted and a woman appeared
Mrs Zoumpoulakis was dressed in black, with a black headscarf tied over her gray hair
Her dark eyes were set deep in their sockets, and the skin beneath looked bruised and swollen, as if she hadn't been sleeping well, or was in pain
He showed her the postcard
He was a friend of Vernon and Allegra, he told her

how to make a bomb

They had said he could stay in their house
Taking the card from him, the woman stabbed at it with a blunt forefinger and started talking rapidly
He had to interrupt her
I don't speak Greek, he said
She pushed the card at him, then muttered to herself and vanished through the curtain of plastic beads
Not sure what else to do, he waited in the empty bar

When Mrs Zoumpoulakis returned, she was wrapped in a black shawl and holding a bunch of keys
She led him across the road
Beyond the church was a passage paved in concrete with crumbling, whitewashed walls on either side
Though it was only a few minutes after seven, the sun had gone
They came to a flight of steps that plunged steeply downwards
There were houses that were vacant or derelict
He could see an olive grove below
Mrs Zoumpoulakis took the steps one at a time, her body turned to the side, as if she had trouble with her knees or hips
He tried to help her, offering an arm, but she ignored him
At the bottom of the steps she turned to the right, along a path of soil and loose stones
In her black clothes there were times when she seemed to disappear
Once, she stopped to rest without him noticing
He almost collided with her

Suddenly she was up close—her old-butter smell, her muttering—and he murmured an apology
Either she didn't hear him or she paid no attention

Finally, they reached the house
Mrs Zoumpoulakis unlocked the door and pushed it open
The air inside the house was surprisingly dry and smelled of burnt wood and candle wax
He could hear the old woman moving about in the dark
There was a scraping sound, a drawer being opened, perhaps, and then a sharp scratch, and her face appeared, disembodied, hovering in the light of a hurricane lamp
She beckoned to him and he followed her into the kitchen
She placed the lamp on the table, next to a green folder with the words TO ARTOPOEIO: INSTRUCTIONS FOR GUESTS on the front
She put the keys beside the folder, then she left

5

Once he had learned how to switch on the electricity, he blew out the hurricane lamp and began to explore the house
At the end of the hall, with its dusty, sensuous pink walls, was a narrow flight of stairs

how to make a bomb

He climbed to the first floor
Off the small square landing were two bedrooms and a bathroom
Wooden beams traversed the ceilings, and the floors were paved with terra-cotta tiles
In the master bedroom the pink was darker than in the hall
The color made him think of foxgloves
The double bed had a black metal headboard, and two windows that both faced south
He was sure it was Allegra's taste that he was seeing
There was no evidence of Vernon, except perhaps for the dog-eared thriller on the bathroom windowsill
He opened a door in the master bedroom and walked out onto a terrace that was built on the flat roof of the kitchen and the storeroom
The trees that stood behind the house stirred in the wind
Holm oaks, he thought
The air smelled of woodsmoke
Clouds hid the stars

Downstairs, in the living room, the windows were set so deep into the walls that there was room for upholstered window seats
On the shelves inside the door were several illustrated guides to the island
There were also books of poetry by Odysseas Elytis, George Seferis, and Kiki Dimoula, most of them bilingual editions
On the far wall was a round, gilt-framed mirror

He saw himself from a distance, and he was small and warped, like a goblin
He hardly recognized himself
He remembered asking Inés if it would be difficult for him, and her saying that it would, and in that moment he knew that she was right
As he kept looking, he thought he saw something pass behind him, across the open doorway
It was more like a shadow than a figure
Air moving down the hall
A draft

Fetching the keys from the kitchen table, he left the house and followed the path that led back to the church
He had noticed a taverna opposite the *kafeneío*, and he was hungry now
A cool wind blew into his face
He thought he heard the clank and tinkle of small bells

The men were where he had left them, and they eyed him as he approached, and with the same absence of expression, as if they had no memory of him, or had never seen him before
He entered the taverna
Two men were sitting in the corner by the TV with plates of meat and chips, and red wine in a vaselike glass carafe
He took a seat at a table by the wall

how to make a bomb

When the waiter came with the menu, he pointed at the two
men, meaning that he would like the same
The waiter nodded and withdrew

There was a moment when the sound on the TV dropped to
nothing and he heard someone singing in the kitchen
Not long after he slept with Anya for the first time, she told
him that she belonged to a choir and that it was performing
Bach's *Christmas Oratorio* in Islington
Would he like to come?
When he saw her in the church that evening, bare shouldered
in a black dress, he couldn't believe he was going out with her
At the wedding in Wiltshire she had seemed so unattainable
He was startled at his luck, his daring

In their early years together, when they shared a top-floor
flat that looked over Primrose Hill, she would sing parts of
Mahler's *The Song of the Earth* while she was cooking
Later, too, after they came into her uncle's money and they
bought the four-story house in Dartmouth Park
There were times when he stood on the stairs that led down to
the kitchen, in a place where he couldn't be seen, and listened to
her without her knowing
Her voice would be quiet, almost thoughtful, and she would
leave long pauses between the phrases, pauses he didn't think
were there in the original music
Wohin ich geh'?

Ich geh', ich wand're in die Berge
Ich suche Ruhe für mein einsam Herz
Where am I going?
I go, I wander in the mountains
I seek peace for my lonely heart
Once, over dinner, he asked her why she always returned to the Mahler symphony
It's just so sad and lovely, she said, and the last part, "The Farewell," is the saddest and most lovely part of all
She told him about the famous English contralto Kathleen Ferrier, and how she sang *The Song of the Earth* in Edinburgh in 1947
On reaching the last word of "The Farewell"—*ewig*, or "forever"—Ferrier's eyes filled with tears and her voice momentarily failed her
Afterwards, in the dressing-room, she was mortified, and she apologized to the conductor, Bruno Walter
He comforted her by telling her that if the members of the orchestra had been great artists, as she was, they would all have been in tears as well
If you listen to that music, Anya told him, you know what it means to be here in the world, and also how it will feel to go
How it will feel to be dead and gone

The waiter arrived with a basket of bread and a carafe of wine
Philip poured himself a glass
The first mouthful was rough and cold, but good
His lamb and chips arrived

how to make a bomb

From the outside, it looked as if he had left her
That was what people would say, and that was without knowing about a Spanish woman called Inés
His absence wasn't in itself a cause for concern
He was always traveling to festivals and conferences, and his research also took him away from time to time
No, people would notice how withdrawn and preoccupied Anya seemed, and they would ask the obvious question
Is everything all right?
If she didn't answer, they would say, *Where's Philip?* and she would sigh and say, *I don't really know*
Or she might say, *Crete*
They were unlikely to be reassured
So far, he had been unable to convey what had happened to him on the way to Bergen airport
Until he could do that, the experience would exclude her
But what if the experience itself—and the impact of that experience—meant that she was *necessarily* excluded?
He pushed his plate away and reached for the wine
If he was thinking about *The Song of the Earth*, it was because he appeared to have turned away from everything about his life that he considered beautiful
His wife, his son
His home
He had gone, and he was wandering in the mountains, and he was wondering if it might be forever

---

Outside again, he fetched his case from the car and started down the concrete passageway towards the steps, the darkness deeper suddenly and whirling all around him
When the leaf on a fig tree touched his face, it felt harsh, even unnatural, as if it was made of cardboard or sandpaper
His nausea returned, but it was more like a memory or a flashback than something happening in real time

On reaching the house, he had to feel for the keyhole with both hands
The key seemed loose inside the lock, like a foot in a shoe that was a size too big, and it took a while to open the door
Once inside, he climbed the stairs
It wasn't even ten o'clock, but he was tired

When he turned out the light, the darkness was intense and absolute
He couldn't see his hand, not even if he held it two or three inches from his face
He listened for noises
Only the wind in the olive trees, the oaks
The wind over the rocks

---

how to make a bomb

He woke in the night believing that he was in London, but when he looked at where the window should have been it wasn't there
There didn't seem to be any windows at all
He felt he might be in a coffin, buried alive, six feet of earth on top of him
He lay still, trying to control his breathing
Then he started to remember
The cheap hotel in Piraeus, the night boat over the Aegean, the drive along the coast to Rethymnon
Then inland, towards the high spine of the island
He pictured Kalivaki as if seen from above
A road winding across rough ground
A cluster of square white houses, like dice thrown against the base of the mountains
The sea a mile to the south, limitless and dark
He seemed to hear Allegra's voice
There's almost nothing there, and yet there's everything
In coming to this place, he might have begun to strip away the aspects of reality that troubled him, all those superfluous and destructive extra layers, but what happened next?
Where to go from here?

6

When he woke again, it was light
He dressed in the clothes he had worn the day before
They were cold from lying on the chair in the corner of the room
Shivering a little, he went to the window and opened the shutters
The sky was a pale glare that hurt his eyes
The area of flat ground in front of the house was covered with dry yellow grass
An olive grove lay beyond
Off to the left, and growing up against the house, were the fig trees Allegra had mentioned
In the distance, the land sloped away towards the coast
Apart from a small church with a tiled roof, he couldn't see another building
He drew the clean air deep into his lungs

Downstairs, he went through the kitchen cupboards
Dry pasta, ground coffee, candles, half a packet of Petit Beurre, some tinned tomatoes, olive oil in a yellow can
Under the sink was a gas cylinder that hooked up to the stove
Walking round to the back of the house, he found the tall brick structure that housed the well
He unlocked the door and switched on the pump
There was a clunk and a whirring, then the distant, urgent rush of water

how to make a bomb

A feather lay on the ground near the well, and he was reminded of a holiday in Spain when Seth was five or six
To give Anya some time on her own one afternoon, he took Seth for a walk
They rounded a point and found a beach he hadn't known was there
A wall reached out at an angle into the sea
Constructed from big blocks of stone, it was all that remained of the ancient port of Empúries, once gateway to the Iberian Peninsula
He helped Seth clamber up onto the wall and they made their way down to the end, a breeze pushing against their backs
Umbrella pines grew on the hills on the far side of the bay
Everything over there was blurred by the heat-haze
Even the trees looked blue

When Seth saw a feather stuck in a crevice in the stone, Philip had an idea
He told Seth to hold the feather above his head, as high as he could, and then open his fingers
Seth did as he said
The breeze caught the feather and away it flew, across the water
They watched until it disappeared into the blue, then Seth turned to him, his features all lit up

It had seemed like such a miracle, the way the feather took off as it left his hand, as fast as something fired from a catapult
They did it again, many times, with a sweet wrapper, a scrap of newspaper, the cellophane from a cigarette packet, a piece of dried seaweed—anything they could find that was light enough
Off they went, each one of them, on a seemingly straight line into the distance, as if they were on a zip wire, and Seth's joy never dipped
It was something to do with the moment of release and the velocity
The first time he tried, it had been a shock
After that, it was anticipation
He knew it was going to happen
And it did

Philip held up the feather and let go, but the air was still and the feather spiraled to the ground
Feathers in the wind
It was something he would say to Seth at bedtime, and Seth would repeat the words, and they would exchange a grin
It had the magic of an incantation or a prayer, it would keep the bad dreams away
For years it bound them together, as a secret might, though it happened much less often once Seth became an adolescent, and then not at all
He checked his watch

The pump had been on for twenty minutes
It was time to switch it off

7

Chiseled out of rocks and dirt, the road to Hora Sfakion
seemed suspended between brown land and blue sea
He didn't think he'd ever been in a place where the human
imprint felt so minimal, so temporary
There was a time before you
Perhaps there will also be a time after you
Kristen's words had a different context suddenly, a new
application
A much more universal meaning

He came round a long bend, and there was the town below,
white buildings cradling the harbor
After he had bought everything he needed, he sat in a café on the
waterfront and opened the guidebook he had brought with him
He read about Frangokastello, a village a few miles east of
where he was staying
In the fourteenth century, the Venetians had chosen the site for
a castle intended to protect them from attacks by pirates and
other hostile forces

Its construction hadn't gone according to plan
Under cover of darkness, local people would descend from the mountains and destroy whatever the Venetians had accomplished during the day
The saboteurs were led by the Patsos brothers, who were eventually caught and hanged, four of them from the castle's turrets, two from the main gate
The castle was completed, and it was still there, almost seven hundred years later
Leaning back in his chair, Philip was reminded of something that Inés had said in the alley behind the flamenco bar
It's a lot to go up against
Should he see the story of the Patsos brothers as another cautionary tale?

By the time he returned to Kalivaki, it was midday, and a strong wind was blowing
As he lifted his shopping out of the car, he happened to glance round
Mrs Zoumpoulakis was on the far side of the road, next to the sign that said ROOMS
One hand clutching her black shawl to her throat, she was staring past him with a look of horror
The wires howled overhead, and the air smelled of rust and ash, as if a burnt-out car had been dumped nearby, among the rocks
He took a step towards her
Mrs Zoumpoulakis, are you all right?

how to make a bomb

Before he could say anything else, she turned away and disappeared into the gap between two houses

After lunch, he made a cup of mountain tea and sat on the front step
The look on the old woman's face had shaken him
He wondered what lay behind it
There was no way of finding out, though, not unless he learned to speak her language
Even then it would not be easy
A weariness came over him
Did the tea have soporific qualities?
He went upstairs and lay down on the bed

When he woke, it was almost five o'clock
He hauled himself upright and put his feet on the floor
His head felt groggy, numb
He drank half a glass of water, then carried a chair out onto the terrace
While he had been asleep, the wind had dropped and the olive trees below the house were still
A low sun shone into his eyes
The presence of the fig trees on the left side of the house and the holm oaks at the back gave the terrace the feeling of a secret space, a kind of sanctuary
The only view was to the south
From midday onwards, in the summer, it would be a real sun-trap

He had a momentary image of Inés sitting on a deck chair next to him in dark glasses and a white bikini
Who knows, I might even visit you

As he shook his head, dismissing the idea as fanciful, he sensed a movement nearby
His first thought was that Mrs Zoumpoulakis had come to apologize or to explain, but when he turned in his chair he saw a man standing in the doorway
The man wore a drab-green sweater that looked like army surplus, navy-blue work trousers, and a pair of scuffed black safety boots with steel toe caps
He was stocky, and his dark hair was thinning at the front
I knocked on the door, he said
He spoke good English, though with a strong Greek accent
The knuckles on his right hand were grazed
You didn't answer, the man went on, as if it was Philip's fault that he was there, inside the house
So you just walked in?
Philip sounded colder and more aggressive than he meant to, perhaps because he had been caught off guard
Yes, of course, the man said
He didn't seem to have the slightest sense of impropriety or guilt
Are you staying here? he asked
Yes, Philip said
I arrived yesterday
He felt instantly that he shouldn't have said so much
There was no reason why he should have to account for himself

how to make a bomb

The man walked to the edge of the terrace, his footsteps so heavy and deliberate that Philip wondered why he hadn't heard him coming up the stairs

He watched as the man leaned a shoulder against the bedroom's outside wall and looked down into the olive grove
It has been very dry, the man said
No rain at all
Philip wasn't sure what to make of this
He said nothing

When the man had had his fill of the view, which he seemed to inhale, like air, he turned to face Philip
I used to live here, he said
In those days it was the village bakery
To Artopoeio
That's what it means
Philip asked if Vernon and Allegra had bought the house from him
Vernon and Allegra, the man said, his tone suggesting that he didn't have much time for the old couple
Are you staying here alone?
Philip nodded
No wife? the man said
No girlfriend?
I already told you, Philip said
I'm on my own

The man walked past him to the back of the terrace and stood still, staring off into the trees

How long will you stay? he asked

I don't know, Philip said

I haven't decided

You haven't decided, the man said

In repeating Philip's words, the man made them sound weak, as though Philip didn't know his own mind

Not wanting the man to think that he felt threatened, he leaned forwards in his chair, his forearms on his knees

Is there something I can help you with?

The man's wide back was framed by the trees beyond

Bad things happened here, the man said

He turned to Philip, a challenge or provocation in the hard set of his face

Still leaning forwards, Philip met his gaze

Bad things, the man said

He was like a third-rate actor delivering third-rate lines, and Philip felt the urge to laugh at him

If he didn't, it was because he suspected that the man might lose his temper, or even become violent

They sat oddly together, the menace and the hamminess

I told Vernon about it, the man said

He didn't listen

Were you trying to warn him? Philip asked

About what? the man said

Philip shrugged

how to make a bomb

Why did you sell the house, he said, if it meant so much to you?
I needed the money, the man said
Philip sat back in his chair
And now you regret it?
Keep asking questions, he told himself
Keep him on the back foot
The man shoved his hands into his pockets and moved towards the door that led to the bedroom, then he stopped and seemed to contemplate the ground
You don't understand anything, he said
Though Philip was tempted to tell the man that he was talking to the wrong person, that he—Philip—wasn't the owner of the house, and that none of this was his concern, he also saw that to be confrontational or dismissive would be to play into the man's hands
It was what he was looking for—or what he was used to.
He had appeared uninvited, he was trespassing, and he hadn't thought to apologize, but it would do no good to point that out
As with a child, it would have the opposite effect
If he told the man to stay away, he would only come closer
At last, he saw a way forwards

What's your name? he asked
The man eyed him, as if he suspected that he was being tricked or fooled
Philip stood up and held out his hand
I'm Philip, he said

The man shook Philip's hand
Niko, he muttered
Any time you want to come and see the place, Philip said, that's fine by me
Niko frowned
Without looking at Philip again, he vanished through the open doorway
This time Philip heard his boots on the stairs

He hurried to the edge of the terrace and peered over the parapet in time to see Niko emerge from the front door
Niko chose to ignore the path that led to the church
Instead, he circled round behind the house and crossed the broken ground where the pump was
It didn't occur to him that he was being watched—or if it did, he didn't care
He climbed the slope and disappeared into the trees, head down, hands closed into fists
What was going through his mind?
Philip couldn't begin to imagine
Dusk was falling, but he sat down again
Niko had walked in through the door and up the stairs as though he owned the place
If he was capable of that, what else was he capable of?

8

The following day, Philip drove east out of Kalivaki
Soon he was passing through the village of Agios Nektarios, where Allegra's mother had once owned a house
He didn't think much would have changed in the years since Vernon and Allegra first started visiting
There were the same tumbledown white buildings, the same men in black shirts sitting in the shade
There was the same sense of nothing going on

After Agios Nektarios, the road plunged downwards, past an EKO petrol station
When he reached the bottom of the hill he turned south, towards the coast
The land had flattened to a thin crust, and the air had heated up
Next to the road were several new haciendas
One had a smooth apricot façade and a row of pillars down one side, a kind of colonnade, like a painting by de Chirico

The road swung to the left and ran parallel to the sea
In the windscreen he saw the castle he had read about, its crenellated walls surprisingly intact
He thought of the six brothers who had tried repeatedly to pull it down

The Patsos brothers, brutally executed by the Venetians
A coach had parked on the dirt outside, and people with iPhones and water bottles were tumbling out
He would visit on another day, he thought, when he could have the place to himself

Driving on, he took a right turning and parked on a cliff top that overlooked a bay
Behind him was a complex of white villas, but it was early in the season and most of them looked empty
Even the nearby taverna seemed closed

He climbed down a flight of steps, between clusters of pink oleander
Short trees with twisted, flaky trunks grew in among the dunes
The sea was ruffled by an offshore breeze, its dark-blue surface flecked with white
Further out, there were strands of violet and purple
When the stones gave way to sand, he took off his shoes and socks and walked barefoot
To the east, a series of promontories reached out into the sea, the orange- and clay-colored rock studded with clumps of greenery

Beyond the strange, short trees, the sand lifted at an angle of forty-five degrees, all the way to the cliff top high above
Sitting at the foot of the slope was a couple in their twenties

how to make a bomb

The woman wore a green sweater and bikini bottoms
Her legs were already brown
Her companion looked much paler, as if he had been on a
different holiday altogether
They stood out, like images that had been upgraded or enriched
It must be to do with the angle of the sun, he thought, and the
way the light was reflecting off the water
The sheer wealth of it
The dazzle

As Philip passed by, the young woman gave him a smile that
was so spontaneous and so candid that he couldn't help smiling
back, but the young man who was with her stared past him,
eyes narrowed against the glare
He moved beyond them, almost to the end of the beach, then
he spread out his towel and sat down
Opening a book of poetry by George Seferis, he began to read
Body, my rich ship, where are you traveling?
Though the lines felt relevant, his mind drifted, and he
imagined himself in Hora Sfakion, next to a kiosk that sold
Greek newspapers
On the front page were two passport-sized photos of the young
tourist couple
Though he couldn't read the article, it was clear that they had
been murdered
Why was he thinking such a thing?
In part, perhaps, because the beach was so deserted
If a crime were committed, there wouldn't be any witnesses

Someone could be killed and nobody would know
Also, the elemental bleakness of the place suggested it
Rocks and sand and water
Nothing else
The sea lay before him, empty of boats, no landfall until the coast of Libya
The taverna, which was half a mile away, was shut, and the villas looked unoccupied
Behind them, the barren plain of Frangokastello, and then the White Mountains, their flanks still streaked with snow, their stark peaks almost ghostly, there but not there
What's more, he had read that violence was innate in Crete, part of the island's character
The people recognized in themselves a natural tendency for passion and excess
Allegra had given him the word for it
Kouzoulada
But there was yet another factor, unrelated to the setting
In the couple he had seen a kind of vulnerability, which was only heightened by the young woman's winning liveliness and charm, and by the diffidence of her companion
It was a quality that a predator would notice, and be drawn to
A quality that might even arouse predatory feelings in someone who had never experienced such feelings before

Putting the book aside, he lay down on his back
The push and pull of the waves, like someone breathing in, then breathing out

He must have slept
When he opened his eyes and looked around, the sun was lower in the sky and he was alone
The young couple had gone
He felt wrong-footed, a little panicky, and quickly gathered up his things and left

9

The next morning he woke at six o'clock
Lying in the half light, his thoughts returned to the couple on the beach
How brightly lit they seemed in retrospect
How doomed
He wished he could talk it over with Anya
Given the context, though, he wasn't sure that she would understand
She might see it as further evidence of instability
Another of his jokes

Once downstairs, he lit the gas under the coffeepot, then he picked up the keys
It was a good time to run the water pump

When he opened the door, a black cat was sitting on the ground outside
It stared up at him, its right ear torn, its eyes the color of turmeric
Another unexpected visitor
He stroked the cat's blunt head
The cat pushed hard against his hand, but didn't purr at all
He liked its uningratiating character, its battle scars
You must be hungry, he said
He fetched some leftover pasta from the kitchen and gave it to the cat, then he sat on the doorstep and gazed into a sky as yet unheated by the sun
The cat must have a connection with the house, he thought
Like Niko

After breakfast, he set up a deck chair on the flat land at the front
He spent the rest of the morning drinking coffee and trying to learn Greek
Sometimes he heard voices in the olive grove below, but he didn't see a soul, and no one bothered him
A sense of ease spread through his body
As a student, he had read Ralph Waldo Emerson's famous essay on nature
Emerson talked about crossing a bare common under a cloudy sky, and the exhilaration that brings with it
In the woods, too, Emerson said, a man casts off his years

10

That evening, Philip decided to eat at the taverna
Curious about the route that Niko had taken, he circled the house and climbed up through the trees
It was already dark, and there was no path, only collapsing drystone walls and terraces of crumbling earth fenced off with rusty wire mesh
One of them had been used as a dumping ground
There were oil drums, coat hangers, door locks, crushed cigarette packets, and bits of smashed roof tile
There was even a TV
He had to tread carefully, watch where he put his feet

Entering a house that had no roof, he picked his way over broken bottles, rubble, and empty tins
The sky towered overhead, milky with cloud
He found a window at the back, just a square hole in the wall, and peered out
Some fifty feet away there was another house

The grass crackled beneath his shoes as he approached
He stopped by a metal gate
From where he stood, he had a view of a kitchen

The bulb hanging from the ceiling had a pink glass shade that cast light onto the table but left the corners of the room in shadow
A door opened and a woman appeared
She wore a black dress, but she wasn't old
Early forties at the most
She had a hard look, as if she had been given very little and expected even less

Lifting the lid on a pot, she stirred the contents, then she turned her head to one side
She was talking to somebody he couldn't see
A man walked in and sat down at the table, under the light
It was Niko
He took a crust of bread and tore a piece off it, then he put it in his mouth and began to chew
Without turning round, he spoke to the woman
She lifted a bottle and a glass off the shelf above the stove and set them down in front of him
Filling the glass, he drank half of it in a single gulp, then he reached for the bread again
What was the relationship between them?
Philip hung in the darkness, his breathing shallow

The woman ladled soup into a bowl and placed it in front of Niko, then she stood back

how to make a bomb

Between mouthfuls, he said something
Once again, he didn't look at her when he spoke
Instead, he stared straight ahead
She took a seat in the corner of the room and began to mend a pair of overalls
When Niko had finished his soup, he wiped his mouth with the back of his hand, then pushed the bowl away and filled his glass again
As before, he gulped down half of it, then continued to stare straight ahead
In the room nothing moved except the woman's hand as she slid the needle through the dark fabric, drew it into the air close to her throat, then slid it into the fabric once again, the silver of the needle glinting as it rose and fell
Philip began to feel that she was hypnotizing him
That he might fall into a trance

Something struck his left hip suddenly and he cried out
A goat stood nearby
Neat leaf-shaped ears, black tufts beneath its chin, eyes so colorless that they looked blind
In the kitchen Niko was on his feet
Philip took a few steps back, casting around for somewhere to hide
A washing machine stood in the long grass
He ducked down behind it, hoping that he wouldn't be visible
The door slammed open, and a pyramid of yellow light fell across the ground

Niko stood in his front yard, shouting in Greek
Crouched behind the washing machine, Philip didn't dare to move
He felt ridiculous, but what else could he do?

When he next looked, Niko was closer, but the woman in the black dress was calling to him from the doorway
There was impatience in her voice, as if she had seen him react like this before
As if he was too easily provoked
Niko shouted back
There's someone out here
I know there is
At least, that was what Philip imagined he was saying
Just then, the goat sidled up to Niko and bleated plaintively at him
Niko swung an arm in its direction and it jumped away
The woman spoke to him again
You see?
It was only a goat
Niko muttered to himself—a curse, it sounded like—then turned and went indoors

Philip stood up and brushed the dirt and grass stalks off his clothes
There was no one in the kitchen window now
He followed a concrete path that meandered between the houses and took him to a flight of steps carved in the rock

He began to climb
Fig trees leaned over garden walls, and he had to bend down or brush the rough, almost scaly leaves aside
On reaching the top, he stepped out onto the road that led through the village

II

The same five men were sitting outside the *kafeneío*
It was tempting to believe that their entire lives were lived beneath that stark, green-white light, that they hadn't moved since the night he arrived
Kalispera, he said as he walked over
No one spoke
The man in the tinted glasses gave him a nod so understated that he wouldn't have noticed if he hadn't been watching closely
I'm sorry, he said, but I don't speak Greek
I intend to learn it, though
Two of the men were playing backgammon, and their eyes didn't leave the board
Another man with a creased and whiskery face looked up at him and then looked down again
None of them gave any indication that they had understood, or were even interested, but he didn't allow himself to feel disheartened

The nod, he told himself
That was a start

He pointed to the only vacant chair and said, May I join you?
The man in the tinted glasses tipped his head back in a gesture that seemed to give Philip the permission he was asking for
It also suggested that he was the group's spokesman
If there was to be any talking to be done, it would be done through him
Philip took a seat
The men shifted on their chairs, not so much to make space for him, he felt, as to adjust to the idea of his presence among them
The waiter came and stood at his shoulder
Ouzo, he said
The waiter went back inside
The two men continued with their game of backgammon while the others watched and smoked
There was the click and snap of worry beads
Every now and then someone offered an observation, or made a remark that sounded critical or derisory
The laughter, if it happened, was always muted, dry

Philip's ouzo came in a tall, straight tumbler with two cubes of ice
He sipped the cloudy drink, then turned to the man in the tinted glasses
Do you speak English?

how to make a bomb

The man gestured with his left hand, the gap between his forefinger and his thumb narrowing to a quarter of an inch, barely enough to let the light through
Hardly any, he was saying
Reading between the lines would be crucial, Philip thought, if he was to spend time with these men
He would have to use his intuition
It was their way to downplay almost everything, but he shouldn't underestimate them, not even for a moment
My name is Philip, he told the man in the tinted glasses
In Greek it's Philippos
The man didn't think to volunteer his own name
Instead, he lit a cigarette and leaned back in his chair, smoke spilling from his pale lips
Probably I shouldn't talk so much, Philip thought
It was enough to be sitting outside the *kafeneío* at the day's end with five local men, enough to be watching the backgammon and drinking ouzo
In the circumstances that was plenty

When he had finished his ouzo, he set the empty glass on the table and looked for the waiter
Alert to every movement, the waiter came and stood beside him, as before
Philip didn't ask for the bill
Instead, he held out a five-euro note
The waiter took the money and put a few coins on the table
Philip nodded his thanks

The waiter turned away and went inside
The entire transaction had taken place without so much as a single word being spoken
Philip felt that he had passed some kind of test
He pushed his chair back and stood up
Kalinikta, he said

He had approached the *kafeneío* wanting a drink, but he had also hoped he might fall into conversation with the men, and that he might find out more about his neighbor, Niko
His expectations had been unrealistic
In retrospect, it was astonishing how little he had learned
He struggled to remember even a single word being addressed to him
But perhaps that was the whole point, he thought as he made his way down the unlit, uneven steps
We have forgotten about silence
How much it can say

He crossed the waste ground outside Niko's house
The front door was closed, and the kitchen curtains had been drawn
His discovery that Niko lived only a short walk away hadn't come as much of a comfort to him, but he still believed that if he was to discourage the man he should be consistently open and welcoming
He should also mirror Niko's behavior by overstepping the mark

His own need should appear greater
If Niko's visit had disconcerted him, it was because it had been so unexpected, but what if he himself employed the weapon of surprise?

12

Back in the house, he thought about the way the men in Kalivaki chose to communicate
Everything was stripped back, pared down
Meaning had to be unearthed
He realized that their behavior had a bearing on his nausea
For him, as for many others, ordinary everyday reality had become unreliable, enervating, even toxic
In Japan, the phenomenon was known as *bunmeibyō*, or "civilization sickness"
Increasing social mobility and rampant large-scale urbanization had had a disastrous effect on human beings, both severing all contact with the natural world, which had given them a sense of perspective and also of belonging, and dismantling the extended family, which had provided them with their principal source of moral and religious instruction
We had been unmoored, cut loose
We were adrift

231

On the other side of the world, Native American tribes seemed to agree
Among indigenous people, there was a profound belief in the importance of relatives
Crucially, they believed that "being related" went beyond the personal
The environment was also a relation
You had the same responsibility to the environment as you did to your community
In fact, the idea of community *included* the environment
In so-called civilization, by contrast, human beings and nature were seen as two separate entities, and land was a passive resource, there to be exploited, plundered

As with any ailment, civilization sickness could be treated
It was a matter of deciding on priorities
When sitting outside the *kafeneío*, he felt some of that hard work had been done
Earlier ways of being weren't necessarily less developed or advanced—or, to put it the other way round, progress could take you backwards
If he spent a small part of each day with those men, it would amount to a kind of re-education
He would be learning something that he used to know, but had been deprived of, or had neglected

He did the washing up, then put his face close to the window
It was so dark that he couldn't see
For all he knew, Niko could be out there, roaming moodily about in his steel-capped boots, his mind tormented by what he called the "bad things"
He didn't relish the idea of waking in the night to find the man in his bedroom, standing over him
After locking the doors, he fastened all the shutters, switched off the lights, and climbed the stairs to bed

13

That night, he couldn't sleep, and he found himself thinking about his father, who had died alone in a bedsit in Hastings
A neighbor had called the police, complaining about the music, and when they broke down the door at one thirty in the morning they found Mr Notman lying on the floor
He had hit his head on the cast-iron grate in the fireplace
He never regained consciousness

During the final years, the only way to be with his father was to sit with him and drink what he was drinking

Usually, it was cut-price chardonnay from Asda or Tesco
He no longer trusted himself to go to pubs
It's too dangerous out there, he would say, a grin wobbling on his face like a plate on a stick, as if the whole thing was a joke
But he had lost his wife, his son, his house, his job

The bullying would come early, towards the end of the second bottle
You think you're better than me, don't you
Or, *You've had it easy*
Or, *You let people walk all over you*
You're weak, you are
You're a victim
Later, as they ventured on to the uncertain ground between the third bottle and the fourth—*You're drinking me out of house and home!*—there would be remorse and self-pity, and sometimes even tears
You don't know what I've been through
You've no bloody idea
He would end up having to comfort his father, telling him that he loved him, and that he understood
Why did he go back, over and over again?
Because he always thought, as he drove through London, on his way to the A21, that this time it would perhaps be different
But it never was

---

how to make a bomb

The record on the turntable on the night of his father's death
was "The Boys in the Backroom" by Marlene Dietrich
It was a song that his father liked to sing at the top of his voice
when he was three sheets to the wind
By then, the look in his eyes would have flicked over like the
fruit in slot machines
Not SOBER SOBER SOBER anymore
DRUNK DRUNK DRUNK
Philip had always been carried along by Marlene's swagger and
bravado, but some years later, when he read the lyrics, he thought he
detected a bitter or sarcastic edge, an undercurrent of self-loathing
And when I die don't pay the preacher
For speaking of my glory and my fame
The song was more like his father than he had realized
It was almost too perfect
My glory and my fame
That was the defiant cry of a man who had done absolutely
nothing with his life—or perhaps, like so many alcoholics, he
had become a kind of legend to himself

Philip got out of bed and opened the shutters
The night smelled of dry grass and cooling rocks, and the sky
was loaded with stars, not only overhead but all the way down
to the horizon
They weren't the meager pinpricks you saw in London
They were wild and lavish, like splashes of white paint or bullet
holes blasted in a piece of splintery black wood
They were astonishing

And suddenly his father was standing beside him
His face was tilted, as if to catch the starlight, and his teeth showed in a tight-lipped smile, and when he spoke his voice was soft with wonder
Isn't that something
For once he wasn't drunk, though it was late

Bless you, Dad, he murmured

14

The following afternoon, he returned to Niko's house and unlatched the metal gate
In the small front yard cactuses stood about in five-liter olive oil tins
The door was open
He didn't hesitate, or even knock
He walked straight in
A passageway ran through the house from front to back
There was a smell of stale sweat
The woman stood at the kitchen sink, washing a pile of fresh greens

how to make a bomb

Niko? he said
She pointed through the wall with a wet hand
He tried the door next to the kitchen, but it was locked
Bouzouki music came from somewhere

He found Niko in the backyard, squatting beside a partially dismantled motorbike, hands black with oil
Nearby was a paint-stained ghetto blaster, an empty coffee cup, and a set of tools laid out neatly on a rag
Kalimera, Philip said
Niko looked up, and his face hardened
How did you find me? he said
Philip shrugged
It's a small village

Standing by the door, arms folded, he watched Niko work
He understood nothing about motorbikes
The sun came out
Niko's scalp showed through his thinning hair

What do you want? Niko asked eventually
I thought we could continue our conversation, Philip said, get to know each other
After all, we're neighbors
I'm busy, Niko said
Philip saw that Niko liked everything on his own terms

He had to be the one who took the initiative
Now that Philip was here unexpectedly, Niko was out of his element, even though he was at home
He seemed younger suddenly, and more uncertain
You told me bad things happened at the house, Philip said
Niko glanced at him, but didn't speak
Philip asked if it was haunted
I didn't say that, Niko said
He was unscrewing a circular metal plate from the engine
It was taking a long time
I don't think I've seen any ghosts, Philip said, though he couldn't help remembering the shadow that had passed behind him in the mirror when he first arrived
I haven't even had any nightmares
Niko sat back, the screwdriver in his hand
He appeared to have realized that Philip wasn't going to leave him alone
It feels very calm, Philip went on
I'm happy there
I'm hoping to stay for quite a while
He walked across the yard and stood in the shadow of a fig tree
After all, it's probably years since the bad things happened
It feels like yesterday, Niko said
He spoke through gritted teeth, and with some force, as if a restraining device inside him had come loose or snapped
Philip waited for him to elaborate, but Niko had turned back to the bike
Why is your English so good? Philip asked

how to make a bomb

No one else round here speaks English
Niko removed the metal plate and placed it on the ground, then he wiped his hands on a rag, rose to his feet, and slumped onto a plastic chair that stood against the wall
I was in the merchant navy, he said
I worked with British crews
You wanted to get away, Philip said
He left the words hanging, somewhere between a statement and a question
Niko didn't seem to understand
Get away?
From the village, Philip said
Because of what happened to you
Because of the bad things
Niko rubbed fiercely at his face with both his hands
Stop talking about that
I would never have known about it, Philip said, if you hadn't told me
It was a mistake, Niko said
Were you trying to scare me? Philip asked
Niko stared at him
Why would I do that?
Philip gave another shrug
I've no idea

He crossed the yard to the back door
Maybe we can talk another time, he said, when you're not so busy

---

Before Niko could react, he stepped back into the house and started down the passageway
He wasn't sure whether his strategy would have the desired effect
In the end, he might have been a little too provocative
Still, he had ventured onto Niko's territory, and he had let it be known that he wasn't someone who could be threatened
He had temporarily reversed the roles
As to what happened next, it was anybody's guess

15

After that, the days began to speed up, one merging into another
The dawn skies still and blue, and then the sun clearing the mountains to the east
The sun warming the rocks
His view of time seemed to have changed
It didn't keep ticking over like a digital readout or the second hand revolving on a clock
It wasn't a measurement of anything
It was merely a space he occupied
He breathed the hours as he breathed the air
They had no power to put him under pressure

how to make a bomb

They didn't make him older
They were just there

One night there was a storm, and he lay in bed and listened to the wind roaring in the trees
The darkness and the wind, he thought
That's all that matters
He might appear to be doing nothing, but what he was actually doing was what Inés had called "paying attention"
He had rejected the framework and the tools he had once relied upon—and relied upon unwittingly, since society achieved so many of its goals by stealth
He was breaking all the old dependencies
He had clicked on UNSUBSCRIBE

But what of Anya and Seth?

For an instant, he felt he was at the top of that tower in Cádiz, looking out over its flat rooftops
The rectangles pink and red and yellow gray
His wife and son were like the whiteness of the city seen at ground level
Still there, but unapparent
Hidden

Once again, he thought of Emerson's essay on nature, and the curious, thrilling phrase the American writer had used
I am glad to the brink of fear

He sat with the men at dusk and drank
He didn't speak
His thoughts came and went rapidly and fleetingly, as clouds do in time-lapse photography
His notebook remained unopened
Blank

16

Late one afternoon, as he drove home after a walk on the beach, the walls and turrets of Frangokastello appeared ahead of him, their stonework orange in the fading light
As always, he thought of the six brothers who had seen the castle as a symbol of oppression
Their punishment, cruel twice over, was to be hanged from the very walls that they had objected to
He couldn't pass the place without imagining those corpses
Those ghosts

And they weren't the only ones

In the course of his reading, he had discovered that, on May 17, 1828, the Turks had slaughtered 358 men in Frangokastello, after a siege that had lasted a week
He had also discovered that the beach he frequented was called Orthi Ammos, or "Standing Sands"
One might think the name referred to the steep dunes that were peculiar to it, but that wasn't the case
Legend had it that, on the day of the massacre, the sand rose up and draped itself over the bodies of the dead
Ever since that time, ghostly figures would be seen at dawn, moving across the flat land near the castle
Some would be mounted, others would be on foot
They were known as *drosoulites*—"dew shades" or "dew shadows"
The Turkish forces who passed through the area towards the end of the nineteenth century mistook them for an army of rebels and fled in confusion
During the Battle of Crete, a German patrol was so convinced they were real that it had opened fire on them
As he approached Frangokastello, he pictured the *drosoulites* picking their way over the plain, warped figures, almost charred-looking, like sculptures by Giacometti
The house where he was staying might not be haunted, but the region was

Beyond the castle was a one-lane turning

On a whim, he followed the road as it led between stands of reed cane and low white buildings

He came to a slipway used by fishermen

Nearby was a car park and a row of wind-bent tamarisks

There was also a taverna with a covered pergola and an outdoor staircase leading to rooms where you could stay

A few people sat about, just gazing at the sea

He chose a table that was out of the wind and ordered a Greek salad and a beer

In the distance was a mauve-gray headland

Lines from *The Song of the Earth* came to him, unsolicited and poignant

I wander in the mountains

I look for peace

When the waiter brought the salad and the beer, Philip asked if it would be possible to make a phone call

The waiter pointed to a thickset, black-haired man in glasses who was sitting at a table by the front wall of the taverna

You can ask, the waiter said

He is the owner

The owner looked up lazily as Philip walked over

In his right hand was a set of amber worry beads, which he swung with a kind of absent-minded nonchalance

What can I do for you?

how to make a bomb

He sounded jaded, like someone who was always being asked for favors
I lost my phone, Philip said
Could I use yours?
Obviously, I'll pay
The owner sighed, then heaved himself out of his chair
Come, he said
He led Philip through a deserted restaurant area and into a small office
On the desk next to the phone were two half-drunk cups of black coffee, a glass ashtray, and a pair of wooden clogs
This is very kind of you, Philip said
The owner grunted and then withdrew

Philip dialed Anya's mobile number
Who's this? she said
In London it was five in the afternoon
She was probably still at work
It's Philip, he said
How are you?
How do you think I am? she said
She thought he was being obtuse or disingenuous
How are you?
He already knew the answer to that question
Any fool would know
He asked if she had received the email he had sent
That was three weeks ago, she said
Three weeks

Through the office window he could see the row of wispy trees at the edge of the property, near the rocks, and the rough sea beyond, its surface all torn up, white rips and slashes in the livid blue
The shiver that shook him had nothing to do with being cold
Are you still there? she asked
Yes, he said
I'm here
Where are you exactly? she asked
Where's "here"?
I told you in the email, he said
I'm in Crete
You have to come home, Philip, she said
I need you
She was only saying what any wife would say to a husband who had taken off without a pretext, with hardly even a warning, and people up and down the country, decent people, they would agree with her, they would all be on her side
Nobody would be on his
I can't come home, he said, not yet
Why not? she said
What's stopping you?
He looked around the office, as if for help
A large-scale map of Crete covered most of the back wall
That's where I am, he thought
It seemed implausible, and yet, at the same time, he could see no other option
You pack your things, Anya was saying, and you go to the nearest airport

how to make a bomb

You get on the next flight to London
What's so difficult?
But then I might just as well have not left in the first place, he said
He could hear the distress in his voice
Something of vital importance was being belittled, brushed aside
I wish you hadn't, Anya said
I wish I'd tried to talk you out of it
She paused
Why are you in Crete, anyway?
What's there?
There's nothing here, he said
That's the whole point
You're talking in riddles, she said
Whenever he tried to convey what he was going through, he felt that he was lying
Worse still, the lie sounded feeble, thin
It was as if he hadn't bothered to invent the detail that would make it believable
You know what, Philip? she said
It's always the same with you
You don't include me in your life
She paused
It's not really a marriage, is it
You just happen to live in the same house
That's not fair, he said
Actually, she went on, talking over him, that's not even true anymore
You don't even live here

Her voice cracked, and she began to cry
Anya, he said
He was pleading with her to make allowances
To understand
No, she said
You shut me out
You *always* shut me out
Fuck you
The line went dead

The receiver in his hand, he stared through the window again
A car pulled up and a couple got out
The man paused, head cocked, to light a cigarette
The woman walked ahead of him to the taverna, a poised figure in a white dress and gold high-heeled sandals

He replaced the receiver and left the office
The owner was sitting by the front wall, as before
I finished, Philip said
The owner looked at him
Is something wrong?
I could use a drink, Philip told him
We have drinks, the owner said
Philip gestured back through the open doorway
Should I pay for the call?
Later, the owner said
Sit down

how to make a bomb

What would you like?
Retsina would be good, Philip said
I'm Philip, by the way
My name is Ioannis, the owner said

When the waiter arrived with his retsina, Philip scanned the menu and ordered a plate of stuffed peppers
A brisk wind pushed at the branches of the tamarisks
Beyond them, out to sea, white spray lifted off the waves in veils
The sun had dropped behind the headland
Soon it would be dark
He poured himself a glass of retsina and drank it down, then he poured himself another
You always shut me out
What could he have done differently?
What could he have said?
If he had told her that he loved her, it would have sounded hollow, like a decoy or a delaying tactic
He drained his second glass and poured a third

The waiter arrived with his stuffed peppers, and he ordered another half liter of retsina
A Cretan family had occupied a nearby table, three generations by the look of it, from a patriarch with a bald head and a bristling white moustache to a young boy with the dark-blond curls of a god

The boy caught him staring and blinked as a cat might
Philip blinked back
The boy grinned, then reached for his Coke
Every time Philip considered returning to London, something in him rose up against the idea, something that didn't even want to entertain the possibility
He loved Anya and Seth, he would never stop loving them, he couldn't imagine not seeing them again, but he was trapped in a double bind of his own making
He needed to resolve it
How, though?

You don't like the peppers?
Ioannis was standing at his shoulder
Philip looked down at his plate and saw that he had barely touched his food
I like them very much, he said
He knew he should eat, if only to prove that what he was saying was true, but his arms felt heavy, and the thought of picking up his knife and fork exhausted him
If you don't like the peppers, Ioannis said, I can bring you something else
No, no, Philip said
I'm very happy with the peppers
It's just that I was thinking
He attempted a smile, but his mouth was trembling, unsteady
You were thinking, Ioannis said

Philip nodded
Ioannis continued to study him, as if he knew something wasn't right and he was trying to determine what it might be
The look was fatherly, which Philip found unnerving, since Ioannis was almost certainly younger than he was
If you eat the peppers, Ioannis said, maybe you will think better, and with that he seemed to decide that he had bothered Philip for long enough and he moved on

Once Philip began to eat, he found that he was hungry
He had almost finished the second carafe
How had that happened?
I must be drunk, he told himself, but the thought was dull and had no impact
The wind had strengthened, and the canvas wall on the west side of the pergola flapped and shuddered
Someone's baseball cap flew off and rolled across the gravel
A little girl ran after it

Later, he asked the waiter for the bill, then sat back with the last of his retsina
He imagined Inés sitting across from him
She had accepted him as someone who was extreme, provisional, and she had given him the space to be that person
She didn't know any different, of course
They had only met in February

It wasn't fair to compare her flexibility and lack of judgment with Anya's exasperation

The waiter returned with the bill and also with a round silver tray containing a carafe of clear liquid and a shot glass
Raki, the waiter said
He smiled, then gestured towards Ioannis
Philip filled the glass
The raki had a vicious, oily taste, something like grappa, only less refined
The last thing he felt like doing was drinking spirits, but he didn't want to appear ungrateful or rude
He knocked it back, then poured another

Once the carafe was empty, he left money on the table and rose slowly to his feet
The toilets were down a passage that was open to the night
The darkness closed around him, the air made up of millions of particles, all jostling
A pale motorboat rocked on the black water
There was no way he could drive

Back in the taverna, he walked over to where Ioannis was sitting
The stuffed peppers, Ioannis said

They were good?
They were very good, Philip said
I made them, Ioannis said
Philip was surprised
You do the cooking?
Ioannis shrugged and said, If I have time
He ground out his cigarette
And the raki?
You like the raki?
That's why I came over, Philip said
To thank you
Ioannis picked up his worry beads and swung them absent-mindedly
Do you have a room? Philip asked
Ioannis looked up at him
You want a room?
Philip nodded
I'm drunk
Ioannis looked at Philip for a while longer, then his shoulders began to move up and down, small movements, but unexpectedly quick, and a wheezing sound came out of him
He was laughing
It's all your fault, Philip said
The raki, on top of the retsina and the beer
Ioannis stood up and went inside, returning moments later with a key
First floor, he said
Sea view
I didn't pay you for the phone call, Philip said

Ioannis gave another shrug, then sat down and reached for his black coffee
Tomorrow, he said

17

Philip was woken by the slam of a car door and a babble of voices
The air in the room was thick and hot
He fumbled for his watch
It was half one in the morning
He could only have been asleep for about an hour
Though he craved a glass of water, he turned in the bed and closed his eyes again
Somebody started knocking on his door
Go away, he shouted
I'm trying to sleep
The knocking grew louder, and more insistent

Dressed in a T-shirt and underpants, he felt his way through the dark to the door and pulled it open
The light was instant, blinding
He had to squint
A woman in raspberry-colored leisurewear stood before him, her eyes puffy and alarmed

how to make a bomb

You go now, she said
She pointed back along the corridor
What do you mean? he said
Go where?
She was already turning away
Leave hotel, she said
There is fire
Behind the woman, a door banged open
A middle-aged couple stumbled out, still half-asleep
A pair of blue flippers fell out of a bag and slapped onto the pale faux-marble floor
The man swore in Greek

Philip stepped back into his room and turned on the light, then he undid the shuttered metal door that led out onto the terrace
Bits of burnt grass and ash were floating in the air
He peered down into the car park
A jeep reversed over a child's shoe and sped off into the night, then two women hurried out of a room somewhere below
They were carrying a piece of luggage each
Halfway to the car, a case burst open, and clothes spilled across the gravel
One of the women let out a wail
He sensed something behind him and glanced over his shoulder
Above the roof the sky was a lurid, hazy red

Back inside, he pulled on his trousers and his shoes and left the room
Downstairs, the man with the flippers told him there was a brush fire to the north of Frangokastello
If the fire jumped the road, the taverna could burn down
Everyone is leaving, the man said
You should leave also

As Philip drove away from the taverna, clouds of smoke drifted across the sky in front of him, driven by the strong wind that was blowing out of the west
He had closed the windows, but the burning smell found its way into the car
He paused at the junction
On the far side of the road the ground was level for about a mile, then it sloped up into the mountains
It was the grass on the flat land that had caught fire
One particular house stood in the path of the blaze, and men were tipping buckets of water onto the wire-mesh fence that surrounded it
He thought he saw Ioannis with a long stick, beating at the flames
Others were out there too, their silhouettes fragile, almost apocalyptic, against the leaping red-and-orange glow
He remembered what Niko had said the first time he appeared
It has been very dry
No rain at all

how to make a bomb

Turning in the direction of Kalivaki, he drove until he was out of range of the fire, then he parked on the verge
Cars roared past, making for safety
He ran over the scorched grass to the house that was vulnerable
The smoke caught in his throat, and he began to cough
In the kitchen, men were taking turns to fill containers from the tap in the sink
A woman pushed a plastic washing-up bowl into his hands
He filled it, then hurried out to where the fire was
Eventually, a human chain was formed, and water was ferried all the way from the kitchen to the fence
When the wind veered, pushing the flames in a southerly direction, towards the taverna, they had to regroup, soaking the grass at the edge of the road
Ioannis passed close to him, a T-shirt tied over his nose and mouth
I thought you were drunk, he said
I was, Philip said
I'm sober now, though
Ioannis chuckled, then moved on

Towards three in the morning the wind dropped and the fire burned itself out
Both the house and the taverna had been saved
Walking back to his car, Philip sat behind the wheel and watched as the men dispersed

He caught sight of his face in the rearview mirror, smears of black on his cheek and forehead
I could drive to Kalivaki now, he thought
He didn't feel drunk anymore, and didn't think he would be a danger to himself or anybody else
At the same time he knew he wouldn't go
He had been caught up in something, and he wasn't ready to turn his back on it
In the taverna all the lights were on, and many of the men who had fought the blaze were gathered round the table where Ioannis had been sitting earlier
As Philip crossed the car park, he stopped to pick up a crocheted shawl and a toy rabbit
Ioannis was in the kitchen area at the back of the restaurant, standing by the coffee machine
Philip put the shawl and the rabbit on the stainless steel counter
I found them outside, he said
Someone might come back for them
Ioannis looked at him
You want a coffee?
I'd love a coffee, Philip said
Can I also have some water?
Of course, Ioannis said, and he pointed to a shelf
The glasses are there
Philip took a glass over to the sink and filled it to the brim
He drank it down in one
Ioannis was putting cups of coffee on a tray
Your name's Philip?

Philip nodded
Ioannis handed him a cup
Sugar? he said
Milk?
Just sugar, Philip said
Ioannis pushed a small tin bowl across the counter
If the fire crossed the road, he said, then he broke off and gestured at the taverna, suggesting that it would have been destroyed
No more stuffed peppers, Philip said
For a few long moments Ioannis failed to react, and Philip worried that he might have spoken out of turn, but then the owner's shoulders began to rise and fall, and this was accompanied, as before, by a series of creaks and wheezes
He was laughing again
He was still laughing as he lifted his tray and started back towards the men

18

Philip was woken by a bar of bright sunlight that reached through the window and across the bed
When he returned to his room at four in the morning, he must have forgotten to close the shuttered metal doors
He showered, then got dressed

Though he had left his clothes on the terrace, draped over a chair, they still smelled strongly of the fire

Downstairs, Ioannis was sitting where he always sat, smoking a cigarette and staring at the sea
Kalimera, Philip said
He had stayed up and listened to Ioannis and the other men, but since they were speaking Greek he had understood almost nothing, only that Ioannis was somebody who people paid attention to, somebody who commanded respect, and when he had finished his coffee he had slipped away
He asked Ioannis if he had slept
One hour, Ioannis said, maybe two
He shrugged
I'll sleep later
He crushed out his cigarette
Philip's eyes drifted towards the headland, a wedge of dark blue in the haze
The wind had dropped to nothing
The day was still and hot

Ioannis asked if he wanted breakfast
I should be going, Philip said
He took out his wallet
How much do I owe you?
Nothing, Ioannis said
Philip stared at him

But what about the phone call?
What about the room?
Ioannis asked where he was staying
Philip pointed to the west
In a friend's house, he said, in Kalivaki
Come and have dinner here sometime, Ioannis said
Maybe I let you pay
His shoulders began to move up and down, and little wheezing sounds came out of him
Smiling, Philip said goodbye and left

As he drove inland, he remembered the phone call with Anya, and his smile faded
It was rare for them to argue, even rarer not to make up afterwards
She had maintained that he didn't include her in his life, and the phrase she had used had an emphatic, all-embracing ring to it, as if she was describing their relationship in its entirety, from the beginning
He didn't feel that was fair or true
Only since returning from Norway had he found it difficult to communicate, and the experience had closed him off from everyone, not just from her
In March, when he tried to let her know what he was thinking, he had been met with complete incredulity
Is this one of your jokes?
It was the type of response a whistleblower might expect
In that sense, perhaps, it was predictable

19

During the next few days he succumbed to a feeling of inertia and despair
Kalivaki no longer seemed like the paradigm that he had seen it as
To think it had brought the words of Emerson to mind!
He managed a hollow laugh
It was merely a far-off corner of the earth where no one had anything to say, and nothing ever happened
It was a vacuum, a dead space

Now came the memory he wanted least
One night in the house in London he had woken from a dream of such extreme violence that he had to sit up in bed and put both feet on the floor
He left the room, Anya still asleep
Out on the landing, some grain or pattern in the silence held him where he was
Instead of going down to the kitchen, as he had been intending to, he climbed the stairs and stood outside Seth's room
The blankness of the door in the dark seemed terrible to him, but he forced himself to open it and it was then that he heard the sound
Each breath Seth took was a rusty, jagged weight dragged over something soft
The air was tearing at his throat

Was that what had brought him to a standstill on the landing?
Could that be why he had woken?
Maybe it even explained his terrifying dream
Then, suddenly, the light was on
Sweat lay slick on Seth's forehead and lacquered his dyed-black hair
His teeth looked gray
Fuck off
The words were murmured, slurred
Two bottles on the floor, both empty
Fentanyl and vodka
How did you know? Anya asked later, when they were in the hospital
I'm not sure, he said
Some kind of instinct, I suppose
Later still, when Seth was out of danger, she said, What made you go up to his room?
You never go up to his room
She sounded resentful
She should have been the one to sense that something was wrong
She should have woken up, not him
He managed not to say what it was in his mind to say
It's lucky someone did

For hours on end, he sat in front of the house and stared out over the olive trees and the barren land beyond
He couldn't read or even move

He couldn't think
All he could do was sleep
Perhaps he should return to London, as Anya had begged him to
Would she take him back, though?
And what about the nausea?
He would have no choice but to see it as an aberration, pretend that it had never happened
If he experienced the same thing again, he would be treated as Jess had said he would be treated, like someone having a breakdown
He would be absorbed into a system whose existence he questioned and whose impact he deplored
If on the other hand he stayed away he would be alone, and who was to say that his life would be worthwhile, or simpler, or even feasible?
Kristen had told him he shouldn't overestimate his own importance
Anya would survive, whether he was there or not
That was all well and good, but what about the effect on him?
What damage was he inflicting on himself?
His family had taken second place to what he was going through
Love had taken second place
He had sacrificed everything—and for what?
For an *idea*

20

Somebody was splashing him
Still half-asleep, he leapt from the bed
Stop it, he cried out
What are you *doing*?
He switched on the light and stood there, blinking
There was no one in the room
He looked down at himself
His boxer shorts and the bottom of his T-shirt were wet
Turning back to the bed, he saw a dark patch
He bent close and smelled, then stood up fast, his face flushing with embarrassment and shame
He seemed to hear his father's voice
Think you're better than me, do you?
Think you're superior?
Well, look at you now

Removing the sheet and then the mattress cover, he dropped both on the floor
The urine had soaked right through
He heaved the mattress off the bed and stood it against the wall, the wet patch facing outwards
Downstairs, he filled a bucket with hot water and added a scoop of washing powder, then he returned to the bedroom and scrubbed at the stain

He changed the water two or three times and kept scrubbing
Nothing like this had ever happened to him before
What was going on?

When he could do no more, he went into the bathroom, took off his T-shirt and shorts, and put them in the washbasin to soak, then he had a shower and dressed
His watch said 4:51
Opening the bedroom window, he leaned his elbows on the windowsill
There was no easing of the darkness, not even in the east
The stars had arms or rays, like the stars that appear in children's stories
They never failed to amaze him

In the kitchen he lit the gas under the coffeepot and turned on the radio, which was tuned to a station that played traditional Greek music
As soon as it was light, he would drag the mattress down the stairs and leave it outside, in the sun
Hopefully, by the time it dried, it would be as good as new
Prizing the lid off a biscuit tin, he found the last two pieces of the baklava he had bought in Hora Sfakion
Black coffee and stale baklava
An early breakfast

Later, in the silence, as a song faded out, he heard a scratching
He went to the front door and opened it
A dark shape pushed past him, into the hallway
Hello, he said
He squatted on his haunches and ran a hand over the cat's coarse fur
I have something to confess
I wet the bed
The response was subdued and mournful, which seemed appropriate
He emptied half a can of tuna onto a saucer, then watched as the cat settled over it, lowering its blunt head
It felt good to have told someone, but the bleakness in his heart remained

21

By half past seven he had hauled the mattress down the stairs and leaned it against the wall next to the front door
He put his nose to the wet patch
He thought he could still smell urine, but maybe it was his imagination

Did you have an accident?

Philip jumped and then swung round
Niko was standing a few yards away, at the southwest corner of the house
Dressed in a camouflage T-shirt, he had a rifle slung over one shoulder and a brown leather bag over the other
He moved closer and propped his rifle against the wall, next to the mattress, and lit a cigarette
As before, he seemed to have no sense that he might be imposing or intruding
His complacency was extreme, almost unnatural

They say you're a hero, he said, his eyes on the olive grove below the house
Philip looked at him
You mean the fire?
Niko nodded
I didn't do that much, Philip said
A hero, Niko said, that's what they're saying
He seemed to wish it wasn't true
Philip asked if he was going hunting
Niko brought his eyes back from the olive grove
You want to know what happened here?
Not really, Philip said
Not anymore
Niko flicked some ash onto the ground
There was a murder

Sorry, Philip said, I don't have time for this
He turned to go back inside, but Niko grabbed him by the upper arm
His grip was fierce
Let go of me, Philip said
Niko's lips parted, as if he was about to argue or protest, but then his grip on Philip's arm relaxed
He shook his head, picked up his rifle
Walked away

22

That evening, in a guide to Crete, Philip came across a photograph of a monastery situated on the side of a mountain, high above the sea
Some of the buildings were the same color and texture as the land they stood on, as if they were trying to blend in
He consulted the map at the front of the book
The monastery was in a place called Preveli, some fifty miles down the coast
I could drive there, he thought
A change of scene might do me good
Anything to shake off the paralyzing sense of desolation

The next morning it was warm by eight o'clock, the air very still and clear, almost glassy
In the villages he passed through, nothing moved
When he reached the petrol station at the bottom of the hill, he ignored the turning to Frangokastello and drove straight on
The road took him through Patsianos, once home to the Patsos brothers
He had tried to learn more about their struggle against the Venetians, but when he looked through the various history books on Vernon and Allegra's shelves the phrases the writers used were pretty much identical, as if they had all drawn on the same source

Before too long, he found himself in the mountains
A few olive trees grew in the crumbling soil next to the road, so ancient looking that they seemed biblical
Higher up, there were pockets of color in among the rocks—the purple of thistles, the yellow of sage
Gradually, as he ascended, the bends grew tighter
Blasts of hot, fragrant air blew in through the open windows
As he rounded a corner in second gear, he stamped on the brake pedal, then leaned forwards, chest against the steering wheel
Scattered across the road were dozens of tomatoes

He switched off the engine and stepped out of the car
There was nobody about
He walked several paces and bent down

how to make a bomb

The tomatoes looked perfect, as if they had been delicately placed on the road
As if some sort of aesthetic had been observed
It made no sense
He stood up and looked ahead, half expecting a flatbed truck to reverse around the bend towards him
Surely the driver would realize that he had shed part of his load?
The spillage could only have happened moments earlier

But no one came

In the harsh light, the green leaves of the olive trees looked silver
The sky was a blank, impenetrable blue
He had the strange feeling of being in an arena
He had been set a puzzle or a challenge, and the stillness was the audience waiting to see what he would make of it
Forces much greater than he was had agreed that he shouldn't be disturbed

He hurried back to his car
In the boot was a plastic bag from the supermarket in Hora Sfakion
Returning to where the tomatoes lay, he began to pick them up, one by one, and place them in the bag

When he had collected all of them, he stowed the bag in the boot
Once again, he had the sense that there were forces present—
gods, he thought—and that he was being watched or
monitored, and that his actions met with their approval

He drove on, still marveling at the sight of the tomatoes spilled
across the road, each one unharmed, immaculate
Even for a nonbeliever, it was tempting to think in terms of a
divine intervention, a sign from the heavens
There had to be a rational explanation
Of course there did
The timing of it, though—and the unlikeliness
The feeling of having been singled out when he most needed it

23

In forty-five minutes, he had reached the Lower Monastery of
St John the Baptist, destroyed by the Turks in the nineteenth
century, and then again by the Germans during the Battle of
Crete
He considered visiting the ruins, but decided to keep going
The image that had caught his imagination was that of the
Upper Monastery, which was still inhabited by monks

He followed the road as it rose up from the valley floor and felt his bleakness and desolation begin to lift

As he approached the monastery, he passed a memorial garden built on the edge of the cliff
There were two statues, one of a soldier, the other of a monk
Both men were gripping rifles
That morning, in the guidebook, he had read about the part the monks had played in World War Two
Although the Germans had threatened the Cretan people with harsh reprisals if they provided the Allies with support or shelter, Abbot Agathangelos Lagouvardos had coordinated rescue missions for retreating Allied troops
In 1941, for instance, lights were used to guide a British submarine into the bay at Limni, below the monastery, and a group of Australian soldiers was successfully evacuated
There were serious repercussions
Many of the monks were arrested, interrogated, and thrown into prison in Chania, but those who remained behind refused to be discouraged
In defiance of the Germans, they continued both to care for Allied troops trapped on the island and to assist guerrilla fighters from the National Resistance movement
As Philip surveyed the rugged slopes, he imagined men filing down a steep path under cover of darkness, the submarine glinting on the water far below

---

He paid a small entrance fee to a wiry, sallow man in a yellow T-shirt and moved on into a courtyard of pale stone, his eyes half-closed against the glare
From somewhere close by came the cry of a peacock
Smooth, sand-colored steps led to the upper level, where a single cypress grew against the balustrade
Next to it stood an old fir tree, a pair of iron bells hanging in its twisted branches, among the cones
He came across a small spring or well and drank from the metal scoop
The water tasted of the rocks, cool and mineral
Later, he sat on a bench in the shade
Below the monastery walls were cages housing various animals, including geese, llamas, hens, and deer
There was also a cross adorned with horns and antlers
A warm wind pushed through the courtyard, past terra-cotta urns containing succulents and oleander
The branches of the fir tree swayed
The voices of other tourists sounded so distant that they might have been the voices of the dead

Before leaving, he walked into the church
Inside were two monks dressed in black robes, each with a *skufia* on his head
There was also a blonde woman with a young girl
Mother and daughter, he thought
He watched as the woman spoke to the older of the two monks

The monk nodded, then reached for a golden cross with a round glass bauble built into it
Moving close to the woman, he placed the cross horizontally against her forehead and murmured a few words, then he turned to the young girl and did the same
The woman smiled and thanked him, then she put a hand on her daughter's back, between her shoulder blades, and steered her past Philip, towards the door
Her face, which didn't seem to register him at all, had an otherworldly calmness that surprised him

Would you also like a blessing?

His attention had been focused on the woman and her child, and he hadn't noticed the monk approaching with the cross
The monk's expression was playful, as if the whole thing was a game, but Philip knew that it was not
Yes, I would, Philip said
There was a hollow, metallic noise as the cross made contact with his forehead, and this also seemed humorous, though the humor had a divine element that he hadn't expected and couldn't have explained
He closed his eyes and stood quite still, the metal cool against his skin
He listened to the words
The fact that he didn't understand the language gave the blessing a dimension it wouldn't otherwise have had—or rather,

it emphasized the unfathomable aspect of a blessing, the sacred mystery from which it came

The words stopped, and the coolness left his forehead
He opened his eyes again
Thank you, he said
The monk nodded, then turned away and placed the cross inside a glass-fronted cabinet

Out in the sunshine again, Philip felt lighter and more anchored
He drove back down the hill and parked above a beach that he had noticed in the guidebook
Megalo Potamos—or "Great River"—was a beautiful place, one of the most beautiful places that he had ever seen
The river, which flowed southwards, out of a gorge, was the deep, dull green of jade
Bending towards him, it ran parallel to a strip of stones and sand before emptying itself into the sea
Dozens of palm trees clustered on both its banks
From high above, they looked like stars

There was no road to the beach
You had to climb down a steep path, then cross the river
He wondered if the Australian soldiers had used this route during their evacuation by the monks

how to make a bomb

Back then, he doubted there would have been steps cut into the rock
The descent would have been perilous, especially in the dark

By the time he reached the bottom, he was sweating
He took off his shoes and socks, then rolled up his trousers and stepped into the river
The coldness of the water was a shock, and it tugged hard at his legs, but it only took a few seconds to get across
Once on the sand, he stripped down to his trunks
He swam to a huge triangular rock that stood at the far end of the beach, close to the shore
Floating on his back, he studied its fractured surface
It looked like an ancient, weathered heart, he thought, a heart that had fossilized, become a monument
He waded out of the sea, then walked back to where his clothes were and lay facedown on the warm stones
Small waves broke close by, making no more sound than someone dropping into an armchair

Later, as he sat at the beach bar, under the tamarisk trees, an idea came to him
He finished his beer, then he paid and left
Arriving at St John the Theologian as it was about to close, he told the gatekeeper that he had a gift for the monks
He held up the supermarket bag of tomatoes, thinking it would be taken from him, but the man pointed through the narrow gate

Go to the church, he said
Somebody is there

The monk Philip found in the church was not the one who had blessed him earlier
He was disappointed, but only for a second
Can I help you? the monk said
Philip said that he had brought a gift
He stepped forwards and showed the monk the bag, holding it open with both hands
The monk took a look, then threw his head back and laughed
Philip had always thought of the phrase "to throw your head back and laugh" as a cliché
It wasn't something that ever happened, except maybe in badly written books
But this particular monk actually *threw his head back and laughed*, so much so that the curve of his top teeth and the pink roof of his mouth were visible
The sight of the tomatoes had made him happy

On the drive back to Kalivaki, Philip found that he was smiling
In gathering the tomatoes and making a gift of them, he had been caught up in some kind of energy or process, perhaps for the first time in his life
He wasn't sure what that energy or process was, only that it had always been there
It was tempting to use a word like "holy"

Its vagueness and enormity felt apt
When he thought of how the tomatoes would provide sustenance, and when he thought that he had been the intermediary, since without his intervention they would almost certainly have gone to waste, he felt a surprising and oddly powerful humility
The story didn't begin and end with him, and it wasn't about him, and yet it proved that he had agency
He might be an outcast, a laughingstock, a kind of latter-day Don Quixote, as Inés had pointed out, he might be a source of exasperation and despair to everyone who knew him, but he could have an *effect*
If he felt comforted, that was why—though "comforted" was too small a word, too soft
"Vindicated" might be closer to the mark

As he followed that empty, sometimes vertiginous road down to the plain of Frangokastello, then up again, through the gritty white villages of Agios Nektarios and Nomikiana, he returned to the moment when he showed the monk the contents of the bag
What startled him, in retrospect, was how the monk appeared to exist on the surface of himself
Far from making him superficial, it seemed like a complex and enlightened state, only achieved by years of discipline and contemplation
He thought of the monk's happiness, and how genuine it had been

Such delight taken in something so inconsequential
He remembered the ease with which the monk had been able to access joy
Apparently aware of everything that led up to that moment—the coincidence, the unlikelihood, the *logic*—he had been able to celebrate it wholeheartedly
That, surely, was the way to live
In a place like St John the Theologian, all ties to the world had been severed
There were no intrusions, no distractions—only sun and wind and stones and prayers and sky
Things could make the impression they were meant to make

24

He slept deeply that night
The next day, he woke up with the idea that he should work on Vernon and Allegra's house
He spent most of the morning in the living room and kitchen, treating the beams on the ceiling for woodworm
The chemical he used was so toxic that he had to wear a mask and gloves
Every now and then, he put down his brush and went outdoors, just to breathe some fresh air
At two o'clock he stopped for lunch

how to make a bomb

Paximadia bread, goats' cheese, tomatoes, and a glass of chilled retsina
A coffee afterwards
The heat lay on the sea, making it look pale, almost white
Something was beginning to crystallize in him, the outline or shape of a decision
He had thought he would spend weeks in the house
Not just the spring, the summer too
With all the swimming and the fresh fruit and the olive oil, he had imagined a fit version of himself, his joints and muscles loose and free of pain, his skin darkened by the sun
Now, though, he wasn't so sure
The vision seemed self-serving, egotistical
It felt too limited

In the afternoon he moved upstairs and treated the beams in the two bedrooms and the bathroom
By early evening, his shoulders ached from painting, and his eyes and nose were smarting from the fumes
He had a hot shower, then walked up into the village, thinking he would have an ouzo with the men, but as he passed Niko's house he noticed that all the lights were on
On an impulse, he knocked on the front door
As he pushed it open, a shadow fell across the passageway
Niko came forwards out of the gloom and asked Philip what he wanted
Niko, Philip said, I'd like to hear your story
He saw that Niko had a wary, almost wounded look

I'm sorry if I was rude the other day, he went on
I was in a funny mood
Niko studied him for a few long moments
Are you hungry?

He led Philip into the kitchen, where the woman in the black dress was preparing dinner
Niko pointed to an empty chair and Philip sat down
The woman looked at him, over her shoulder
Kalispera, Philip said
She murmured a few words that he didn't understand, then she went over to a cupboard, returning with a plate, a knife and fork, and a glass
As she reached past him to set his place, he smelled her sweat, which had the bitterness of vinegar
Niko spoke to her, and a liter bottle with no label appeared on the table between them
He pulled the cork out and poured two glasses of red wine
This is very generous of you, Philip said

Niko drank, then put his glass down on the table and began to speak in a voice that was flat and unemotional
The murder happened in front of your house, he said, where the olive trees are
That's where my mother killed my father
Philip stared at him
My father was a violent man, Niko went on

how to make a bomb

He beat my mother every day
One time he hit her so hard that her shoulder was dislocated
She couldn't use her arm, but he forced her to work
When I tried to help her, he pulled me away
She must learn, he said
He looked past Philip, towards the window, and Philip had the sudden feeling that there were two of him, one sitting at the table, listening to Niko, the other standing outside, by the gate
Later, Niko said, my father would be tender
He held her hand or stroked her hair, and tears would be running down his face
What have I done?
I'm sorry
I didn't mean to hurt you
Niko drained his glass and poured himself another, then pushed the bottle across the oilcloth to Philip
His eyes had darkened, but his lips were pale, bloodless
The tenderness was worse than the violence, he went on, because we didn't know where it came from, or how long it would last
When he was like that it was quiet in the house, it made us all relax, we almost forgot
What did she do, Philip asked, to make him so angry?
If she was late serving dinner, Niko said
If she looked at him the wrong way, or she didn't look at him
People like that, it doesn't matter what you do
The violence, it always happens

The woman spoke to Niko and he half turned in his chair and said something abrupt
She asked if I'm talking about the past, Niko told Philip
The woman spoke again
This time she sounded more insistent
She says it does no good, Niko said
I told her that you're living in the house, but she says it's nothing to do with you, and anyway, it's over and done with, it's water down the drain, it's old bones in the ground
Maybe she has a point, Philip said
Niko was shaking his head
It made us what we are, me and my sister
Philip looked at him
She's your sister?
Niko nodded
She's seven years older
She looked after me when our mother and father were gone
She still looks after you, Philip said
Niko nodded again
Yes

Dinner was a piece of grilled meat, potatoes cooked in oil, and some local greens known as *vlita*
Once Niko's sister had served them, she retreated to a chair in the corner and took up her sewing, just as she had on the night when Philip stood outside the window
He asked Niko what his sister's name was

how to make a bomb

Anatolia, Niko said
At the mention of her name, Anatolia glanced up, then she shrugged and went back to her mending
Won't she join us? Philip asked
Niko told him that she preferred to eat alone

After the meal, they retired to the backyard, where they sat against the wall on plastic chairs
The evening was warm and still
Niko uncorked a second liter of red wine, then produced a packet of cigarettes and held it out to Philip
Philip thanked him and took one
Niko reached across and lit the cigarette for him, then lit one for himself
He leaned back, smoothing a hand over his hair
Tell me about the murder, Philip said
Niko looked at him sidelong
You're very complicated
Philip laughed
Why do you say that?
I don't know what you want, Niko said
He dragged on his cigarette, then flicked the filter with his thumb so the ash dropped to the ground
Maybe you also don't know
He filled their glasses and put the cork back in the bottle, hitting it gently with the heel of his hand, then he began

It was the end of April, and there was thunder in the mountains
A ferocious wind blew out of the east
Locals called it the Big Tongue
It usually lasted for several days and drove everybody mad
During that time, he ran down to the coast
The land ended abruptly, dropping thirty feet into the sea
Waves pounded at the base of the cliff, the gray water topped with foaming white
Through the spray, he saw a trawler halfway to the horizon, it was rising and falling, one moment it was there, the next it was gone, he worried it might sink
But then his viewpoint twisted and he was on the boat and he could see himself, a lone figure standing on the shore
He was the one who was in danger, he remembered thinking
He was the one who needed rescuing
The roar of the water and the wind was so loud that if he spoke or even shouted he couldn't hear himself
He shouted and kept on shouting, there was more inside him than he had realized, things he hated and didn't have the power to change
In the middle of it all, the rain swooped in across the land like a handful of something cold flung from a great distance
Striking him full in the face, it snatched the breath out of his lungs
He was wet through in seconds
He turned and hurried home
The rain came after him, it was in his eyes and ears and down his neck, but he ran on

how to make a bomb

The rocks were slippery, and he lost his footing more than once
By the time he reached the olive grove, he had a stitch
The crash of the storm should have hidden any other sound, but he thought he heard a cry of pain
He looked through the rain-streaked air and saw his father with just a singlet on, his thick arms dangling
His mother stood nearby
One of her eye sockets was a cup of blood
The cup was filled too full, though, and the blood was spilling down her face, her throat, all down her front, it didn't show, her dress was black
She was holding a rifle level with her waist
When his father made a lunge at her, the gun jerked in her hands
The harsh, flat noise came after
His father jumped backwards, it looked funny, like a party trick, a cartoon on TV
He wanted to laugh out loud or clap
How did you do that?
Can you teach me?
Then his father was lying on the mud, one leg bent under his body, mouth wide-open

After that, his memory had gaps and holes in it
He was in the house and his mother was holding him against her very tight and she was shaking
Some of the blood from her eye had dripped onto his shirt
His father was outside, in the storm

His mouth was full of rain
They'll come for me, his mother told him, and I'll have to go with them
He didn't understand that his father was dead and that he would never see his mother again
What happened to your eye? he asked
Nothing, she said
She tried to laugh, but it didn't work, not with all that blood on her face
She pulled him hard against her once again
She was still trembling
Are you cold? he asked
A little, she said
What about you?
I'm fine, he said

I'm fine
Niko repeated the words, then brought his glass of wine up to his mouth and drained it

In court, he went on, his mother chose not to defend herself
She refused to show remorse
I killed him, she said, and I'm glad I killed him
I should have done it earlier
No sooner had she spoken than her dead husband's father stood up and shot her
He had smuggled a gun into the courtroom

She died half an hour later
Things like that happened back then, Niko went on, though I knew nothing about it at the time
Anatolia told me later, when she thought I was old enough
A moth bounced off the bare bulb above his head
His face was in shadow
I'm so sorry, Philip said
Niko lit another cigarette
According to the law of blood, he said, our families are equal now
That's how local people look at it
He shrugged
I'm sorry, Philip said again
Their conversation had nowhere else to go
After finishing the wine, he thanked Niko for his hospitality, then he stood up and left

On his way back through the house he stopped by a half-open door
A double bed took up most of the room, and the bedside lamp with its red shade gave off a light that was muted, confidential
Propped against a stack of pillows were several dolls
Their eyes and hair looked realistic, almost human, and they were dressed in elaborate outfits made of satin, lace, and velvet
Anatolia was kneeling on the far side of the bed with her head bowed
He could hear her voice—subdued, monotonous

Not wanting to interrupt her prayers, he stepped away and moved off down the corridor

25

In the morning he packed a few essentials into a bag
The plan that he had sensed as an outline or a shape a few days earlier had assumed a concrete form
It had also acquired an urgency
Hoisting the bag over his shoulder, he climbed up through the tangle of undergrowth behind the house
After receiving such unexpected hospitality, he didn't think he could disappear without letting Niko know

He walked in through the open door
There was no one in the kitchen, but the radio was on and a pan of stock or soup was bubbling away on the stove
He found Anatolia in the backyard, in the wind and sun, hanging out the washing
Niko? he asked
She shook her head, then said a few words that he didn't understand
He signaled that he needed something to write with

how to make a bomb

Back in the kitchen, she handed him a pencil stub and an old shop receipt
He scribbled a note to Niko and gave it to her, then he hesitated
He realized that she was watching him
She seemed perplexed, as if she couldn't imagine what else he might want
He had drawn her close without intending to, the space between and around them suddenly more intimate
He felt anything was possible just then, in the cool half dark of the kitchen
They had stepped to one side of time, both of them together, both at once, like two people dancing, and that knowledge held him there for even longer
How strange and wonderful that life could open up like that, he thought
Scenes there shouldn't have been room for
Moments that hadn't been factored in, or even foreseen, since they owed their existence to the miracle of pure chance
If only I could *make* that happen

And then, out of nowhere, he found the words he had been searching for
Evfaristó poli echthés nichte
Nóstimo fagitó
Thank you for the other night
Excellent food

Her face cleared, and she smiled at him, not something he had imagined that he would ever see
Since she made a point of remaining at the edge of every situation, as if she didn't trust herself, or didn't quite belong, he had assumed her capacity for joy had been taken from her
He was glad she had proved him wrong

26

As he drove out of Kalivaki, his mind flew on ahead of him
He saw himself at the entrance to the monastery, the gatekeeper pointing to a pale-yellow building in the lower courtyard
He would find the abbot sitting at a desk in a high-ceilinged room
On the wall behind him there would be a painted wooden icon
Otherwise the room would be bare
As he drew near, the abbot would look up from the book he was reading
He would notice the blown pupil in the abbot's left eye
It was the monk who had blessed him with the cross on his first visit
You were here before, the abbot would say
As before, his manner would be playful on the surface, but serious beneath

how to make a bomb

Philip would nod
Last week, he would say
You were kind enough to give me your blessing
And this week? the abbot would say
What can I do for you?
I was just wondering, Philip would say
Could I stay here for a while?

Before the abbot could reply, he would describe what the monastery meant to him
During the days prior to receiving the blessing, he would say, he had been plunged in a state of profound despair
He didn't think he had ever felt so low
More than once, he had found himself in tears
He had even wet the bed
In an attempt to extricate himself, he had decided on a change of scene
The choice of the monastery as a destination had been arbitrary, almost incidental
He had expected nothing
Expectation required energy, and he'd had none of that

He would describe how he had discovered the tomatoes lying on the road, all of them in perfect condition
They had taken him out of himself when that was precisely what he had needed
He felt that he had witnessed a sort of miracle

Though he recognized that the tomatoes were a gift, he would tell the abbot, he hadn't known quite how to use that gift
All he had understood was that they were valuable, and that they shouldn't be wasted, and since they had graced him with their presence, since he was the one who had been chosen, as it were, he had to assume responsibility for them
To begin with, he would tell the abbot, that fact that the tomatoes had appeared seemed enough in itself
He had gathered them with care, as if from the vine, then he had got back into his car and driven on
He visited the monastery, as planned
He swam in the sea
He drank a beer under the trees
One thing flowed into the next, and everything was easy, idyllic
He felt that he had returned to the world
No, that was wrong
He felt that he had *been returned*
What had happened was something he'd had no say in and no power over
It had been bestowed on him

He would look into the abbot's face—his tolerant, amused expression, his damaged eye
I felt blessed, he would say, even before you blessed me

---

how to make a bomb

It was while he was on the beach, he would go on, that he realized he should give the tomatoes to the monastery
It would be a modest act, and yet, at the same time, it seemed audacious
He wasn't even sure if monks accepted gifts from strangers
But he drove back to the monastery, and the gatekeeper directed him to the church, and the tomatoes were duly handed over
How to explain what he felt at that moment?
It didn't cross his mind that he was being considerate
or generous, he would say, or that the monks might be appreciative
No, it was more as if he had finally discovered the role that he was supposed to be playing
He had not only taken part in a process
He had brought it to fruition
For once, he was fully woven into the fabric of existence
In using a phrase like "the fabric of existence," he ran the risk of sounding pretentious, he knew that, but it didn't seem inappropriate, since his actions had a spiritual or even cosmic aspect, having more to do with that which was heavenly than with the things of the earth
As the wine and the wafer were symbols in a Mass, he would tell the abbot, so the tomatoes were symbolic, they had been used to make a point, and he began to wonder if there had been times in the past when he had failed to understand that some kind of gesture or contribution was required of him
Had his life been one long history of inattention, a catalog of missed signals and opportunities gone begging?

And how would it feel if he lived with such heightened awareness that he was *always* woven into the fabric?

Once again, he would look into the abbot's eyes
Is that what it's like for you, Father?
Or perhaps it would be better to keep that kind of thought to himself
He shouldn't be too familiar
Certainly he shouldn't seem impertinent or cocky

What I was given on that day, he would go on quickly, was a sense of perspective
Nothing that happens is so bad that it can't be accommodated
That was my feeling
And that feeling came from here
He would gesture at the room, but his gesture would pass beyond the walls to include all the buildings and all the men who lived and worshipped there
I'll always be grateful to this place, he would say, even if you turn me away
And if you do turn me away, I'll understand
Thank you for allowing me to speak
As he fell silent, he would see the abbot rise to his feet
Come with me, the abbot would say

how to make a bomb

Philip had been so deep in his imaginings that he had forgotten to keep an eye out for the bend in the road where he had found the tomatoes
Up ahead, he saw a sign that said RODAKINO, the blue metal riddled with bullet holes
He was already halfway to the monastery

He pictured the abbot leading him towards a building that he had noticed on his first visit
Its stone façade was as pockmarked and scarred as the mountains that rose behind it, though clouds of pink and scarlet oleander grew around the doors and window frames
He would be shown into a room that was small and bare
There would be an iron bed, a table and a chair, and a cross fixed to the wall with a nail
If he opened the shutters, there would be a view of the land behind the monastery
The splintered rocks, the empty sky
Here you will find peace, the abbot would say, or words to that effect
It would take Philip a few moments to realize that he was being granted the favor he had asked for, and his sense of relief would be so great that he might fall to his knees

As he entered the village of Rodakino, he shifted into second gear

He passed a sheep that had been hung upside down from a tree's horizontal branch
A man was working at its belly with a knife
The blood looked fierce and glossy in the sunlight
Peering through the windscreen, he noted the barren mountain ridges to the north
Up there somewhere, in the 1800s, local men had raised a Greek flag in defiance of the Turks
This was not a place that liked to compromise

27

By two o'clock that afternoon he was in the little seaside town of Plakias
He ate lunch in a restaurant that overlooked the beach
Once again, his mind ran on ahead
He pictured himself in the monastery at night, near the church
The cypress tree rose above him, its spear-shaped foliage black against the sky's dark blue
A breeze came up close and pushed itself against his body
He thought of an animal, invisible but gentle
He would sleep with his door open
Apart from him, there were no strangers in the place
He couldn't come to any harm

He would attend as many services as he could, since they would lend a structure and a rhythm to his days
Unable to follow the Greek, he would focus on the sound it made instead
He would notice how certain phrases were repeated
He might begin to understand how prayer could wear a path through your mind, as water wears a path through stone, and how, if you prayed for long enough, and with sufficient intensity and concentration, all your thoughts would take that path, and you could keep all other thoughts at bay
Prayer created a desired absence, a calming emptiness
Prayer brought peace

During daylight hours, there would probably be work for him to do
Every morning, before the tourists arrived, he could sweep the courtyards and the steps, and in the late afternoon, when everyone had gone, he could water the plants in their terracotta pots
He could also help in the kitchen or the garden
He would see the tasks as gifts
Gradually, he would begin to substitute his own language with the language of the monks
Glory to you, our Lord
Holy Mother of God, save us
Lord Jesus Christ, have mercy on me, the sinner

Glory to God
There were any number of permutations, and he would learn each one of them in Greek
If he talked to the monks while performing his daily chores, he would use blessings to the exclusion of all other speech, as they did
Nothing else was needed

Would he keep a journal?
He could call it *Seven Days in Preveli*
It would be a record of his insights and impressions
His entries would be simple yet profound, and who knows, there might even be epiphanies
That, surely, was why he had been drawn to the stationery shop in Piraeus, and why he had purchased the blue notebook
But when he saw himself sitting at the desk with a pen in his hand he couldn't imagine what he would write
He felt a long way from words
Oddly, this was a feeling of richness, not one of poverty
Feeling empty felt like being full

Gazing out over the bay of Plakias, he smiled to himself
The idea that he might keep a journal was obviously rooted in old habits, redundant modes of thinking
Blank pages
That would be the most faithful account of time spent at the monastery

28

Pushing his plate aside, he reached for the postcards he had bought
He wrote the first one to Vernon and Allegra
He wanted to reassure them that their house was in good order
Once again, he thanked them for allowing him to stay
It came at exactly the right time

He wrote a second card, to Seth
The other day I was thinking how we stood on that wall in Spain and watched the feather and the seaweed and the bits of paper fly across the bay
Do you remember that?
It was one of the moments in my life when I was happiest, and you seemed happy too
I love you very much, Seth
Feathers in the wind!
Dad

He imagined Seth reading the card in rainy Manchester, lines appearing on his forehead, lips tucked into his mouth
Displays of parental affection always baffled him

Finally, he wrote to Jess
I was hoping you might do something for me
On my way to Crete, I lost my phone, and I'm having trouble getting through to Anya
The last time we spoke, she said I had shut her out
Could you have a word with her?
I thought you might be able to explain what I'm doing
Just give her your version of what I told you in the British Library
He looked up, pen in hand
He knew how Jess would respond
Anya won't listen
She doesn't like me
Also, she'll realize that you're behind it
She's not stupid
She'll think we're plotting against her
He sighed, then bent over the card again
I know it's a lot to ask, but please try
I can't think of anyone more capable than you
There's no one I trust more

After posting the cards, he walked back to his car
He had parked in the sun, and the interior was stifling
The steering wheel almost burned his hands
Opening the windows, he leaned back

how to make a bomb

He pictured his last morning at the monastery, the sky white but with a suggestion of brown, like scalded milk
He would find the abbot in the shadow of the gatehouse
I want to thank you for taking me in, he would say, and his voice would be unsteady suddenly, as if he was speaking at the funeral of someone he had loved
You realized how much it meant to me
And also when you blessed me with the cross, you realized how much it meant
He would take out several folded fifty-euro notes
I'd like to give you this, he would say, though what you gave me can't be bought
We gave you nothing, the abbot would say
Everything you received, you found for yourself

No, wait, Philip thought as he turned the key in the ignition
That sounds too secular
He drove along the seafront, then turned inland, past a white hotel
By the time he reached the village of Lefkogeia, he had a sentence that felt appropriate, in character

Everything you received, you received through the grace of God

29

In his imagination he had just left the monastery
In reality he was about to arrive
Up ahead, on the cliff top, he saw the memorial garden with its two bronze statues and its bursts of oleander
When he rounded the next bend, the weathered gray-and-yellow buildings would be visible
Suddenly, he had a vision of his Fiat Panda coming along the road towards him, two versions of himself, each traveling in the opposite direction
For a moment, he wasn't sure which one seemed more real
Which one he would rather be

At the entrance, the same man was on duty, only this time he was wearing sunglasses
I would like to stay here, Philip told him
The man lowered his eyes, and an ambiguous smile showed at the edges of his mouth
In broken English, he told Philip that there was only room for the monks
In that case, Philip said, I need to talk to the abbot
This is very important to me
The man reached down with one hand and adjusted the position of a piece of paper on his desk

The abbot is not here, he said
In Rethymnon
Was he lying?
Philip couldn't tell
He asked if he could talk to someone else
The man was still moving papers about, but not, Philip felt, to any great purpose
There is a monk in the church, the man said
You can go there
That enigmatic smile again, as if he knew something that Philip didn't

Philip climbed the steps to the upper courtyard and entered the church
A monk was placing candles in a waist-high votive stand
He had thinning, curly hair and a full beard
Philip had never seen him before
He told the monk that he was hoping to stay at the monastery
He was a pilgrim, he said, and he was seeking refuge
The monk listened as the gatekeeper had listened, with his face turned a little to one side
When Philip had finished, he shook his head
He tried to say something, but his English wasn't as good as the gatekeeper's, and Philip didn't understand
He guided Philip back to the door and pointed at another monk, who was sitting in the shade beneath the fir tree
This was the person Philip should speak to

As Philip approached, the monk rose to his feet
He wore glasses with severe, black frames, and gave off an air of authority that was absent in the other monks
He looked almost daunting
Philip greeted him and repeated his request
The response was the same
We have only monks here, he told Philip
There is no room
Perhaps I could talk to the abbot, Philip said
The monk gave a shrug
Today he is in Rethymnon
Philip asked if the abbot spoke English
The monk laughed dismissively, almost condescendingly
No, he said

In simple language, Philip described how he had been suffering, and how he had paid the monastery a visit, and how, by complete chance, he had received a blessing
Since then, he told the monk, everything had changed
He had returned because he would like to experience once again the peace and beauty of the place
The monk was shaking his head, slowly but emphatically
There is no room here, he said, only for monks
We are only five
So I can't even stay the night? Philip said

how to make a bomb

I don't need a bed
I can sleep on the floor
The monk looked past him, into the sky, his eyes untroubled, expressionless, impenetrable as doors with no handles
Only monks, he said
A peacock close by let out a shriek

Philip looked away, wishing he could summon a convincing argument
Nothing came to him
He was claiming to be a pilgrim seeking refuge—but that wasn't true, not really
What he wanted was to be put back in touch with the feeling the blessing had given him, that trancelike, almost paradoxical mixture of lightness and being anchored
He wanted that feeling for longer
Ideally, he wanted it forever
At the same time, he was looking for a simple, uncluttered way to live
In a monastery like Preveli, all the unnecessary and oppressive layers had been stripped away
The surface was just the surface, and reality was one pure thing
It occurred to him that feeling grounded and also weightless might be consequences of such a life
If they wouldn't let him stay, though, he had no chance of finding out

He looked back just as the monk was moving off
It's really not possible? he said
He could hear the despair in his voice, and hoped that it might have some effect
The monk considered him, unsmiling
Not, he said

In his imaginary appearance at St John the Theologian, Philip had allowed for the fact that he might be turned away
He had even told the abbot that he would understand
The actual experience felt different
This wasn't the monastery that he had visited before, and it wasn't the monastery that he'd imagined either
Perhaps this was the true monastery, though
Unyielding and fierce

He didn't know what to think as he drove back to Kalivaki
His mind felt bruised, but also numb
Was it conceivable that the monks had seen into him more deeply than he saw himself?
Had they detected something equivocal, or wanting?
In his fantasy version of the monastery, the monk who had blessed him had turned out to be the abbot
He had also spoken English
He had welcomed Philip, and had given him the nourishment that he had craved
It had been too simplistic, too far-fetched

It had been naïve
Ironically, the words that he had put in the abbot's mouth on the last morning, the words he had thought too secular, had been accurate after all
Everything he found, he would have to find for himself
He allowed himself a rueful smile

30

That night, back in the house, he woke up in a sweat, his heart beating with such force that his vision seemed to pulse
The door to the roof was open, and a man was standing in the gap
Hello? Philip said
The man shifted his weight from one foot to the other
He didn't speak
Philip thought at first that it was Niko
As his eyes adjusted, though, he saw that the man was dressed in black robes and a black *kalimavkion* with a veil
He had a full, dark beard, and a metal cross hung around his neck
He held a rifle at an angle across his body
Since the moon was behind him, his face was hard to make out, but he didn't look like any of the monks that Philip had seen at the monastery

He leaned up on his elbows
Who are you?
The monk shifted his weight again, his breathing slow and steady
The belt of bullets he was wearing gleamed
He appeared to be waiting for Philip to come to some kind of realization, but he wouldn't answer any questions
He wouldn't even open his mouth

When Philip woke again, the door to the roof was closed, and it was dark
Hello? he said
Are you still there?
He reached out and turned on the bedside lamp
Blinking in the glare, he saw that he was alone in the room
His watch said 4:11
He lay back against the pillow, but didn't fall asleep again until it was almost dawn

31

That day the wind burst out of the mountains, big scoops of it
Outside the house, the trees were hurled about, the sound of their leaves like waves crashing on a beach

He wondered if this was the Big Tongue that Niko had spoken of
When the rain came, it flew sideways through the air, almost horizontally
Hardly any landed on the ground
He tried going for a walk, but soon gave up, worried that he might be blown off his feet, or hit by a flying object

As he looked idly through the shelves in the downstairs room, he came across a history of Cretan religious institutions
If he hadn't noticed it before, it was perhaps because the gold letters on the spine had flaked or faded
He took the book over to a window seat
Inside, he found a chapter on the monasteries at Preveli

First, he read about Abbot Ephraim Prevelis, who had played an active role in the rebellion against the Turks in the late eighteenth century
Accused of killing a Turkish janissary with his bare hands, he was eventually acquitted
The cross Philip had been blessed with had been made by silversmiths when Ephraim was abbot, and was notable for the large crystal built into the handle
The monks of Preveli had carried the cross into battle with them, as other soldiers carry flags and banners, both to identify and to inspire them

Lost in a clash with the Turks at Amourgeles in 1823, the cross ended up in the hands of Genoese sailors, who bought it in a market in Heraklion
While passing through the waters off Preveli, their vessel became mysteriously becalmed
Only when the sailors returned the cross to its rightful owners were they able to continue on their journey

Something similar had happened during World War Two
In 1941, German officers looted the precious relic and loaded it onto a plane in Chania with the intention of flying it to Athens, but the plane wouldn't take off
The cross was transferred to a different plane
That plane wouldn't take off either
A few days later, in circumstances that were never recorded, the cross found its way back to the monastery
Philip lifted his eyes from the pages of the book
The plane that wouldn't leave the ground
The ship that wouldn't sail
Both the German army officers and the seafarers from Genoa appeared to have fallen under a spell
In wrongfully acquiring an object that didn't belong to them, they had forfeited their power

Next, he read about Melchizadek Tsouderos, another inspirational abbot

It was Tsouderos who had hoisted a flag on the hills above Rodakino in defiance of the Turkish invaders

Though he must have known that he was jeopardizing his own life and the life of the monks in his charge, he purchased weapons and stored them at the monastery, and also organized a local militia

Throughout the second half of the nineteenth century, the monks of Preveli regularly participated in revolutionary activity against the Turks

This long tradition of resistance provided the background or precedent for the courageous stand Abbot Lagouvardos took against the Germans in 1941

The statue on the cliff top was a memorial to Lagouvardos, and to the Allied troops that he had helped to save

Leaning back, with the book open on his lap, Philip thought once again about the monk who had appeared in the night

For holy men, dreams were the devil's vehicles, conveying temptation, illusion, and deceit, but he found it hard to dismiss or disregard what he had seen

He couldn't help remembering how Inés had responded to his dream about Clive, his childhood friend who had died

It's the message, not the messenger

In the case of the man standing patiently in his bedroom doorway, the two seemed inextricably linked

And there was something else

An armed figure had also featured in Niko's story
What had his mother been thinking when she followed her husband down into the olive grove?
Why had she taken a gun with her?
He thought he knew
It was the only way to make things stop
You try everything else, and then you reach for a weapon

Something came to him just then, and it came whole, like a soap bubble floating up into the air
See how swollen it looks, how iridescent
How full of possibility
See how it softly explodes, leaving no trace of itself behind
It was like a secret note that self-destructs the moment it has been deciphered
He felt giddy suddenly, off-balance
At last his dream about the monk made sense to him
It didn't matter that he had been turned away from the monastery
He had learned what he needed to learn

The storm had passed on
The wind had dropped
He opened the door and stepped outside
The sun shone in his eyes

A bell was ringing in the church
The smell of wet rock
Wet stone

The figure who had appeared to him didn't stand for contemplation and simplicity, or even for an unwavering sense of discipline
He didn't represent the nonmaterial life either
He wasn't a symbol of a world that was free of acquisition and consumption
No, his silence spoke of something else entirely

If your cause is just, you take up arms

32

The following morning, he went looking for Mrs Zoumpoulakis
He found her near the church, with a large, blue plastic bag of wild herbs
I'm leaving, he told her
She stared at him, her jaw tense, dark loops of skin beneath her eyes

I'll bring you the key, he went on
Tomorrow probably
She muttered a few words and shook her head, and he thought he knew what she was thinking
I'll never understand these foreigners, however long I live

That evening, after packing, he passed Niko and Anatolia's house
The place was in darkness
The dolls would be lined up on the bed in their fine clothes, their glass eyes glinting
Had Anatolia found comfort in them when she was a girl and her parents were at each other's throats?
Had she used them to block out the violence?
And what were they to her now?
Did they help to keep the past at bay, or had they become some kind of compensation for not having a family of her own?

On the main road, the usual men were sitting outside the *kafeneío*
Philip ordered an ouzo, then turned to the man in the tinted glasses
I'm leaving tomorrow
He stumbled a little over the Greek
You don't stay for the summer? the man said in English
Philip stared at him
You speak English?

how to make a bomb

The man's only answer was to light a cigarette
Philip tasted his ouzo
My plans have changed, he said
There's something I have to do
The man appeared to consider him
You will put out another fire?
The other men laughed quietly, as if they were on their own, and enjoying a private joke
To a greater or lesser extent, it seemed they all spoke English
He had to admire their slyness, their inscrutability
Something like that, he said, only this fire is bigger
Much bigger
The men shifted on their chairs
They hadn't grasped his meaning, and he wasn't about to enlighten them
He couldn't help relishing his one small moment of ascendancy
He had never got the better of them before

Finishing his ouzo, he signaled for the bill
The waiter slanted his eyes at the man with the tinted glasses
Philip looked at the man
Did you pay for my drink?
The man tilted his head back quickly
Philip thanked him, then he rose to his feet and went round the table, shaking hands with each of the men
Finally, he shook hands with the man in the glasses
After all this time in the village, he still knew nothing about him

He didn't know where he lived or who he lived with
He didn't even know his name

On his way back to the house, he took the long way round, the route that he had followed when he first arrived
It was dusk, but the sky clung to the last of the light
The land glowed with a peculiar, dull intensity, and the sea was the silver blue of a dress in a fairy tale
As he turned down the concrete path that led to the steps, Inés appeared ahead of him
She was looking over her shoulder, her black hair falling past her face
She could have been holding him to a promise that he had made, a promise that would be honored out here, in the dark, or sometime later, when they were in the house, or she might simply have been checking that he was still behind her, that he wasn't lost
A shiver passed through the world, though the fig trees that curled above her didn't move
I thought something might happen between us, he said
She was still looking at him, over her shoulder, a smudge of shadow at the corner of her mouth
It did, she said
Something did happen
She was wearing the black shirt and the white jeans that she wore on the night she invited him for dinner in her apartment, the night he told her that he didn't want anything from her
It wasn't what I thought, he said

She moved on, beneath the overhanging trees
I miss you, Inés, he called after her
I think of you
She was laughing suddenly, her eyes alive, her hair drifting across her open mouth
You don't think of me at all, she said

When he came round the corner of his house, Niko was sitting on the doorstep
I heard you're leaving, he said
Is that true?
Philip asked him how he knew
My aunt told me, Niko said
Mrs Zoumpoulakis
Wait a minute, Philip said
Mrs Zoumpoulakis is your aunt?
Niko nodded
She's my father's sister
This new information sank in slowly
The man Niko's mother had murdered was the brother of Mrs Zoumpoulakis, but not just that
Mrs Zoumpoulakis was also the daughter of the man who had smuggled a gun into the courtroom, and shot Niko's mother
She lived within the confines of a vendetta, and would constantly be wondering if more blood was about to be shed
No wonder she stood on the street, staring horror-struck at nothing

If she had agreed to act as caretaker for the house, it was probably because she wanted to retain some kind of physical connection with the tragedy
In that respect, she and Niko were the same
And suddenly he thought he understood why Anatolia had kept the dolls
Perhaps they were the only beings that she could rely on
After all, they were unlikely to be taken from her, and they could not be killed

Niko had picked up a twig and he was drawing a circle in the dirt between his feet
It's very sudden, he said
He seemed to understand that Philip had a secret agenda, and thought it was something he should be privy to
Have you eaten? Philip asked
Niko drew a second circle in the dirt, then shook his head
How about some dinner? Philip said
I'll cook for you

IV

softly explodes

I

He landed in London on a Tuesday afternoon
The sky was a clutter of white and gray, and the air had a sweaty smell, like the onions in hot dogs
He felt besieged by announcements
Health and safety mostly
If you see something that doesn't look right, speak to staff or text the British Transport Police
The trouble was, none of it looked right
What was he supposed to do, report every single thing he saw?
He missed Crete
Its raw simplicity, its lawlessness
Its fragrance

On the Gatwick Express he found a seat next to the window and picked up a crumpled copy of the *Metro*
The headline on the front said MONSOON BRITAIN
Apparently it would be the wettest June on record
He folded the paper, let it drop

how to make a bomb

The grind and screech of wheels on the track, the low babble of passengers
He closed his eyes and fell into a doze

When he arrived at Victoria, he left the station and walked down Vauxhall Bridge Road
An energy drinks can rolled past his foot
A crinkly, hollow sound
On the pavement spat-out chewing gum had been trodden into discs
A man in a suit approached
Philip's eyes were drawn to the neatly knotted tie, with its alternating stripes of frost blue and salmon pink
He experienced a moment of vertigo as other possible designs bombarded him
He had to stop and gag
The man gave him a look of mild disgust and hurried past
On the plane Philip had steeled himself against what was to come, but it had only heightened his apprehension and his hypersensitivity
You have to adapt, he told himself
Acclimatize
Remember why you're here

Some weeks ago, when Inés asked if he would write something, he had been unsure
Since then, his thoughts had taken a radical new turn

He wanted to critique the world that he was living in, but he also wanted to dismantle it
He would definitely be writing something
A polemic—or better still, a manifesto
At the same time, he knew that words alone weren't going to be enough
That was the lesson he had learned in Crete

He headed south on Vauxhall Bridge
In front of him was the MI6 building, a faux-Aztec fortress of poured concrete and triple-glazed green glass
To the west, late orange sunlight colored one side of a cylindrical tower block
It was rumored that an entire Russian Orthodox chapel had been taken up in the lift, piece by piece, and assembled in a penthouse belonging to the fertilizer tycoon and Putin crony Andrei Guriev
London was a laundromat for dirty money, now more than ever, billions a year
The Thames swirled past below, opaque and devious

As he came down off the bridge, Vauxhall bus station stood before him, its stainless steel roof reaching into the sky like a huge surreal pair of silver skis
Behind the station, almost lurking in its shadow, was a five-story Travelodge
Travelodge was a chain of hotels that seemed to pride itself not just on being ordinary, but on having no character at all

how to make a bomb

The elision of "travel" and "lodge" troubled him briefly, it was so obviously made-up, someone's bright idea, but staying there would guarantee a certain anonymity
And there was another advantage
He had never lived or worked in Vauxhall
He had only ever passed through on his way to somewhere else
If he was going into hiding, this was a good place to start

He pressed the button by the intercom
The door slid open
Reception was in the basement, the lighting stark as a supermarket or a detention center
The man behind the desk wore a name badge on a lanyard
MALCOLM
He had cropped gray hair, and his face was chapped, as though it hurt him to shave
Philip asked if he had a room
The man looked at him
You have to book online, he said
I can't book here? Philip said
The man shook his head
It's because of the area, he explained
Anybody could walk in
He paused
We have to protect the rooms
Ironically, he looked like someone with a criminal record
Nothing too serious

Possession of a controlled substance, low-value shoplifting
A bit of mindless vandalism

The thing is, Philip said, I lost my phone, and I don't have a laptop with me
Malcolm looked past him, into the lobby
As there's no one here, he said, I could do it for you if you like
That would be very kind, Philip said
Consulting his computer screen, Malcolm asked how many nights he would be staying
Philip had to think quickly
Four, he said
He gave Malcolm the information he needed, including the billing address for his credit card
With his missing phone and a home address that was only a few miles away, he was worried he might appear suspicious
Say something normal, he thought
Reassure the man
What time's breakfast, Malcolm? he asked
If you want our unlimited, all-you-can-eat breakfast, Malcolm said, you have to pay extra
Unlimited, Philip thought
All-you-can-eat
I'll leave it for now, he said
Malcolm tapped at his computer for another minute or two, then placed a blue key card on the counter
Third floor, he said

how to make a bomb

Once in his room, Philip stood at the window
Beyond the bus station's glinting roof was an apartment complex with a façade of reflective, pale-green glass
To the left was the tower he had seen from Vauxhall Bridge
He had an image of the Russian oligarch sitting in his very own chapel, six hundred feet above the ground
Yawning, he faced back into the room
He was tired after all the traveling, but he was hungry too
He hadn't eaten since Heraklion

Back on the ground floor, he moved through the glass door and out onto the street
He could hear someone singing
The voice floated through the drafty spaces of the station like the spirit of the place itself, but the feeling of estrangement seemed aimed specifically at him

He found himself on a wide road, heading east
Before too long, he came to a Spanish restaurant-bar that was built into the brick arches of a railway embankment
Taking a small table by the wall, he ordered tapas and a large glass of house white
At a nearby table four women in their twenties were getting drunk
He finished his wine and ordered another

His food arrived
He had boarded the flight to London in a rush of adrenaline, knowing what needed to be done
As yet, though, he had no idea how to accomplish it
Should he have stayed away until he had a plan of action that was fully formed?

He saw himself standing outside his house in Dartmouth Park
A figure brushed past in a black leather jacket
It was Jess
He was with her as she climbed the steps to the front door, with her as she rang the bell
Anya appeared, her hair tied back, no makeup
Philip isn't here, she said
If Jess was startled by the hostile tone, she gave no sign of it
I know, she said
That's why I came
Anya walked off into the house, leaving Jess to close the door behind her
In the kitchen, Jess leaned against the stove, arms folded
I'm not sure he'll be coming back
Anya stared at her
What makes you say that?
I spoke to him, Jess said
Did he tell you he wasn't coming back? Anya asked
Jess shook her head
It was something I felt
She moved to the window, thumbs in the pockets of her jeans

how to make a bomb

He's on a journey that excludes us
Us? Anya said
What do you mean, us?
Jess turned from the window
I don't expect to see him either, in case you're wondering
This journey you're talking about, Anya said, what's the destination?
Jess gave a shrug
If I knew that

Sighing, Philip brought his eyes back into focus and met the gaze of one of the young women at the nearby table
He hadn't been staring at her—at least, not intentionally—but she gave him a hard, sneering look, then spoke to the young woman sitting next to her
He heard unpleasant laughter and began to sweat
His plan might be vague as yet, but he couldn't afford to draw attention to himself
From that moment on, he made a point of ignoring the young women, and the next time he hazarded a glance in their direction they were studying their phones
He paid his bill and left

Outside, it had begun to rain
Cars rushed past, the hiss of tires, the shiny red ribbons of their brake lights on the tarmac
In the distance a siren swooped and howled

Everything sick, he thought
Everything in pain
He crossed the road, then moved through the bus station
A girl was hunched on a square of cardboard near the steps that led down into the tube
Her face was pinched and pale
A runaway
After what had happened in the Spanish place, he didn't want to risk approaching her
His actions could be misinterpreted

Back in his room, he took out his notebook and his pen, then sat down at the desk
He stared at the blank wall in front of him
First of all, he would have to dispel the idea that he was a man of a certain age who was going through a crisis
He didn't feel "left behind" by technology, and he wasn't longing to return to a childhood that might or might not have been idyllic
This wasn't about Luddism or nostalgia
Buried deep in the etymology of the word *manifesto* was the Latin word *infestus*, meaning hostile, and it was true that he was envisaging a fierce attack on the current state of things, but it had to come across as original and poised, the product of a reasonable, clear-thinking mind, not the ranting of some lunatic on the fringes of society
When people finished reading what he had written, he wanted them to say, *Yes, of course*
That's how it is

Why didn't I realize before?
The taxi driver in Cádiz had asked if he was an anarchist, and he had laughed
He wasn't laughing now
He picked up his pen
How to begin?

2

He was woken by a drunk man singing "La vie en rose"
Standing at the window, he couldn't see where the voice was coming from
He looked at his watch
2:19
Lights showed in the apartment complex at the foot of Vauxhall Bridge
Two men in white shirts stepped onto a balcony
Clouds of smoke poured from their vapes
Behind the men, shadowy figures were dancing to music that he couldn't hear

When he woke again, it was light, and he could hear the buses pulling in and out of the station and the low-level mutter of commuters

London, he thought
He was only six or seven miles from where he lived, but this was a different city, alien, unknown
The expensive, aquarium-like apartments with their late-night party people
The rough sleepers on their cardboard squares
La vie en rose

That morning, a young woman with a name badge that said PRECIOUS was on Reception
He asked her if there were any electronics shops in the area
She advised him to take a bus down Wandsworth Road—the 77 or the 87—or else he could walk
It was only ten or fifteen minutes
He could do a deal, she told him, especially if he paid in cash
He thanked her for being so helpful
After buying a takeaway coffee from the Little Waitrose next to the hotel, he withdrew some money from a nearby ATM and headed west on foot
It was one of those London mornings that was neither hot nor cold
The air was still and heavy, the sky a solid gray
Planes rumbled overhead, unseen
Most of the buildings were made of grimy brick, and the green of the trees looked dusty, dull
He felt as if he was walking in his sleep

---

how to make a bomb

In his mind he returned to the house in Dartmouth Park, Anya at the kitchen table, Jess over by the window

When I told you he wasn't coming back, Jess said, I might have been exaggerating

If he does come back, he'll be a different person

He'll have different priorities

She adjusted her jacket and faced back into the room

He'll want a different life

I don't know what that means, Anya said

I don't either, Jess said, not really

It's all just speculation

But it's as close as I can get

He asked you to come and see me, didn't he, Anya said later as she showed Jess to the door

I tried to get out of it, Jess said

Anya gave her a watery smile

I can imagine

When Jess reached the bottom of the steps, she looked back up at Anya

For what it's worth, she said, you should know that he still loves you

He has never stopped loving you

Anya's eyes narrowed

Did he ask you to say that?

No, he didn't, Jess said

I thought of it myself

She paused
It's true, though

The pavement widened, and Philip came to a shop with a sign that said MOBILE PHONE AND LAPTOP
He pushed on the door, which jangled, and the man standing behind the glass counter asked how he could help
Philip said he was looking for a laptop
A laptop? the man said
You talking reconditioned?
The door jangled again, and Philip felt the air around him tighten
A man had just walked in
He came and stood next to Philip, hands flat on the counter, palms down
He wore an off-white polo shirt and low-slung jeans, and had a spider tattooed on the back of each hand
Mind if I go first? he said
I'm on a double yellow
Philip asked how long he would be
Not long, the man said
You want me to watch your car for you? Philip said
The man turned to face Philip
You'd do that?
Why not? Philip said
It's no different to standing here
The man looked at Philip hard, weighing him up, then he

walked to the door, opened it, and pointed to a white van
twenty yards away
Philip held out a hand
You'd better give me the keys
The man gave a disbelieving laugh, then he looked past Philip,
at the man behind the counter
Is this guy for real?
The man behind the counter shrugged
If I don't have keys, Philip said, and the police turn up, I won't
be able to move your van
You'll get a ticket
Is that what you want?
The man put his face close to Philip's face
Are you scamming me?
I'm just trying to help, Philip said
You in here, me out there—it's a better allocation of resources
The man's face opened wide, and his teeth showed
Okay, he said, but if you nick my van I'll hunt you down and
break your fucking legs
Philip's eyebrows lifted
Did you get that from a movie?
The man looked at the floor and grinned and shook his head,
then he took out his keys and thrust them at Philip
I'm serious, he said

Out on the street Philip leaned against the van as if it was his,
the keys making a sharp shape in his right hand

He was pleased with the initiative that he had shown
The spontaneity
Did you get that from a movie?
He had hardly recognized the person who had spoken
It seemed he was capable of anything

Looking left and right, he glimpsed a man in a black hat and a dark-blue jacket with reflective silver stripes
A traffic warden
He glanced towards the shop, but there was no sign of the van's owner
Slipping behind the wheel, he turned the key in the ignition
A talk show burst out of a speaker in the door
He muted the volume, then headed east
He wouldn't go as far as Vauxhall
The one-way system that encircled the bus station might prove difficult to negotiate, and he didn't fancy getting caught in it
After a couple of minutes, he swung across the traffic, into a side street, and parked by a pub called The Nott

He turned up the volume on the radio
A man was talking about his experience of domestic violence
She completely lost it, pulled a knife on me
On the dashboard was a copy of that day's *Mirror* and a pair of sunglasses

Next to him, on the passenger seat, were two cans of Red Bull, a receipt book held together with an elastic band, and an unopened packet of Smoky Bacon crisps
Could this be my life? he wondered
What would that feel like?
Am I actually capable of becoming anything I want to be?
At that moment, he realized that stealing the van was a very real possibility
In a sense, he had already stolen it
All he had to do was *go on stealing it*, which he could do by not returning to the shop
He had no use for a van, though—did he?

He roused himself
How much time had passed?

When he approached the mobile and computer shop, the owner of the van was already on the pavement, head jerking this way and that
Philip pulled into a space, then sounded the horn
Over here, he shouted
The man pushed off the curb and into the traffic, jaw muscles tight, one hand outstretched to stop the cars
I thought you fucked me over, he said to Philip when he reached the van
His face was bubbling with violent thoughts, like an electric kettle that had failed to switch itself off

Didn't you see the traffic warden? Philip said
No, the man said
Okay
He wet his top lip with his tongue
I owe you one, all right?
Taking out a business card, he handed it to Philip
ROSS JAMES, it said
RJ LONDON SCAFFOLDING LTD
There was an address in SW11, and a mobile number
You're Ross? Philip said
The man nodded
If you ever need some scaffolding, he said

Philip watched from the pavement as Ross blasted the horn twice and pulled out into the traffic
If you ever need some scaffolding
He shook his head, then slid the card into his pocket

3

It was two o'clock by the time he got back to the Travelodge
The man in the shop—Sabbir—had sorted him out with a basic smartphone and a reconditioned laptop
At Reception, he asked Precious for the Wi-Fi code

how to make a bomb

Up in his room, he ordered a takeaway, then he sat down at the desk and set to work on his manifesto
He began with a detailed, almost forensic account of his journey to Bergen airport
He described his perceptions, and how they had impacted on him
In treating the card reader, the metal poles in the tram, and the billboard with the snowcapped *A* as universals, he aimed to show how people are unrelentingly exposed to an infrastructure they haven't chosen
The words came easily, as if they had been waiting

We have been seduced or coerced into an existence that is completely factitious, he wrote
We have been trained to perform a series of actions that aren't natural to us
We're like the seal with its brightly colored ball
The tiger on its tub
Why do we agree to play along?
Because, like circus animals, we're rewarded
Since the pre-Christian era, if not before, those in power have known that one way to appease their subjects is to allow certain benefits to trickle down
The runaway consumerism of the recent years has been achieved not just by destigmatizing debt, but also by promoting it
We've ended up with things we haven't earned, and can't really afford
Things that make us feel up-to-date

Things that keep us quiet
Electric cars, flatscreen TVs, iPhones, home extensions, drones
At the same time, we're constantly told that the system's fit for purpose, it's the only one that works, there's really no alternative
Any evidence to the contrary is concealed or discredited, using powerful tools like advertising, tabloid journalism, and social media
The real fake news isn't news that isn't true
It's news someone doesn't want to hear, let alone believe
Perhaps what they're telling us is right, we think to ourselves
That's what life is like these days
We should get used to it

He paused for a few moments, lifting his eyes to the window, then he began to type again
The artificial reality that surrounds us and the unnatural forms of behavior that it requires or provokes are not in our interest
They're in the interest of businesses that prioritize growth and profit while disregarding the environmental consequences and the human cost
We're not just being monetized
We're suffering as a result
The betting shops and fast-food outlets that dominate our high streets are purveyors of addictive behavior and poor health
The prevalence of electronic devices has rendered us less active

Physical ailments have surged accordingly, as have psychological disorders
The promise that we will feel connected to the world, that we will all be brought closer together, turns out to be hollow and superficial
We're more likely to feel isolated, or fall prey to envy and depression, and there's no doubt that our personal information will be exploited for financial gain
But that's not the worst of it
When reality makes us ill, it continues to feed off us
Young people with mental health issues fuel the drug conglomerates, not to mention the markets for complementary medicine and therapy
Care homes filled with those afflicted by diseases of the modern age—Alzheimer's, Parkinson's, dementia—provide investors with extremely healthy dividends
Society resembles Cronus, king of the Titans, famous for devouring his own children

He was about to contrast "civilization sickness," as the Japanese call it, with Native American ideas of community when he saw the outline of a conclusion
He opened a new file
Why should a nation's success be linked to economic performance, he wrote, when it could be measured in other, far more human, ways?
In a steady-state or degrowth version of society, evils like

poverty, pollution, and inequality would stand a better chance of being eradicated
We would produce less and consume less
We might have less income, but we'd have more freedom
No one would feel "overlooked" or "left behind," a perennial complaint in so many Western countries
The air would be quieter and cleaner
Our children would be happier and more healthy
There would be more birds, and we would hear them when they sang

He looked up from his laptop
Above the apartment complex with its reflective windows, the cloud cover had broken up and patches of pale blue showed through
Soon it would be evening
Was he being impossibly naïve?
Was his thinking in any way original, or was he simply dredging up old arguments?
Was the whole thing just too big to overturn?
He shook his head
That was what they wanted people to believe
He boiled the electric kettle and made himself a coffee with the sachets provided, then he sat down again

Every now and then, he asked himself why he didn't simply join Extinction Rebellion or the Dark Mountain Project

He could participate in organized events—closing bridges, disrupting public transport, blocking airport runways
Such actions were effective, and also logical, since they simulated the forms of chaos climate change would bring about
He shared many of XR's beliefs and aims, not least to challenge the capitalist model as a socioeconomic system and to call out a political leadership that had normalized mendacity, incompetence, and bluster
XR had the authorities worried
He had seen reports from the right-wing think tank Policy Exchange in which the movement was accused of trying to sabotage democracy and the British state
He could add his voice to those of the activists
He could get his hands dirty
He could become one of the so-called arrestables
Why was he so determined to go it alone?

If he threw in his lot with XR or Dark Mountain, he would be perceived as yet another white, middle-class, middle-aged male convert to the cause, not exactly what the movements were crying out for when they were being criticized for their lack of diversity
He was under no illusions as to what he represented, but this was about more than feeling superfluous or inappropriate
It was about how the idea had come to him—his Damascene moment on the way to Bergen airport

His vision was personal and idiosyncratic, and his approach should reflect that fact
It seemed that he was, in many respects, the "Ingenious Gentleman" Inés had compared him to
Smiling, he reached for his cup of coffee
He had allied himself with a fictional character rather than with a movement, a cadre, or a cell
Somehow that felt right

Operating as a free agent, though, he still had to choose between violent and nonviolent protest
Once again, his thinking had been dictated by his demographic
He could glue himself to the railings of Downing Street or spray the statue of Churchill with fake blood or throw an egg at the prime minister, but he was still a fifty-something white man, and none of it would make the news
He remembered reading an interview with the human rights lawyer responsible for coordinating XR's legal team
Part of the point, the lawyer had said, was to link distant and abstract destruction with tangible things which people care about
That was the type of action he was contemplating

4

Towards eight o'clock, he left the Travelodge and walked east
That afternoon, by chance, he had come across some footage of the 1993 Conservative Party conference in Blackpool
He had been struck by how dusty and colorless pre-Internet society had looked
As he approached the tapas place, an idea came to him
He had been thinking that he would publish his manifesto online, as text, but what if he also made a video?
Feeling energized, he pushed the glass door open

Table for one, sir?

The waiter who stood beside him, menu in hand, was the waiter who had served him the night before
He looked into the man's round face
There was a diffidence, but also something dogged or intractable, the sense of purpose that had brought him to this point and kept him going
He couldn't take this man for granted
Not this man, not anyone
Incidental characters had important parts to play
After all, hadn't Inés been incidental at the beginning?

He asked the waiter what his name was
Ernesto, the man said

Once Philip had ordered, he sat back
He felt happy with the progress he was making, particularly with his use of circus animals as a metaphor
His entire thesis originated in the moment when that young Norwegian woman unthinkingly touched her travel card to the card reader
Everything he objected to was contained in that one image

After dinner, he walked back to his hotel, his head buzzing from the wine
At a junction, he stopped to let a car go past
As it disappeared beneath the railway embankment, the glow of its brake lights showed him a figure crouching in the tunnel, on a narrow strip of pavement, her legs drawn up against her chest, her forehead resting on her knees
He moved closer
She was wearing a thin, green parka with the hood up, and her long, pale hair hung down, almost to the ground
She was sitting on a square of cardboard
Was she the girl he had seen the night before, near the steps that led down into the tube?

---

how to make a bomb

He sat beside her, his back against the wall
At first nothing happened, but then she seemed to sense his presence
She lifted her head and looked at him
Her face was colorless, her eyes were rimmed with red
She was younger than he had expected, only sixteen or seventeen
I don't do blow jobs, she said
He stared straight ahead, waiting for the shock to pass
Good, he said at last
I'm glad
She asked him what he wanted
I thought we could talk, he said
Talk?
She let out a laugh
There was no humor in it, only bitterness
All this, he said—and he gestured at the tunnel and their diminished view of the world beyond—they'd like us to think it's the way things have to be
It isn't, though
She was cold and tired, she'd probably been sitting on that piece of cardboard for hours, but he sensed a low flame of curiosity
I'm not happy, he went on
I don't fit in
She looked at him again
Same, she said
I don't know why you're here, he said
Perhaps you ran away from home, or perhaps you don't have a home

Perhaps you don't have anyone who cares about you
He paused
Or perhaps you want to be sitting in this tunnel
Perhaps it's a choice
It's not a choice, she said
Who in their right fucking mind would choose to sit in a tunnel?
He nodded
You shouldn't be here, he said
It's wrong
Sounds like you want to do something about it, she said
I'm going to, he said
It's just, I haven't quite decided what
He stared at the tunnel wall—the tattered flyer for a gay club, the green stain made by dripping water, the mottled bricks
The girl's head was resting on her knees again, as if she was dispirited by his lack of direction
As if she had hoped for something more
All he could see was her lank hair, a hand with bitten fingernails, and one surprisingly delicate ear
I'll think of something, he told her, but he didn't sound convincing, not even to himself

Got any change?
She spoke without lifting her forehead from her knees
No, he said, but I do have money
He took out his wallet and removed some notes—three tens, a twenty, and a five—then he held them out to her

how to make a bomb

Her head came up
You're giving me all that?
Why not? he said
She stuffed the notes into a pocket in her parka
Thanks
That'll help a lot
He asked what her name was
Mary, she said
He laughed
What's so funny? she asked him
I didn't think people your age were called Mary, he said
Your parents must have been old-fashioned
She was looking straight ahead, at the dark, damp tunnel wall
I don't know what they were
Though what she was saying had a sour, resentful edge, it had the ring of truth about it
A truth that was hers, but also absolute
We never know our parents
We're not really interested, not when we're young, we can't afford to be, it would hold us back
By the time we're ready to ask questions it's too late
They're gone

You didn't say your name, she said
He told her it was Philip
She sniffed, then dragged the sleeve of her parka across her nose
Not exactly modern
He smiled

What will you do? he asked
Find a hostel, she said, get something to eat
I could buy you something, he said
I've got a credit card
She shook her head
You've done enough
He felt an overwhelming sadness all of a sudden, as if she were not a stranger but his daughter, a daughter he had failed to protect
I'll be all right, she said
Don't worry
He climbed to his feet
His back was stiff, and he had pins and needles in his legs
Good luck, Mary, he said
She gave him a nod
You too

Back in his room in the Travelodge, he went back over the encounter
Whatever trouble she was in, £55 wasn't going to solve it
He drew the curtains, then he sat down at the desk, opened his laptop, and read the last few lines that he had written
Sickness, medication, pollution, sickness
We have created a vicious circle in which we have agreed to live
Our own poisoned labyrinth
Outside, a group of men were chanting
It was someone's birthday, or else a football team had won
He leaned back in his chair

Consumer societies consume themselves, he thought, like snakes devouring their own tails
Typically, the Ouroboros was seen as a symbol of eternity
It was also believed to represent fertility—the cycle of life and death
In his thesis, though, it symbolized the opposite
A system that was actively cooperating in its own demise
A way of being with no future

5

He woke at dawn and sat by the window, watching people move through the bus station below
A man in trainers sprinted for a bus, but the bus left before he could reach it
The man wheeled away, head tilted back, eyes closed
His despair seemed out of proportion to what had happened
He might have lost an item of great value that couldn't be replaced or missed an opportunity that would never come again

Another man arrived at the closed door of a bus as the bus was pulling away
He ran alongside in his black North Face jacket, banging on the glass with the flat of his hand

Hey, he was shouting
Stop
Then he shouted louder still
Fucking *stop*
When the bus continued to accelerate, he howled into the morning air like a soul in torment
He had been denied something he had set his heart on, something on which everything depended, and he had been denied it for no reason
Or perhaps he had been denied it because he was seen as undeserving or insignificant
Or perhaps he had been denied it out of spite
His fury and hopelessness in the face of this rebuff seemed biblical
The phrase "gnashing of teeth" came to mind
To ascribe such importance to something so relatively trivial was clearly an overreaction, and yet Philip didn't feel he could belittle or ignore the suffering that the people involved so obviously experienced
It seemed symbolic of some far greater loss
Perhaps it was even a symptom of the sickness that he had diagnosed
What kind of world was it where the failure to catch a bus took on the appearance of a tragedy?

Of all the characters he observed that morning, the most poignant were those who turned away with no expression when the door stayed closed and the bus set off without them

how to make a bomb

They did their best to hide the evidence that they had been
hurrying, that they had attempted something and fallen short,
not because they didn't care about what had just occurred, or
because they weren't feeling the fury and hopelessness of the
man in the North Face jacket, but because they suspected that
they were being watched
They didn't want to appear to have made a fool of themselves,
and so they pretended that it didn't mean anything
The idea that you had to pretend that something unimportant
didn't matter
This was a whole new accretion of psychological damage
A whole new level of absurdity

At breakfast round the corner, his thoughts returned to St John
the Theologian
The brightness of the sun in the upper courtyard
The cool gloom in the church
The speed and ease with which the unexpected blessing had
unburdened him
Memory as mirage, shimmering, unbelievable
In the monastery he had caught a glimpse of the simple,
unmediated existence he had been looking for
If there was peace in that place, though, there was also war

Outside again, he walked round to the bus station
He stood in the middle of the concourse, beneath the stainless
steel roof, and closed his eyes

He breathed as the monk who had appeared to him had breathed, deeply and steadily, out and in, and was aware of something beginning to accumulate
It felt like certainty, he thought, or power
He was alive to the people moving all around him
This only added to his stillness
He imagined looking down at himself from his window on the third floor of the Travelodge
What he saw wasn't the historian Philip Notman in his brown suede jacket and his jeans
Instead, he saw a figure dressed from head to toe in black
A figure wearing a *kalimavkion*
A figure with a rifle
In the context of a London bus station, he looked as unlikely as a superhero from a comic book

He returned to where he stood, his eyes still closed, the power and the certainty still in him
This is the pure thing that I need to hold on to, he told himself
This is what
He staggered sideways suddenly and almost fell
His eyes opened in alarm
A man in a cheap suit was rounding on him
Half his takeout Starbucks latte had slopped out of its paper cup and onto the concrete
Small beige puddle
What the fuck are you doing, just standing there? the man said

how to make a bomb

He shook the coffee off his hand
Idiot
What am I doing? Philip said
He felt a calm that was supreme, and a surprising capacity for menace
You really want to know?
The man's face fluttered and flicked over
It was like seeing the destination change on a departures board, outrage replaced by dumb bewilderment
Dickhead, the man said
Prick
Philip took a step towards him
It was the first time he had moved in several minutes, and it was potent, almost seismic
He had the strangest sensation of irresistibility, like the Chinese martial arts expert who holds up a hand, palm facing out, and sends his opponent flying across a room
You really want to know what I'm doing? he said
I'll tell you
Fuck off, the man said, but he seemed wary now, and he was backing away
He wasn't in a hurry anymore
All that haste had been unnecessary, meaningless
Philip smiled to himself
One man standing perfectly still
That was all it took

He turned slowly, just as a City Tour bus pulled in
An Asian couple sat on the top deck, its cutaway roof exposing them to low, gray skies and flecks of rain
No one else had braved the weather
On the side of the bus was an artful jumble of images, the sights that people would see if they bought a ticket
St Paul's Cathedral, the Gherkin, Tower Bridge
The London Eye
Big Ben
The bus had come to a halt nearby, and it was standing sideways-on to him
Its position seemed calculated, intentional
What did it remind him of?
Suddenly he knew
In his writings, Priscus described the Huns arriving on the shores of Lake Maeotis in the early years of the fifth century
They assumed it was impassable, like the sea
At that moment, a deer appeared
Stepping into the water, the deer stopped and seemed to look at them, over its shoulder, then it moved forwards
Following this unexpected guide, the Huns were able to cross the lake on foot
They found themselves in Scythia, a land of plenty which they hadn't known existed, and which they conquered shortly afterwards

As he stood by the City Tour bus, he realized that a possibility was being presented to him

how to make a bomb

He was looking at a number of iconic British monuments and buildings
If one of them were to be destroyed, or even damaged, it would be the lead story on broadcast media throughout the world
A plan that radical would require a degree of covertness and vigilance he hadn't bargained for
The Vauxhall Travelodge would no longer do
He needed to go underground
He searched his pockets for the business card Ross James had given him
RJ LONDON SCAFFOLDING
Like Allegra's postcard of the house in Crete, it represented an opportunity
An offer
He typed Vauxhall bus station, the address of the scaffolding yard, and "get directions" into his phone
The 156, it seemed, would take him close

Half an hour later, he was walking down Prairie Street
Terraced houses made of liver-colored brick, grubby net curtains in the downstairs windows
A down-at-heel but plucky atmosphere, as if life would be lived no matter what
He passed a corner shop and turned right, into a cul-de-sac
The air was damp and close, and he was sweating
A path sloped up to a footbridge

In the blue-gray haze, he could see the city skyline—the tower where the Russian oligarch had a penthouse, the distant spire of the Shard beyond
Down to his left, and wedged between two sets of train tracks, were several corrugated-iron structures
The whole area looked hidden, unstable, temporary
A sort of shantytown or no-man's-land

He came down off the bridge
Ahead of him was a grimy Victorian tunnel, much narrower than the one where he had found Mary
It seemed to be the only way of accessing the area by car
He followed a road round to the right, past a tire merchant's and a waste disposal business, and there in front of him was RJ London Scaffolding
In the yard was a two-story shed with long wooden boards and gray metal poles stacked horizontally on shelves
Next to the shed was a prefab office
As he approached, the door opened and Ross appeared
An older man was with him
Shaved head, big belly
Cigarette
Ross was studying Philip's face, trying to work out where he had seen him before
A train rumbled past on the embankment high above

---

how to make a bomb

We met yesterday, Philip said
I'm the one who didn't steal your van
Ross spoke to his colleague
I'll handle this, Gary

Philip waited until Gary had disappeared into the shed
You said to contact you if I needed scaffolding
Ross was looking dubious
You need scaffolding?
Not exactly, Philip said
I do need help, though
Ross shook his head
You've come to the wrong place, mate
This isn't the Samaritans
Philip grinned
Ross, he said, as if they knew each other, just hear me out, will you

Ross shifted his weight from one foot to the other
Probably he was wishing that he hadn't got into debt by accepting a favor he hadn't even asked for, but what intrigued Philip was the way Ross's body language was echoing that of the monk who had appeared in his dream
It was as if he—Philip—was following a trail that led, implausibly, from a monastery in Crete to a builders' yard in Battersea

He had come to the right place, no matter what anyone might say

He told Ross that he was looking for somewhere to stay
Ross was shaking his head again
I'm running a business here
Philip interrupted him
That's why it's perfect
I need to lie low
Ross's phone buzzed, but he ignored it
You on the run or something?
Philip had prepared for this moment, knowing that he would have to have a story to tell
I left my wife, he said, and I don't want her to find me
He took a step closer to Ross
I can pay
Ross turned his back on Philip and walked away
He appeared to be thinking

Philip surveyed the empty yellow skips, the potholes filled with last night's rain
The wind lifted, and a loose piece of metal clanged
Another train went past
You owe me one, he said
Ross looked at him over his shoulder
You left your wife?

how to make a bomb

Okay, Philip said, she kicked me out
Ross moved towards him fast and put a raised finger in his face
Don't fucking lie to me
Philip stood his ground
I'm sorry, Ross
I was embarrassed
He looked at his feet, then looked at Ross again
Can you help?

Ross thought for a while, then jerked his head
He led Philip into the shed, through a corrugated-iron flap at the back, and out onto a blunt triangle of land
A small caravan stood among the weeds and nettles, its outer skin faded and peeling, its original color hard to determine
Opening the door, Ross told Philip to take a look
Philip climbed inside
The reek of damp and mold burned his nostrils
At one end of the caravan were two cushioned benches with a wooden table in between
He parted the curtains
The view was of the embankment, which curved southwards, an iron bridge no more than fifty yards away
In the front half of the caravan there was a fridge, a stove, another built-in table, a cupboard for hanging clothes, and a freestanding electric radiator
Even if the curtains were closed, light would filter through the plastic skylight in the roof

---

He stepped down into the undergrowth, where Ross was jabbing at his phone with a forefinger
Interested? Ross said, not looking up
Philip dusted off his hands
How much do you want?
One fifty, Ross said
Cash
A month? Philip said
Ross laughed softly
A week
He was surveying the area with distance in his gaze, as if it was a deer park or the grounds of some stately home
Prime location, isn't it
No one's going to find you here
Philip reached back inside the caravan and flicked a switch
Nothing happened
Is there power? he asked
Ross told him that he could run an extension cord out from the shed
That was what he did before, when he used it as an office
The good old days, Philip said
Ross grinned

As they walked back to the yard, Ross asked when he wanted to move in

At the weekend, Philip told him
Ross gave a nod
There was a toilet behind the office, he said
If Philip wanted a shower, he could use the leisure center on Sheepcote Lane
They had a sauna too
What happens at night? Philip asked
Everybody leaves at about six, Ross told him
After that, the gates are padlocked
You'll be shut in
Philip asked whether he could have a key
I don't know you, Ross said
You trusted me with your van, Philip pointed out
Ross looked at him steadily
Okay, he said, but if you fuck me over
You'll break my legs, Philip said
I know

6

He spent that afternoon and most of the next day buying items for his caravan and arranging for their delivery
On Friday evening, when he returned from dinner, he checked the tunnel under the railway

He was relieved to see that it was empty
As he cut through the bus station, though, he noticed a figure slumped against a pillar next to the waste bin
Mary?
She lifted her forehead from her knees
You again, she said
There was only weariness, and a vague and grudging recognition, but that was all he had the right to expect
He had no idea how it would feel to live that life
You're not in the tunnel, he said
She looked at him with no expression, her lips the same color as her face
You don't miss a trick, do you
His heart felt heavy suddenly, as if everything he attempted was destined to fail
As if none of it was worth the bother
He should go home, and be with his wife and son, and carry on writing a book about someone nobody had ever heard of

Perhaps she picked up on his sudden change of mood and felt responsible for it, because she spoke again
I had a night in a hostel, she told him, then the money ran out
She glanced over her shoulder, towards the main road
I got scared in that tunnel on my own
There are more people here
Also, some heat comes up the steps
She was talking about the entrance to the Underground

how to make a bomb

Not much, he said
You're shivering
She shook her head with a kind of slow despair
I said some heat comes up
I didn't say I wasn't cold
Stand up, he said
You can't stay here all night
She seemed wary, and also obstinate, but his insistence had brought her to her feet
Shoulders hunched, she clutched the points of her elbows and looked around, as if she felt exposed
Now she was upright, he saw how thin she was
Stalklike wrists and neck
Stick legs
He took out his phone and googled "travelodge vauxhall"
I'm getting you a room in my hotel, he said
You can have a hot shower and dry your clothes
You'll have a proper bed
She was still looking at him warily, but also with a kind of resignation, as if she suspected something bad was coming but didn't know what she could do about it
I'm getting you a room, he said, that's all
I need your name
Mary McDaid, she said
He asked how old she was
She didn't answer
I'm going to say you're eighteen, he told her, otherwise we'll have a problem

---

In the lobby, Precious was on duty
Philip walked up to the reception desk and told her that he had booked a room
You already have a room, she said, then she yawned, one hand lifting to cover her mouth
Each nail was painted a different color and frosted at the tip
It's for my friend, he said
She looked past him at Mary, who was standing close to him, almost behind him, as if he was some kind of shield
Probably there was a clause in the Travelodge terms and conditions that gave staff the right to turn away people they judged to be unsuitable
He was determined not to let that happen
Is she eighteen? Precious asked
She can't stay in a room by herself if she's not eighteen
She looked at Mary again
I need to see ID
I'll vouch for her, Philip said, then he leaned towards Precious and lowered his voice
She's been living on the streets
She needs help
If there's any trouble, Precious said, they could sack me
He told her there would be no trouble
He gave his word
Precious brought her eyes back to his, and though her expression hadn't altered he sensed a softening in her

how to make a bomb

She reached behind her and slid a key card across the counter to Mary
You're on the first floor at the back, she said
Mary's hand closed around the card, her knuckles standing out like dull-red marbles
He asked if she was hungry
She shook her head
Just tired

When they reached the first floor, he said good night and carried on up the stairs
He was tired too, he realized
Hey, Philip
He stopped and looked over his shoulder
She was below him, by the fire door, in her soiled green parka and her dirt-stained jeans
Thank you, she said
It was the first time he had seen anything resembling a smile, and she suddenly seemed even younger
He didn't want to think about what might happen to her tomorrow or the next day
How little we can do, he thought
Almost nothing, really
Will you be all right? he asked
Her nose was dripping, and she wiped it on her sleeve
I told you before, she said
You don't have to worry about me
I bought you breakfast, he said

You'll be hungry in the morning
Her smile was still there, though it was slightly crumpled now, as if she felt for him, or even pitied him
Those who help often seem more vulnerable than those who are being helped
On the road outside, a siren yelped, then wailed
Good night, he said again
Sleep well

Back in his room on the third floor he stood at the window
An ambulance flashed past
Chips of blue light flickered and skidded across the stainless steel roof below
You don't have to worry about me
That was easy to say
Still, he felt better than he had in days

7

He was awake before dawn, and by half past seven he was standing at Reception in the basement
Checking out? Malcolm said
Philip nodded
Malcolm asked if he was going far

how to make a bomb

Philip told Malcolm he was heading north, which wasn't true
This is how you disappear, he thought

When he had paid his bill, he reached into his jacket pocket and took out an envelope
On the front it said MARY MCDAID, ROOM 124
Inside was a note listing hostels that might take in an eighteen-year-old homeless woman, together with their addresses and phone numbers
He had also given her his phone number
If she needed someone to talk to, he told her, she could always call

He passed the envelope to Malcolm, asking him to make sure Mary received it before she left
Is this your friend? Malcolm asked
The look he gave Philip was knowing and unsavory, as if he thought he had the goods on Philip
As if he was saying, *I'll keep your dirty little secret*
Don't do that, Malcolm, Philip said
Do what?
Now Malcolm was acting all innocent
Philip sighed
Why don't you try sleeping out there, he said, on a piece of cardboard?
Malcolm flushed
I got her a room for the night, Philip told him

It's not much, but it's something
Sorry, Malcolm stammered, I didn't mean
Just give her the envelope, Philip said

8

When he reached RJ London Scaffolding, a beaten-up, dull-gold Honda was parked outside, and the man with the big belly was unlocking the gates
As he returned to his car, he gave Philip a cold stare
Boss know you're coming today?
Yes, Philip said, he knows
He moved across the yard and into the shed that housed the planks and poles, then on through the corrugated-iron door and into the triangle of waste ground beyond
It was damp in the caravan, and dirtier than he remembered
Dead flies lay in crunchy, glinting heaps on the Formica table and in the sink, and there were stiff brown patches on the carpet, as if someone had spilled sauce or soup
Every surface felt sticky to the touch
He had been so excited by the prospect of a new, concealed life that he had blinded himself to the state of the place
One hundred and fifty pounds a week
He thought he'd probably been had, but Ross had sensed his need, his desperation

how to make a bomb

Sitting on a plywood bench, he flicked one of the light switches
Nothing happened
He stared out through the window
He could hear men talking in the shed
The dull clang of metal poles
This was his fifth day in London, and he still hadn't contacted Anya
She didn't even know he was back
He pushed his face into his hands and stayed in that position with his eyes tight shut
In the darkness he could see a dim petrol-blue horizon, like the sea at night
The truth wasn't something he could tell, and what else was there?
He had used up all the excuses he could think of

Phil?

He took his hands from his eyes
The inside of the caravan seemed heightened, as if viewed through a color filter

Phil!

He rose from the bench and poked his head out of the door
Ross stood among the weeds in a gray hoodie
You settling in? he said
I don't have any power, Philip told him
Ross grinned, then lit a cigarette
Are you going to be one of those pain-in-the-arse tenants, always whingeing about something?
You told me there'd be power, Philip said
Ross said he'd sort it out
Where are the nearest shops? Philip asked
Through the tunnel and straight on, Ross told him
There's a supermarket, Thai takeaway
Laundrette
He dropped his cigarette and trod on it
Everything you need, Phil
All mod cons

In the early afternoon, when Philip returned from the laundrette with clean curtains and cushion covers, he found that Ross had been as good as his word
With an extension cord in place, he was able to boil water
As he set to work scrubbing the surfaces, he imagined Anya appearing at the corrugated-iron door in a short-sleeved summer dress and a pair of trainers
She moved through the undergrowth with her head lowered, only looking up when she was a few feet away
Her expression was dreamy, almost absent, as if she was on her own

how to make a bomb

I think I got stung, she murmured
Where? he asked
She showed him the raised white marks on her ankles and on the back of her hands
I'm sorry, Anya, he said
I should have warned you about the nettles
He took her in his arms, the woman he had fought for all those years ago, the woman he had loved ever since
She allowed him to hold her for a few moments, then she stood back and gazed past him, towards the railway bridge
You're really living here?
He nodded
I did a deal with Ross
It's costing me a fortune
He laughed
Ross? she said
Who's Ross?
He runs the place, he told her
I don't think you'd get on
He paused, then looked around
Where's Seth?
He's in the car, she said
Leaving Anya where she was, he walked through the shed, across the yard, and out onto the cobbled road
The sky was white, the light fierce and yet diffuse
He could see Seth in the windscreen of Anya's old Saab, but oddly it was Seth at fourteen, his dyed-black hair falling across his forehead, earbuds jammed into his ears
Philip waved as he walked round to the passenger side

It's good of you to come, he said
Seth was busy taking in the corrugated-iron fencing, the dumped fake-leather three-piece suite, the stack of used car tires
What are you doing in this shithole, Dad?
Philip smiled
You really want to know?
Seth squinted up at him, lazily curious
I'm making a bomb, Philip said
Seth's eyes flared
What?
Leaning on the open window, Philip looked left and right as if to make sure that nobody was listening
I'm making a bomb, he said
Don't tell your mother

He emptied a bucket of water into the weeds, then stood looking out across the railway tracks
He didn't want another phone call with Anya
He needed to see her
If they were face-to-face, there was a chance that he would find the right words
That was his hope

A Southern Rail train went past, next stop Vauxhall, then Waterloo
One of the windows framed a man in his middle years
Balding, overweight, gray suit and tie

Their eyes met, and the man gave him a smile and a quick thumbs-up

He stood in the weeds with his bucket as the train vanished round a curve

I see you, the man was saying

You're not alone

In the caravan again, he looked around

The cushions were zipped into their covers and the curtains were back on the windows

The carpet was no longer crusted with spillages and stains

His sleeping bag had arrived, and he had laid it lengthways on one of the bench seats

The smell of old dirt and neglect was gone

He nodded to himself, then stepped out of the caravan and locked the door behind him

In the office, Ross had both feet on his desk, his legs crossed at the ankle, a bag of crisps open on his lap

He looked up as Philip entered, a loose grin on his face

Wife track you down yet?

So far, so good, Philip said

Why did she kick you out, anyway? Ross asked

Philip remembered how Ross had put a finger in his face when he first appeared—*Don't fucking lie to me*—and an image of Inés came to him, two in the morning in that convent in Jerez, the glow of her body in the dark, the feel of her skin on his

Inés was not a lie

I was seeing someone else, he said

Ross crushed the empty crisp packet and lobbed it into the wastepaper basket in the corner

You don't seem the type

Philip thought about that for a moment, then he nodded

I agree

So how come you're not with her, Ross went on, your bit on the side?

It's over, Philip said

Or perhaps it never really began

He couldn't help smiling

He was wondering how Inés would react to being called a "bit on the side"

I don't know what there is to smile about, Ross said

Sounds like you messed up good and proper

She was Spanish, Philip told him

She had this black hair

Came down to here

He placed a hand sideways against his ribs

It was so shiny it looked wet

So what are you saying? Ross said

It was worth it?

Philip nodded

Yes

Then he thought of his wife and son, Anya with a nettle rash on her bare legs, Seth in the car, staring up at him, his face the color of sour cream

No, he said

He sighed
I don't know
Opening his wallet, he took out the £150 he had withdrawn from the ATM that afternoon and handed it to Ross
My first week's rent, he said

9

That evening, he began to film his manifesto
He kept it simple, the beige velour curtains forming the background, the lighting offered by the desk lamp low and focused
The first time he watched himself, he found his suntan disconcerting
Gradually, though, he began to realize that his new appearance might have advantages
He could pass for someone who spent the day outdoors, someone who was in touch with nature —a gardener, for example, or a fisherman
Given the content of his manifesto, this seemed apt
Did he appear to be speaking from a caravan?
Only to someone familiar with caravans—and anyway, so what if he did?
It suggested a life lived on the margins, a voluntary exile, a voice that had not been listened to, but was now demanding to be heard

The summer night closed around him, and there was just the circle of lamplight on his worktable and the warm air smelling of buddleia
One southbound goods train came thundering across the bridge towards him, so loud that he felt it might jump its tracks and burst through the caravan's thin metallic skin
The silence was never really silent
There was always a distant roar or rustle, a sound that was like restlessness, someone turning in a bed

At eleven, he yawned, then clicked on SAVE
He lay down and read a poem by Kiki Dimoula, which he had copied out by hand while he was in the house in Crete
There was a line he kept returning to, a line he found consoling
No end is articulate

Later, when the light was out and he had zipped himself into his sleeping bag, he counted the seconds between trains, and in the end he slept, though he was woken more than once by the scratching of birds' feet on the plastic skylight

10

The following morning he replayed what he had recorded the night before

It's as if we've been unconscious for a hundred years, like the princess in "Sleeping Beauty"

Not the Disney version, but the source of the Disney version, "Sun, Moon and Talia," which was written by the poet and fairy tale collector Giambattista Basile

In the original story, Talia was raped by the king while she was asleep

That's what has happened to us

We've been taken advantage of

We've been raped while we were sleeping

He pressed STOP

Was he being too harsh, too provocative?

Was it pedantic to mention the origins of Sleeping Beauty?

It was so important to get the tone right

He had to be passionate without being hysterical, authoritative without being professorial, sincere without being dull

Most important of all, he had to be human

He might be planning something extreme, but he was an ordinary person

He was Everyman

He was Notman

Seconds after pressing PLAY on the Sleeping Beauty segment again, the door to the caravan opened and Ross's head appeared

Philip jumped, then slammed his laptop shut

I heard voices, Ross said

What are you, Philip said, schizophrenic?

Ross bared his teeth

You're funny, you are

You're a real scream

You could've knocked, Philip said

Ross climbed into the caravan and settled on the other side of the table

Mind if I smoke?

Philip fetched an empty juice bottle and put it in front of Ross

Ashtray, he said

Ross lit up

When I heard voices, I thought you had your Spanish bird in here

I thought you might be up to something

I already told you, Philip said

It's over

And anyway, she lives in Spain

Ross smiled, as if he knew better, and oddly, in that moment, Philip imagined Inés sitting on the bench next to Ross and looking around, then moving a strand of hair out of her eyes and reaching for his lighter so she could light a cigarette

He had to close his eyes to banish her

how to make a bomb

When he opened his eyes again, Ross was watching him
You're a dark horse, aren't you, Phil, he said
He thought Philip was lying about his Spanish bird
He didn't believe the affair was over
Positioning his cigarette above the juice bottle, he tapped some ash into the neck
I'm not the one who's schizo, he said
You were talking to yourself
I was working on a lecture, Philip told him
I'm a historian
What kind of history? Ross asked
My last book was about the Merovingians, Philip said
Ross dropped his cigarette into the bottle and watched it fill with smoke
What's the Merovingians?
They were the kings of Gaul back in the Dark Ages, Philip told him
Ross grinned
Like *Game of Thrones*?
Kind of, Philip said
You want to hear a story from that time?
Ross nodded

In the second half of the sixth century, Philip said, a king called Clothar the First held court in a village northeast of Paris
It was there, on the banks of a river, that Clothar's subjects would assemble, and these gatherings would be followed by

feasts where deer and wild boar were roasted on spits, and wine was served from oak barrels

It was also there, in a secret apartment, that he kept triple-locked chests containing jewelry and gold

Ross lit another cigarette and sat back, eyes intent on Philip and glittering, as if he had just been handed keys to all the treasure chests, and would soon be rich himself

When Clothar wasn't away fighting his enemies, Philip went on, he would move from one royal estate to another, choosing new mistresses wherever he went

He had a wife called Ingonda, who came from a poor background

Though he continued to sleep with other women, he was passionately in love with Ingonda, and lived with her in complete harmony

One day, Ingonda went to Clothar and said, My lord, you have been gracious enough to call me to your bed

Perhaps you would now be still more gracious and consider the request of your humble servant

I have a sister, Aregonda, who is employed in your service, weaving and dyeing fabric

I beg you to be so good as to procure her a rich and brave husband, so that I may suffer no more humiliation on her account, but rest easy in my heart

Is that how they talked? Ross asked

Yes, Philip said

According to the sources, anyway

Intrigued by Ingonda's words, he went on, Clothar set off for the domain where Aregonda lived

how to make a bomb

On discovering that Aregonda was just as beautiful as her sister,
Clothar installed her in the royal apartment and married her
Some days later, he returned to Ingonda
Sweet one, he said, I have granted the favor you asked of me
I looked for a man who was rich and brave, but could find no one richer or braver than myself
I have therefore made Aregonda my wife
Ross was laughing in disbelief
He wanted to know how Ingonda reacted
She showed all her usual calmness and self-possession, Philip told him
Let my lord do as seems right and appropriate, she said, just so long as I lose none of his affection
They were together until she died ten years later, in AD 546

Ross picked up his cigarettes and his lighter
Seems like you learned a thing or two from Cloth-ears or whatever he was called
At the door of the caravan he paused
There was that loose grin again
Except he wouldn't have been kicked out by his missus, would he?

Philip sat still and listened until he heard Ross close the shed door behind him
He couldn't allow himself to be caught off guard like that again
What if he had been working with explosives?

He would have to wedge the shed door shut from the outside
The next time Ross wanted to surprise him—and he was sure that Ross had done it deliberately—he would have to hammer on the corrugated iron
Shout Philip's name
And if Ross asked why he was barricading himself in, he would say that privacy was important to him, and that he didn't appreciate being disturbed
Telling the story of Clothar and his many women had been an exercise in smoke and mirrors
He wanted Ross to see him as a bit of a philanderer
He wanted Ross to think his Spanish bird was visiting—or some other bird, perhaps—because that was the "something" he was up to, that was his dark secret, dark horse that he was

11

To finish his video, he needed to add a title and a strapline
The only person he could trust was Jess, but it was a risk to call her, even on his new phone
He had to make sure the police couldn't connect him with Jess—or with anyone else, for that matter
He was already worried that he might have implicated Ross
Would the authorities believe Ross when he told them that he didn't have a clue that he was harboring a terrorist?

how to make a bomb

He googled hotels in south London
The five-star Rafayel was on the river, about a mile away
If he had no luck at the Rafayel, there was always the Crowne Plaza
It was next door, more or less
He packed his laptop into a plastic bag and left the caravan

Twenty minutes later, he arrived at the hotel
Revolving glass doors spun him into a lobby that was a brash mix of animal-print sofas, exotic blooms, and ultraviolet lighting
He told the woman on Reception that he had lost his phone and asked if he could make a local call
Of course, she said
She showed him to the house phone, on a nearby desk
It's nine for an outside line, she said
He thanked her, then dialed Jess's number
Jess answered almost immediately
Who's this?
It's Philip, he said
I'm back from Crete
He paused
I'm staying in south London at the moment
The silence told him that Jess didn't know quite what to make of that
You didn't go home? she said eventually

No, he said
Not exactly
Why not? she said
Why didn't you go home?
He looked out across the lobby, with its pools of purple light
Jess, he said, I need your help
She told him that she was busy all afternoon, but she could meet him in the café at the British Library at six thirty

After leaving the Rafayel, he walked to Clapham Junction, where he bought a pair of cheap sunglasses and a dark-blue sweatshirt with a hood
He ate a sandwich in the station, then he caught a train to Victoria
The corrugated-iron shantytown appeared on his right, some distance below
He glimpsed the triangle of waste ground
It was a London where the feral and the opulent rubbed shoulders, the Rolls-Royce parked on Sheepcote Lane, a fox tearing at a rubbish bag nearby
That's where I'm living now, he thought
That's home
Intoxication mingled with sharp stabs of unease

Once at Victoria, he transferred to the tube and traveled north on the Victoria line
He was going to the library, as he had so often in the past

This time, though, he wouldn't be reading any books
He was no longer a historian
He was not that man
Something struck him suddenly, something so obvious that he couldn't believe he hadn't thought of it before
He laughed out loud, just once, in astonishment
The elderly woman sitting opposite was looking at him with concern and also with a certain fondness, as if she thought him eccentric but harmless
I just had a brilliant idea, he told her
She leaned forwards and tapped him on the knee with the fingertips of one hand
Good for you, she said
He opened Notes on his phone and wrote "A Notmanifesto," then he put the phone away again
A Notmanifesto
In employing a negative, it suggested repudiation and rebellion
His manifesto was *against* something
Also, since it incorporated his surname, it instantly identified the work as his
On top of that, he had come up with his very own portmanteau
It seemed that his stay at the Travelodge had taught him something after all

The train slowed as it pulled into Kings Cross
As he took the escalator up to the street, he pulled the sweatshirt hood over his head and put the sunglasses on

Ideally, he didn't want to be seen at all, by anyone, but he was living in a surveillance culture
There were half a million CCTV cameras in London alone
If you traveled from one end of the city to the other, you were likely to be recorded more than thirty times

Once in the library, he kept his hood up while he checked which part of the building was the least overlooked
This wasn't something he had ever thought about before
He had moved through the world unthinkingly
That degree of freedom now seemed like a luxury, and also like a form of blindness
He had agreed to meet Jess in the café, even though it was no longer serving, but now that he saw it he felt that it was too brightly lit
Instead, he decided to wait near the top of the escalator, where the lighting was much dimmer
Luckily, there were two seats side by side, both unoccupied
He sat down and opened his laptop
It was almost five o'clock
He would go through his manifesto one last time
He didn't think that he and Jess would be visible while they were sitting in that darkened area near the escalator—not clearly, anyway—but they would be seen when they walked into the library, and also when they walked out again
He had arrived before her
He would have to make sure that they left separately as well

how to make a bomb

At twenty to seven, Jess appeared at the top of the escalator
He called her name and she came over
When she was sitting next to him, he leaned close to her and spoke in a low voice
Does anyone know we're meeting?
Philip, she said, are you all right?
He asked her what she meant
You look completely different, she told him
The hoodie
I've never seen you in a hoodie
Jess, he said, please listen
We don't have long
He told her he had made a video
It was an account of what had happened to him in Norway and during the weeks that followed, and the thoughts he'd had as a result
He took out a piece of paper and handed it to her
"Unreal," she said
Is that the title of the video?
He nodded
It's reality itself that has become unreal, he said, but there's also a slang meaning
It's unreal that things are the way they are
Like, *How did this happen*?
Okay, she said
Under the title, he said, I want a strapline that says *A Notmanifesto*

Jess laughed
It just came to me, he told her, as I was on my way here
I can't believe I didn't think of it before
He paused
Would you be able to add the title and the strapline to the opening frame?
She nodded
I didn't want to involve you, he said, but I couldn't think who else to ask
She wanted to know if he had thought of using tags
He didn't understand
A tag communicates the essence of your content, she told him
If your video was about how to make a speech, your main tag would be something like "public speaking tips"
It's a crucial ranking factor in YouTube's search algorithm, and it's the algorithm that determines which videos the viewers are offered
To maximize the views your video gets, you need a tag that sends it to the top of the platform's search results
Philip was sure that the violent action he was planning would be the reason why his video attracted viewers, and that it would prove a hundred times more effective than any tag he might use, though obviously he had to keep that knowledge to himself
Don't bother with the tags, he said

Inserting the title and the strapline in such a way that Philip was satisfied took almost an hour

how to make a bomb

When Jess had finished, she closed the laptop and passed it to him
I'm sorry, he said, but I can't stay
He suggested they should say goodbye outside
She should leave first
He would meet her out of sight of the cameras, in the cut-through that linked the forecourt of the library with Euston Road
If she thought he was behaving oddly or being melodramatic, she didn't let on

She was standing by the sandwich place when he arrived
Something I forgot to ask, he said
Did you see Anya?
She hunched her shoulders, and light caught on her leather jacket, making parts of it look white or silver
I went to your house, she said
She wouldn't let me in
Did you talk to her? he asked
Jess looked away from him, into the traffic
I tried, she said
She pretty much slammed the door in my face
How did she look? he asked
Pale, she said
Like she hadn't slept

A group of students brushed past, talking over each other, phones in their hands

---

I haven't told you everything, he said
I can't
It's hard, though, because I want to
He studied the ground, wondering what else he could say
It wouldn't be fair on you
Stepping close to her, he put his arms round her
Thank you for helping me today
He held her tight, and for longer than he would normally have done
When he stood back, she had an uncertain, almost plaintive look that wasn't typical of her
What are you going to do, she said, really?
I should go, he said
He pulled his hood up over his head and moved past her

From Kings Cross to where he lived was about an hour on foot
On warm summer nights, he often chose to walk home from the library
His route would take him round the back of St Pancras International, then over Regent's Canal, and on through Camden Square
He knew it off by heart, he didn't have to think
Sometimes he stopped for a drink at the Rose and Crown, which was twenty minutes from his house
He wouldn't be stopping that evening, though

He needed to see Anya
It wasn't something he could put off any longer

12

As he headed north, his mind flew forwards into the dark, and on into the days that would come after
Their soundtrack was the wince and clatter of passing trains, the clang of scaffolding poles in the corrugated-iron shed
The hiss of June rain on the weeds and nettles
He saw himself appearing at the leisure center every morning for a shower
The woman on Reception with the bad knee always spoke to him
All right, love?
He saw himself existing on food that he didn't need to cook
July would bring a change in the weather
It would be hot in the caravan, he was in a metal container with the sun beating down, but he would keep the door shut and the curtains drawn
Sometimes he would sleep through the afternoon
His face would grow paler
What are you going to do—really?

Now that his manifesto was ready to upload in all its forms, he
would devote himself to working on the explosive device
To what extent would he be able to use regular search engines
to acquire the information he needed?
He suspected it might be more accessible than he imagined
But you couldn't google "how to make a bomb" without raising
a few red flags
His phone calls, texts, and emails could be intercepted
He remembered reading that Anders Breivik spent two
hundred hours studying bomb-making recipes online and a
further two months making the bombs themselves
He didn't have the luxury of that much time
The clock was ticking

There would be moments when he felt a hand wrap itself
around his brain and squeeze
His whole body would be seized with panic
Calm down, he would tell himself
Just breathe
The fact that he was acting on his own was in his favor
He didn't have any "associates"
He wasn't part of a "cell"
Also in his favor were certain aspects of his identity
He was a middle-aged white male
He was heterosexual
He was university educated
He was Christian

how to make a bomb

Like a false nose and a stick-on moustache, these attributes
would help to keep him hidden
They more or less amounted to a disguise

He saw himself researching materials and beginning to compile
a "shopping list"
Using skills acquired during his career as a historian, he would
cross-refer between various e-book manuals and anonymously
written sets of instructions
Would he venture into the darknet?
Probably not
His presence in those explicit and often contaminating sites
and chat rooms would attract even more attention
While conducting his research, he would constantly be
reminded of how the world would react to him
What he was contemplating was referred to as a "lone actor
terrorist attack"
He would be known as a "lone wolf"
In tabloid newspapers and on social media, knee-jerk words like
"evil" and "monster" would inevitably be used

He could already imagine the drawbacks and pitfalls of a
potential "shopping expedition"
Security had tightened since the 7/7 bombings in 2005
The people who worked at the relevant outlets might have been
sent on courses that taught them how to recognize suspicious
behavior

If he bought what were seen as precursor chemicals in the manufacture of homemade explosives, he might well be reported to the authorities

If possible, therefore, he should buy the necessary ingredients in smaller, more reassuring quantities, and he should vary the wholesale and retail outlets that he used, never appearing at the same outlet twice

If challenged, he would have excuses ready

I run a hairdressing business

I make fireworks

I own a farm

Fortunately, his target was specific, and the device required would be relatively small

To write his manifesto, he had drawn on his years as a historian

In the same way, his background in science would prove invaluable when it came to assembling a bomb

He was aware of the difficulty and the dangers, having read about the number of "own goals" suffered by IRA bomb-makers during the Troubles

It was all too easy to blow yourself up

He would almost certainly settle on triacetone triperoxide—or TATP—as the ingredients he would need had many different uses, and were distributed and sold through hundreds of suppliers

The accelerant and the detonators could also be made from household items that were readily available

He might even be able to order everything on Amazon

how to make a bomb

Ideally, he would conduct a trial run
As a boy, his mother had taken him for long walks in Ashdown Forest
Since it was the largest free-access public space in the southeast of England, and easily accessible by car, it wouldn't be hard to find a remote spot, away from people

He imagined a night when he was close to perfecting the device
His head felt jangled, and his thoughts were hectic
Even after the trains stopped running, they sliced and rattled through his dreams
He woke to a darkness that seemed to be pulsating
The caravan's thin walls creaked with the cold of the early morning dew
He sensed movement in the undergrowth outside
Despite all his precautions, had the authorities managed to tap his phone and monitor his purchases?
Had they found out where he was living and sent an Armed Response Unit to apprehend him?
Even now, specialist firearms officers in night-vision goggles and bullet-resistant jackets could be fanning out across the waste ground
Even now, they could be easing towards the caravan and flattening themselves against the exterior, semiautomatic weapons at the ready
He leapt out of his sleeping bag and flung the door wide-open

The black bulk of the shed loomed against the western sky, its door wedged shut with an ironing board that he had found on Sheepcote Lane
The weeds stood motionless and silent
He could smell their bitter smell
Lying down again, he closed his eyes, but slept no better

His mind leapt forwards once again
It was a Sunday in July, more rain was forecast
The time had come
He uploaded his video, then googled it
The opening frames held on a black-and-white photograph of a microwave with a cracked glass door
He was obviously invoking consumer culture and the phenomenon of planned obsolescence, but the image worked on another level too
Just as the door of the microwave appeared to be contained by the window of YouTube, so the window of YouTube appeared to be contained by the screen of whatever device people were using to view the video
The Russian-doll effect was like a visual rendering of his perception that behind every manufactured item were a thousand other versions of that item
Superimposed on the stark image of the microwave in spaced-out red block capitals was the title of the video
U N R E A L
Below it, and also in red, though smaller, were the words *A Notmanifesto*

how to make a bomb

A tapping started on the roof
He was glad of the bad weather
It would keep people indoors
Off the streets

He watched his video from beginning to end and gave it a thumbs-up, then he closed the laptop
One view, one like
His eyes moved to the sports bag on the floor
The rain was growing heavier
The roar on the roof shut him in and made him feel safe
He had to fight the urge to stretch out on a bench seat and close his eyes
He thought of Talia, and how she had been raped while she was sleeping, then he thought of Seth in hospital, a tube down his throat to help him breathe
He reached for an open bottle of Sauvignon and drained it
The wine was tepid, acidic
After taking a last look around, he picked up the bag, switched off the light, and left the caravan
He doubted he would be coming back

On the bus to Vauxhall, his phone rang
He looked at it, surprised
His phone never rang
When he answered, a small voice said, It's Mary

He was so focused on his own undertaking, so deep in the moment, that it took him a few seconds to make the connection

You forgot me already, she said

He shook his head

I would never do that

Her silence told him she was unconvinced

You're not back in that tunnel, are you? he said

She seemed to laugh, though she could have been sniffing

He had never seen her without a runny nose

No, she said

I found a place to live

I'm having counseling as well

I'm doing fine

That's good to hear, he said

Well, anyway, she said

I just thought I'd call and tell you

Mary, he said, you're going to be all right

I'm proud of you

Once again she didn't speak, though this silence felt softer

He pictured her trying to process words that she might never have heard before

You know something? she said

That was the first time I ever stayed in a hotel

He emerged from his imaginings and looked around

Up ahead, the Boston Arms rose into the sky, with its cupola and its wrought-iron weathervane

how to make a bomb

He was only minutes from his house
He thought of Mary's spikiness and her frayed courage and
feared his intervention had done nothing to improve her lot
The phone call that he had imagined was just wishful thinking
He passed the Spaghetti House, then the secondary school, all
concrete slabs and narrow panes of glass
The road began to climb

He had lived in Dartmouth Park for fifteen years, and yet he
seemed to have little or no connection with the place
Still, when he reached his turning, he didn't hesitate
The clouds had broken up, and a smudged moon kept sliding
sideways, as if he had been drinking
High up, the wind would be blowing hard
A jet stream, perhaps
He thought of how it would push at the walls of his caravan,
and how the desk lamp would tremble
The circle of light it cast on the Formica table would tremble
too, and that trembling had given him a feeling of security
No one will ever find you here

Straddling the hill, the road was level for the first two hundred
yards
He lived at the point where it sloped downwards
Until the early nineteenth century, the area had been famous
for its dairy farms, and sometimes, while walking to the tube in
the morning, ghostly sounds would come to him

The lowing of cows as they were being milked
The dull clank of metal churns
He looked ahead to where his house was
Though he had tried to imagine how it would be to see Anya, he really had no idea
Her unpredictability prevented him from knowing
Was it the unknown in her, he wondered, that he loved the most?

In his mind he fast-forwarded into the future once again, to the imagined culmination of all his efforts
The night of the bomb
At Vauxhall bus station, he transferred to a 77 going east and got off two stops before the terminus
He turned into Chicheley Street, and there in front of him was the Millennium Wheel, known to most people as the London Eye
Since it wasn't in Westminster and wasn't guarded by the police, it was easier to approach than either Big Ben or the Houses of Parliament
It was also more vulnerable and more susceptible to damage than most of London's iconic structures
Situated in a small public park on the south bank of the river, it had the advantage of being a little out of the way
Timing was important too
At ten o'clock on a rainy Sunday night, it seemed unlikely that many people would be around
There would be less chance of casualties

how to make a bomb

As he stared upwards, he let out a muffled exclamation
If the Eye was seen as a symbol of the industrial revolution
and of the constantly turning world, it was also an expression
of hope for the new millennium, since it had been completed,
against all the odds, in the final days of 1999
More recently, however, it had been sponsored by Coca-Cola
The soft drinks giant had been one of the foremost architects of
the manufactured reality that sickened him
He might have had practical reasons for choosing the Eye, but
the intuitive or subconscious thinking behind his decision had
been unerring
Now that it glowed a deep, rich Coca-Cola red, there wasn't a
target in London that was more appropriate

From where he stood, against the sidewall of the old County
Hall building, he could see the cable backstays extending all the
way to the top of the wheel's frame
According to his research, they had been woven by Tensosecky,
an Italian company that specialized in the manufacture of
cables for suspension bridges
Anchored to the ground, they were housed inside a tough,
transparent casing
If they could be made to snap, there was a chance the wheel
would topple sideways, into the river

The moment he left the shadows with the sports bag, he would
be visible

No one could approach within fifty yards of the London Eye without being recorded by one camera or another
It didn't worry him if he was identified, or even apprehended, but he had to have time to act before that happened
With one deft movement, he would hoist the bag onto the roof of the transparent case
He would wedge it against the base of the cables, then step away
Once at a safe distance, and after checking to ensure that there was nobody in the vicinity, he would detonate the bomb

What would that be like?

A flash, and then a flat bang
The blaring of a car alarm
Someone somewhere screaming
Shoved hard in the chest, he staggered backwards
Had he stood too close?
An acrid stink fused with the smell of a damp night
The burning and the rain

He looked up, one hand shielding his eyes
The cable backstays had been severed by the blast
His breath tight in his throat, he watched the wheel hang in the dark, quite motionless
Slowly, it began to tilt away from him
Then it stopped

how to make a bomb

The red glow fizzled, sputtered, and went out
There was a crack, and then a splintering, and the circle of the wheel appeared to flatten
As it crashed into the Thames, demolishing the pier, a boom shook the air
Spray leapt up and fell back, as if exhausted

Blue lights whirled across the bridge

He hadn't expected such a swift response
Pinned to the ground, his face was forced sideways into the paving stones
His hands were cuffed behind him
He felt that one of his shoulders might be dislocated
The rain still falling
He could taste it in his mouth
Blood too
Officers in Kevlar body armor shouting
Their sturdy boots, their automatic weapons
You don't have to say anything, but it may harm your defense if you don't mention
He talked over the voice
Behind your words, he said, are all the other words you might have used
Behind your guns
The voice told him to shut it

Did you watch my video? he asked
I said, shut it

What would happen that evening, and the next day?
What would the papers say?
TERROR STRIKES AT HEART OF LONDON
LONDON'S NIGHT OF TERROR
Or they might be more specific
BOMB DESTROYS LONDON EYE
Or even, more emotively
LONDON BLINDED

He had stopped outside his house
The curtains were drawn in the front room, and no light showed through the gap
He stepped back into the space between two cars
His heart fluttered inside his chest, less like flesh and blood than feathers, something that might take wing
There was a light on upstairs, on the first floor, in the room Anya used as a study
He moved across the pavement and opened the gate
Instead of climbing the steps to the front door, he walked round the side of the house and down the narrow passage that led to the garden
After so many weeks away, it seemed insensitive to walk into the hall as if nothing had happened

how to make a bomb

At the same time, it felt too formal to ring the bell
If he went round the back, it would be less presumptuous, and less abrupt

Light from the kitchen spilled across the grass towards the damson tree
He moved over to the window
There was Anya, sideways-on to him, standing at the sink
She wore a knee-length, dark-green dress he hadn't seen before, and her hair was tied back, held by a clip or a barrette
She was drying a water glass
He had spent so long either remembering or imagining her that she didn't seem entirely real
If he stood there watching her, that perhaps was why
He was adjusting to her presence
But then he began to feel that he was taking advantage
On a kind of impulse, and before he could properly think it through, he called her name
Her head came up and when she saw him she let out a cry and threw the glass away from her
It landed on the floor at the base of the fridge and shattered
He went to the back door and opened it
Sorry, he said, I didn't mean to frighten you
She was leaning on the edge of the sink, propped on her forearms, her head lowered
Fucking hell, Philip, she said
He took a step into the room, then stopped
Are you all right?

Did you cut yourself?
What are you *doing* here? she said
She used a wet hand to move a strand of hair out of her eyes and looked at him sidelong
Are you even real?
That's what I thought when I saw you through the window, he said
I couldn't quite believe it was you
How long were you out there, watching? she asked
He had to lie or she would get angry
Not long, he said
She straightened up, one hand against her collarbone
My heart's going really fast
He asked if she wanted to sit down and was about to fetch a chair when she put a hand out, palm facing him
Leave me alone
I'll wait for you in the garden, he said
Come out when you're ready

He sat on the bench under the damson tree, its branches weighed down by misty, blue-black fruit
On summer evenings, after putting Seth to bed, they would often sit in the garden with a bottle of white wine
They'd be there for hours, talking
That was something their friends used to say
You two—you never stop talking, do you
He glanced towards the kitchen window
There was no one in the room

how to make a bomb

The block of impassive yellow light, the water glass in fragments on the floor
He didn't know if she would do what he had suggested
What if she failed to appear?
He let his head tilt back

The clouds were moving fast, like debris in a river that had swelled with recent, heavy rain

Sometime later, the back door closed and he sensed her approaching, though he didn't turn to her until she sat down at the far end of the bench
She had put on a black cardigan over her green dress
Her hair was loose
You're really tanned, she said
He nodded
I was in Crete
I told you
She looked at him quickly, then looked away
It's all right for some
It wasn't a holiday, he said
What was it, then? she asked
He stared off into the dark
Somehow he had to walk the line between not lying and not telling the truth
If it seemed to her that he was keeping things from her, if she felt excluded, even in his presence, he would lose her

---

She reached into the pocket of her cardigan and took out a packet of cigarettes, then she lit one and blew a thin stream of smoke into the air in front of her

When did you start smoking? he asked

When do you think? she said

He asked if he could have one

She held out the packet and the lighter

He took a cigarette and lit it, then he put the packet and the lighter on the bench between them

He asked whether she had spoken to Seth

Two days ago, she said

He's fine

Does he know about me? he asked

He knows you're away, she said

She looked at the glowing tip of her cigarette, then put it to her lips and took a drag

He said he'd had a weird card from you

Philip smiled

I don't know if it was weird

I told him I loved him

She shrugged

That's what he said

She flicked some ash onto the grass

Obviously, he doesn't know you're back

I didn't know either—until just now

I haven't been back that long, he said

He shifted on the bench

how to make a bomb

Actually, that's a lie
I got back about two weeks ago
Her head turned sharply towards him
I thought about calling you, he said, but I couldn't work out what to say
I thought it would be better to come and see you
And frighten me half to death, she said
I'm sorry about that, he said
I didn't mean to frighten you
She took a last drag on her cigarette and studied the end of it again, then she threw it into a flower bed, where it lay among the plants, still smoldering
It wasn't like her not to respect her surroundings
He worried that she might treat herself with the same carelessness and vehemence
I never meant to put you through all this, he said
It just happened
It just happened, she said, and gave a hollow laugh
That's great
She turned to face him, one leg folded under her
So what's the plan?
Are you coming home?
Eyes lowered, she touched a fold or wrinkle in her dress
Where are you staying, anyway?
He leaned forwards, forearms on his knees, and watched the smoke unravel from his cigarette
None of her questions could be answered

Do you remember how you courted me? she said
It's an old-fashioned word, I know, but it *was* old-fashioned, what you did, how you behaved
Like something from another time
Stuntman, he said
He smiled, then shook his head
You wrote me letters, she said, remember?
You wrote the most beautiful things, and I believed them all
She laughed again, but it was soft this time, and wistful, as if she had been naïve back then, easily influenced
It wasn't true
She had been strong-willed and self-possessed from the very beginning
It seemed to him that she had always known herself
During those autumn months, when he was writing to her, there had been moments when he doubted he would be able to win her over, moments when he almost gave up, lapsed into silence
I used to mean something to you, she said
You still do, he said
No, she said, and she was shaking her head
You don't *tell* me anything
Her voice was quiet, but the tone was scalding suddenly, and furious
Anya, he said, I'm trying to protect you
Protect me? she said
From what?
She looked away into the sky
Maybe I don't want to be protected

how to make a bomb

He looked where she was looking
The moon had risen higher, and it was more misshapen, like someone screwing up their face
It used to be me and you, she went on, the two of us against the world
What happened to that?
He took a breath and let it out so slowly that he could feel his heartbeat in it
I'm planning something dangerous, he said
She laughed out loud
For fuck's sake, Philip
Have you listened to yourself?
She shook herself, then wrapped her cardigan more snugly around her body

Loneliness descended on him like a snowfall, delicate and cold

In that moment, oddly, Anya seemed to move to a different level, as if all the things they had said so far were trivial, irrelevant, things that needed to be cleared out of the way in order that the real things could be expressed
She reached out and took hold of one of his hands
Come home, Philip
We need you
She paused
I need you
He looked down at his hand in hers

It would be so easy for him to turn his back on everything
The manifesto, the caravan
The bomb
His unexpected appearance at the house could be transformed into a homecoming
He would look at her and say, It's not too late?
And she would say, Thank God, and the breath would rush out of her, as if she had been holding it ever since that day in March, when he flew to Seville
And he would say, It was a kind of madness
I see that now
He would walk into the kitchen, open the fridge and take out a beer, as men do in TV dramas or in films, and she would follow him, closing the door to the garden behind them
He would sit on the sofa in the living room, and she would sit beside him
They wouldn't say too much
There would be a time for talking, but for now it was enough to be in each other's company, their silence a new silence, sure of itself, unquestioning
Later, they would go to bed
Later still, perhaps, they would make love
Perhaps Seth could be persuaded to come down from Manchester for the weekend, and the three of them would go out to dinner
How was Crete? Seth would ask
Crete? he would say
It was an absolute disaster
He would start to laugh, and soon they would all be laughing

how to make a bomb

A family reunion, the first in ages
A happy ending

During his time away, he had been under a spell, like someone in a fairy tale, and all the people he had met, from Inés Vaquero de Ayala to Mary McDaid, they were all made-up characters, imaginary beings
He would downplay the whole episode
He might even try to persuade himself that none of it had happened
When he thought about that time, he would shake his head
What had he been thinking?
In the end, though, perhaps he would come to see it as a necessary process, a kind of purging or cleansing
A stepping stone to the place where he now was
The only part of it that he would admit to was the unnerving journey from Bergen to London, but it was a wobble, a glitch, one of those things that you can never quite explain
It had happened, and he wouldn't think about it again
It was like writing in the sand, and ordinary life, like the sea, would soon rush in and wash it all away

Did I do something? Anya was saying
If I did, I'm sorry
You didn't do anything, he murmured
Is it because you think you're not loved? she asked
She tightened her grip on his hand

You *are* loved, Philip
You're very loved
She looked at him again, and there was urgency in her face, and supplication
Come home, she said

If he could just say yes, he thought, if he could manage to articulate that tiny, slightly elastic-sounding word, it would mean that he had snapped out of the trance
If he agreed to return, if he stood up from the bench and walked into the house with her, she would forgive him
He knew that
They would be stronger than before—stronger than they had ever been
They had been tested, and they had come through
Nothing they faced in the weeks and months and years that lay ahead would be so difficult
If they could survive this, they could survive anything

At some north London dinner party in the future, he would tell the story, and he would watch the eyes of the people at the table widen in horror and disbelief
I was about to blow up the London Eye, he would say
I wrote a manifesto, I made a bomb, I had it all planned, right down to the last detail, but I went to see Anya, and Anya talked me out of it
He would give his wife a searching look

Was there still something about her that he hadn't understood?
Anya saved me, he would say
It would be a story he often told, a story he embellished with each new telling
It would become one of the great stories of his life
Philip Notman, terrorist
Imagine, he would say, and he would look at the people sitting round the table, and his eyes would be as wide as theirs

Anya was still gripping his hand, trying to bring him out of his thoughts, trying to anchor him in the present, where she was
Come home, she was saying
Just come home
We love you
And I love you, he said
He brought her hands up to his face and kissed them
I love you very much, and I love Seth
I always will
None of this was ever about that

He rose from the bench

You're going, she said
You're really going
I think I have to, he said
Go then, she said

And don't come back
She was on her feet suddenly, and she had moved past him, beyond the damson tree
I'll pretend that you were never here
There was no one at the window
No one in the garden
He was outside her field of vision, it was as if he had already left
She had closed herself against him
There was no one in the garden, she went on
I imagined the whole thing
She might have been rehearsing what she would say to the authorities, or to a court, while under oath
She needed to have her story straight
She would go over and over it until she knew it off by heart, until she believed that it was true
Until every last trace of him had been erased
I was washing up, she said, and a glass slipped from my hand and smashed
I went outside and had a smoke
I do that sometimes, if I'm upset
I was out there for ten minutes, fifteen at the most
Then I got cold and went back in
She lit another cigarette
She was still facing away from him, her eyes fixed on the darkness at the end of the garden
Her hair moved in the breeze
My son wasn't there, she said
It was just me in the house
I was alone

how to make a bomb

The single tear that ran down her cheek seemed to come from nowhere, like rain from a clear sky
She blew smoke into the air, and blew it fiercely, as if she wished that she had nothing to do with it, as if she wanted it as far away from her as possible
She wiped her face with her left hand
I was alone, she said
I'd been alone for weeks

Though it was hard for him to leave without saying another word, he knew that he couldn't interrupt her
He couldn't still be there when she turned round
Her imagined version had to be the real one, and he had no place in it
He walked back down the passage at the side of the house
He didn't feel anything
Was this absence of feeling a deficiency, or was it the emptiness of true purpose, the emptiness of prayer?
Exhilaration and heartbreak and regret would come later, perhaps, or perhaps he was more thoroughly prepared than he had realized, and they wouldn't come at all

He closed the gate behind him, then set off along the street
Above the trees, fast-flowing clouds
A small, misshapen moon
His body was moving automatically, of its own accord
Gunfire burst from an upstairs window

The rattle of bullets, then a frantic swirl of trumpets and guitars
Their next-door neighbor was watching a film
He wondered which film it was
He couldn't think
There was a flat bang as the bomb went off, and he smelled the burning and the rain
He saw the wheel crash into the glittering black water of the Thames
But his imagination had been limited, convenient
It had hidden things from him
The people injured by the blast, the people who were dead
It had showed him the white spray rising gracefully into the night and the blue lights whirling on the bridge, but it had spared him the body parts, the stumps
There had been no mess, no blood
No anguish
And what of the effect on Anya and Seth?
He had told himself that he was acting on their behalf, but they would have to live with the consequences
They would forever after be associated with a monster
They would be seen as monsters too

His pace had slowed

The clouds, the moon
The shifting trees
His footsteps on the paving stones
His breathing

how to make a bomb

The idea that he would spend the night in a caravan in
Battersea seemed unbelievable

Someone called his name, and he turned round
A figure was standing ten yards away, half in moonlight, half in shadow
Anya? he said
As he moved towards her, she held out her phone
It's Seth, she said
He wants to talk to you
How strange, he thought
Seth never rings
He took the phone from her and put it to his ear
Seth, he said, what is it?
Is something wrong?

rupert thomson is the author of thirteen critically acclaimed novels, including *The Insult*, which was shortlisted for the Guardian Fiction Prize, and chosen by David Bowie as one of his 100 Must-Read Books of All Time, *Death of a Murderer*, which was shortlisted for the Costa Prize, and *The Book of Revelation*, which was made into a feature film by the Australian writer/director, Ana Kokkinos. His memoir, *This Party's Got to Stop*, won the Writers' Guild Non-Fiction Book of the Year in 2010. He is a Fellow of the Royal Society of Literature, and has contributed to the *Financial Times*, the *Guardian*, the *London Review of Books*, *Granta*, and the *Independent*. He lives in London.